The Throgmorton Legacy
by
Trudie le Beau
ISBN: 978-0-9933714-9-3

The Throgmorton Legacy

The Throgmorton Legacy
by
Trudie le Beau

ISBN: 978-0-9933714-9-3

Published by

i2i
PUBLISHING

i2i Publishing. Manchester. UK.
www.i2ipublishing.co.uk

October 1781

HMS *Huron* has recently left Portsmouth after undergoing minor repairs in preparation for her journey, with all haste, to the West Indies where she is to rejoin the British fleet, now under the command of Sir George Rodney.

Buoyed up by victories in the Caribbean where they had successfully captured several British held islands, the French fleet has now joined forces with the Spanish and are threatening to invade and recapture Jamaica, which has been under British rule since it was wrested from Spain in 1655. Naval involvement in the American Revolutionary War, and the ongoing action in the Lesser Antilles has taken a severe toll on the British Navy, both in ships and men, and *Huron* is badly needed to bolster the fleet in their attempt to thwart this new threat.

Huron is a seventy four gun third rate ship of the line in His Majesty's Navy and, as is usual in time of war, the navy is short of ships and men. The *Huron* now prowls the southern coastline of England like some great carnivorous beast searching for prey in every fishing port and village in her path. News of her imminent approach spreads like brush fire before her so that all able bodied men melt away from their homes until the danger of impressment has passed. Although only experienced mariners are supposed to be recruited, tales abound of men with no knowledge of the sea being tricked or taken against their will.

Naval pay is pretty fair, as are the food rations, but conditions at sea are notoriously harsh, and only a fool would voluntarily risk life and limb and allow himself to be torn from his loved ones, not knowing if or when he would ever see them again.

On her last tour of duty *Huron* had lost thirty five of her crew. Some killed in action, some overboard and several had died suddenly and inexplicably, hence her need to trawl for replacements.

Her Captain, Mr. Hector Coutts, neither knows nor cares about the fate of those he has lost. He has no interest in his crew;

his only concern is the smooth running of his ship. As far as he is concerned the five hundred or so seamen on board are good for one thing and one thing only – to enable him to follow and complete his orders, thereby pleasing his masters and furthering his career. He is an ambitious, driven man – a glory hunter.

Prologue

He crashed through the undergrowth, the only sounds in his consciousness the hammering of his heart, and his gasping ragged breathing as he ran, desperate to escape his pursuers. Oblivious to the thorns and branches tearing at his legs and face, terror drawing the last vestige of strength from his exhausted body, he ran blindly on. The sound of the shot was synonymous with the blow that catapulted him tumbling head first into a small ravine. He lay momentarily in the moss covered hollow gritting his teeth against the pain in his back, trying to make sense of what had happened.

He wiped his eyes to clear away the sweat and tears and saw in the dappled sunlight that he was lying in the bed of a stream completely concealed from above by the sapling cobs and hazels that he had cursed for impeding his escape just moments before. The Gods had been kind to him; the youthful boughs had merely bent to accommodate his passage and sprung back leaving no indication that they had ever been disturbed. He saw that part of one bank had been eroded, leaving a hollow between the exposed roots of an old overhanging Beech. Clenching his teeth against immense pain he squirmed into the earth cocoon, the effort making him vomit bile before a merciful blanket of oblivion descended to give him momentary relief.

Too soon he regained consciousness to the sound of cracking twigs and rustling leaves as his pursuers approached. He dared not move and lay with his head in the bile soaked mud, every muscle in his body as taught as a bow string. He tried to control his ragged breathing and prayed that the murmuring stream would cover the sound.

"Well where in hell's name is the bastard then? I tell you

Cooper, if you've finished him I'll flay you alive. Not likely though is it you cretin! I'd bet a bloody blind man full of grog would be a better shot than you."

At the sound of the hated voice that he knew so well, the contents of his bowels turned to water evacuating involuntarily into his already wet trousers; the wretch making stench filling his nostrils.

'Oh Lord no! Please don't let them come near.'

"When I get my hands on that whore's brat I'll make him long to meet his maker. He'll beg me to finish him before I'm done. By Christ he'll not escape me again. I'll make him squeal just like his black monkey mate. He'll squeal so loud for mercy they'll hear him as far away as London Town, the snivelling bastard."

So they had found Junti, poor devil.

"God's teeth! He can't have got that far ahead of us. Use that one eye of yours, you useless bastard, and look, look!" The two hunters thrashed around in the undergrowth for several minutes becoming more and more frustrated, seeing no sign of their quarry. "The only way out of this bloody wood is to follow that stream, but which way? I reckon he'll be too scared to turn back so we'll carry on ahead. Oh this bloody cassock is a fucking nuisance." He heard material ripping. "Roll it up and stuff it in your shirt and let's get going; if that bastard gets away I'll have your other eye out, you bloody cretinous idiot."

Cooper's voice, "Yes Cap'n."

The sound of searching gradually receded as his pursuers tramped further downstream, but he lay immobile not daring to move a muscle. He lay prone for hour upon hour, drifting in and out of consciousness, not daring to leave cover until night fell. Eventually, scared witless but fighting down his fear he ventured out from his shelter, ears cocked for the slightest sound. He became aware of a low keening sound and realised through his haze of pain and angst that it was coming from him.

"Oh Christ help me, what am I to do? Oh Christ. Oh Christ - aarrhh."

The pain in his shoulder was almost more than he could bear but his fear of being captured by Cyrus Mallet overrode everything else. Shock and fever had set in but fighting to control his delirium, he managed to follow the stream in the moonlight having sense enough to move in the opposite direction to that of his enemies. He trudged along in the shallow water as best he could, collapsing at times under the weight of pain in his back. He was soon soaked through, knees and hands grazed, but no matter, he must go on.

As night turned into day the stream left the shelter of the wood and he was now in open meadow. Exhausted he crawled up the shallow bank to the nearest bush big enough to give him cover throughout the daylight hours. Working his way under the bramble on his belly he came upon a freshly dug hole and hoped it had been made by a rabbit; he'd heard that foxes would tear a man to shreds if cornered and he was in no shape to fight off so much as a mouse. As he lay, his head in the soft, sweet smelling grass he watched a large brown rabbit sporting a top hat and black jacket fastened with brass buttons pop out of the hole.

"Hello there Eli, and what can I do for you? Would you like a nice glass of cold ale and maybe one of the wife's pork pies?"

"Aye, that would just do me nicely," he said just as darkness closed in around him once again.

He came to around dusk chilled to the bone, shivering uncontrollably. Wracked with pain he scrabbled his way from under the bush and hauled himself onto his feet using almost the last of his fast depleting physical reserves. He thought he could make out lights in the distance and forced himself to head towards them staggering, sometimes falling and crawling on lacerated knees. He must have shelter, he was so cold.

The beacon of light that drew him shone from a small cottage and, thankful for the full moon he saw across the yard, merciful heaven, a barn. The huge wooden doors were fitted with a heavy duty hasp and staple and secured with a wooden peg. He bit his lip against the torture of moving his arms and slowly, moving the peg from side to side, managed to pull it free. He heard a dog growl from somewhere inside but was beyond clear thought - he just knew he had to have shelter - maybe some straw to lie on.

He staggered into the barn and collapsed into temporary oblivion. He had no idea how far he had travelled or for how long, delirium had set in and he remembered nothing more until seeing the boy with the lamp.

Chapter 1

Jake lay propped on one elbow, listening, ears straining.
Something had woken him and his first thought was for
Jess. He hadn't slept well for the past few nights as she was
in pup and he was anxiously waiting for her to give birth.
She usually slept at the foot of his bed but had chosen to
spend the last two nights in the barn. Pa said this was
normal and she just wanted some peace and quiet when the
time came. Jake had gathered a pile of straw and covered it
with an old blanket to make a nest for her and her pups so
they could be warm and snug. It pleased him that she had
taken to it and would rummage around, preparing for the
day. Yes, there it was again! Jess barked and then gave a
low growl - maybe she was in pain!

Jake had loved Jess since the day they had found her; a
little brown ball of fluff whimpering and cowering under
the leg of a market stall. Ma had taken pity on her and
gathered her up as no-one else seemed at all interested in
the poor little mite. She thought too that Jake could do with
a companion. Their home was fairly remote and apart from
coming into Poundsmill on the occasional market day they
rarely saw anyone. Of course she had once thought that
Spinnaker Cottage would be filled with the sounds of half a
dozen children, but that was not to be.

"Here Jake, tuck your shirt into your pants and put this
little 'un in to keep her warm. We could do with a good dog
and it looks like she could do with a home."

The boy was only too pleased to oblige and in no time
the little scrap had stopped shivering and lay calm and still
in her new sanctuary. From that moment, heart against tiny
heart, a bond had formed between the two and he and Jess
had become inseparable.

Jake just had to go to her, she may need him. He threw back his covers and was down the stairs, barefoot and lighting a lantern in the scullery in the blink of an eye. He picked his way across the yard, the ground cold and hard beneath his feet, thankful for a full moon. He found the barn door hanging slightly ajar. Pa usually locked it last thing to keep the chickens safe but he must have forgotten tonight - good job he had heard Jess then. He held up the lantern and could see her on the straw bed, laying very still and panting heavily - it had started then - perhaps he should go and wake Pa. As he stood undecided, something seized his ankle in a vice like grip making him scream out dropping the lantern in his fright and leaving him in darkness save for a shaft of moonlight streaming in through the door.

"Steady now lad, I mean thee no harm. I just need to stay here for the night - I need to rest." Jake yanked his leg trying to free it, desperate to escape, thankfully, the stranger's grasp loosened and Jake made a lunge for his lantern. "Please lad, just let me be. I'll be gone in the morning but I must rest tonight." With the aid of the moonbeam, Jake was just about able to see the muddy blood soaked hand that had gripped him so tightly.

He was still staring transfixed, when Pa burst in, shotgun at the ready. "Jake, where are you boy? I heard you shout, what's wrong? Is it Jess?"

"No Pa, there's a man here and him is bleeding; he wants to stay here tonight - says he needs rest." Pa took a few careful steps further into the barn to get a view of the shadowy figure at Jake's feet. With only the moonlight to see by he could just make out an elderly man, white hair scraped back from his ashen face. His rough wool shirt was caked in dark dried blood, the hand at Jake's feet red and slick now with bleeding that had started anew. "He looks half dead Pa, what shall we do?"

Pa knelt down to get a better look "He's still just about breathing lad. I don't think we've much choice but to get him inside and let Ma do what she can for him. Go and fetch her; it's going to take three of us to carry him, and then stoke up the fire and put on a pan of water. I reckon your Ma will need some to clean him up."

There was no need to wake Ma; she was already coming across the yard. As she entered the barn she stopped dead as though she had walked smack into the door.

"Good God in heaven what is that stink?" Jake blurted out what had happened and said he was just going in to stoke the fire for Pa. "Well them filthy pants has got to come off afore he goes indoors."

Ma nimbly undid the stranger's belt, removed his boots and slid the offending articles off. "They are only fit to be buried somewhere. Here Pa, be careful where you hold 'em but just throw 'em outside for now."

Jake stoked the fire and set a full kettle to heat. He cleared off the kitchen table too as there was nowhere else downstairs to lay a man half dead, and Ma could see to him better there. Then he hurried back to the barn. Pa did as he was bid with the filthy trousers and, with the stranger naked from the waist down he, Lizzie and Jake part carried, part dragged their burden across the yard towards the kitchen. Breathing heavily John kicked the door aside with a crash and they lay him on the flagged floor.

"Good lad, well done Jake," said Pa. "That's it; we'll get him onto the table and see to him there." With one final heave the stranger lay spread-eagled and they finally had chance to take a good look at him.

He appeared to be well past middle age; his skin was

quite smooth, reminding Jake of soft leather gloves, but there were deep creases across his forehead and around his mouth pulling it down. This gave him an air of deep pathos. Ma gently cut through the rough wool shirt that covered his upper body to expose an unusually muscular chest for a man of his age. He was very thin and his ribs were quite visible but the muscles in his shoulders and arms were still defined. Ma dipped a cloth into a little of the water which was warming on the fire and swabbed him down. As she washed away the blood they all saw a marble sized lump just below his left collar bone. Ma asked Pa to help her lift him slightly and, as she had expected she saw a round hole in his left shoulder.

"It's as I thought, the shot is there just below his skin. It won't be hard to get that out but I think it has shattered the bone. Nothing we can do about that but bind it, but we must get that piece of lead out or he'll die of poisoning." Ma had grown used to using a knife over the years when treating their livestock and, once she felt her blade had heated sufficiently, she opened the stranger's shoulder and flicked out the ball of shot with the tip of the knife in a matter of seconds.

There was only a small wound back and front which she doused liberally with a saline solution hoping it would ward off any infection, although even after her best ministrations she doubted that this poor man would live. She then bound the shoulder as best she could, leaving the dressing loose, so that the wound could drain, as it healed in the course of time.

It seemed to have been a long night and the old cock was crowing when at last Ma had done what she could for the stranger. He had been shot in the back and the bullet had smashed into his clavicle breaking it in the process. With luck the bone would mend, provided he wasn't carried off with a fever. Lizzie then proceeded to clean the lower half of the stranger's body using plenty of lye soap. Unfazed she got John to hold him on his side so that she could clean between his buttocks which were encrusted with stubborn foul smelling detritus. John, trying not to retch made a mental note to swab the table liberally when they had done. He wasn't sure he fancied eating from it ever again. Lizzie then washed down the dirty, blood encrusted legs and rubbed a comfrey balm into the many scratches. They decided that, as he couldn't stay on the kitchen table, the best thing would be to get him up to a bed while he was still unconscious. As Ma said it would be a lot less painful for him than moving him when he was awake.

It was a real struggle manhandling the dead weight up the narrow staircase; Pa carrying the shoulders and Ma and Jake a leg each, but eventually they made it and he was put into Jake's bed. Leading from Jake's room there was another up in the attic which they called the hidey hole because the door to the staircase was cut into the wall and almost impossible to detect. The staircase, however, was so steep and the door so narrow that manhandling the sick stranger up to it would be an impossibility. They left him sleeping soundly, naked so that Lizzie could tend to him more easily over the coming days. Jake didn't mind this new arrangement one bit as he loved to be up there in his 'secret' room, imagining he was a buccaneer righting wrongs and freeing maidens from distress.

It was only when they came back down and Ma was heating up yesterday's broth for breakfast, that Jake remembered Jess. "Oh Pa! Poor Jess, I've left her all on her own at the very time she might need me." He ran to the barn calling her name and found her, still in her bed, but nuzzling four little bundles. She wagged her tail when she saw Jake, rolled on her side to let the pups suckle, and closed her eyes - she had had a long night too. "You clever girl Jess, you did it all on your own. I'm so sorry that I left you. Now, you just have a little nap and I'll fetch you a bowl of fresh milk." Jake ran from the barn scattering the chickens as he went, bursting to tell the good news.

It wasn't until the next evening that the stranger began to stir. Jake had crept into his room and was watching him when the rheumy blue eyes suddenly opened. Although he seemed to be looking around Jake realised that he was far from being conscious of his surroundings. He began to mutter and toss his head from side to side obviously in some nightmare world; the look of terror on the old man's face frightened Jake and he rushed downstairs. "Ma, he's calling out something awful about sons of the devil and such and sweating and he is wet through."

"That's the fever started then," said Ma. "If he dies we'll have to get news of it to the magistrate; if he gets through it then we can find out who the devil he is and what brought him to these parts."

Chapter 2

'These parts' were in the county of Somerset, mid-way between Plymouth and Bristol. Jake's Pa, John Edward Faraday, had come to the village of Poundsmill as a young man in 1764 looking for work as a carpenter. He had learned his craft from his father, helping out almost as soon as he could talk. He had proved a quick learner and had a feel for wood, treating it with care as though it were a living thing. Tall and dark with laughing blue eyes his arrival had caused quite a stir amongst all ages of the female community. He certainly had a way with the ladies and was happy sewing his wild oats whilst earning a reasonable living doing mostly repairs to the buildings and farming equipment around Poundsmill.

Over the next four years or so his reputation as an excellent craftsman grew and eventually he was summoned by the renowned architect Sir Edward Villiers to his grand estate which covered a few thousand acres. Sir Edward had designed a new folly for which he needed windows; he also required a craftsman of some skill to repair damaged furniture and replace mouldings and cornices at the main house which had been owned by the Villiers family for the last hundred and fifty years. John was taken on and paid nineteen shillings a week, a not inconsiderable sum. He found the work rewarding though his employer was a very demanding man, but he never found John lacking. He expected and got the best from everyone around him so praise from him, which happily John received on a fairly regular basis, was praise indeed.

Sometimes taking a break from the exacting work, John would hitch a lift into the little hamlet of Henfield where he enjoyed a pint and chit chat with some of the locals.

On one particular day he was sitting outside The Green Man Inn savouring his mug of ale, relaxing in the peace and quiet of the place and listening to the droning of bees and darting insects when he saw a diminutive figure emerge from a grey stone house which fronted the village green. Always having an eye for the ladies he watched as she crossed the open space in front of him, taking in the line of her shoulders and her tiny waist. She was not the prettiest girl he had ever seen but her face was very pleasing and there was something about her that made him want to know her. She became aware of him staring and turned to look at him. "Hello there," he said suddenly feeling tongue tied and stupid, "my name is John."

Elizabeth Sarah Bridges had been aware of his eyes on her and had been ready with her rebuff but somehow, when she looked into the eyes of this bold young stranger, she felt drawn to him and simply said, "Hello, my name is Elizabeth."

It would be fair to say that from that moment they were mutually attracted; she with his obvious physical attributes and his easy manner, he with her sensuous presence, and lustrous dark hair which shone the colour of chestnut in the sunshine. John was used to coquettish, simpering girls fawning around him and found Elizabeth's open no-nonsense gaze and straightforward manner very refreshing. During the course of their next few meetings (on the village green in view of all in order to observe propriety) John found that his Lizzie, as he liked to think of her, had a feisty character, a quick mind and was charming and innately kind hearted. She also seemed completely unaware of her many female charms and without guile, which John found an endearing characteristic. In fact the more he discovered about her the harder he fell in her thrall, he was well and truly smitten.

John learned that Lizzie was companion to a Mrs. Forster, a widow of two years. When her husband had died, in order to alleviate the crushing loneliness of life without him, she had cast round for someone to live in. Elizabeth was anxious to gain some employment as her father had also recently died and she and her mother were finding it almost impossible to make ends meet. Mrs. Forster was a reasonable employer and enjoyed teaching Lizzie the rudiments of the three r's. She had to admit to herself that her paid companion was a very quick minded girl and she found it very rewarding to see her pupil drink in all new knowledge as fast as it was served up.

When Lizzie had some free time though, she loved watching and learning from cook who showed her how to make all sorts of dishes; her own mother had no interest in the culinary arts, so she was a complete novice. Cook, Mrs. Simmons, a widow of some ten years, showed her how to preserve meats and fruit, bake bread, prepare game and much more. Soon after meeting John, her employer, the said Mrs. Forster, gave up the struggle of living the life she had merely endured without her husband, leaving Lizzie and cook once again without work or income. Lizzie was sad to have to say goodbye to Queenie (Simmons) as she had become very fond of her but fate took a hand when John recommended her for a vacancy at Feston Park house where she was at last able to fulfil her true potential catering for the large and frequent dinner parties given by his lordship.

When they were courting Lizzie and John would sometimes steal a half day on Sunday and take a picnic onto the seashore. It was during one of these magical times they had alone together that they came across a derelict old cottage tucked down in a hollow, just about a hundred yards inland. There had at one time been a fence enclosing a large parcel of land but now only a few rotten old posts bore witness to its existence. The cottage was almost overrun with ivy and they had to fight their way through the waist-high thistles and grass which tugged at their clothes and pricked any unprotected skin. They were instantly intrigued by the place which seemed to radiate a sad air of loneliness and they both felt that somehow they and the house belonged together; that it had been waiting for them.

John forced open the front door, which was hanging on one very rusty hinge, and holding hands they walked over the threshold. It wasn't grand in any way, small and unprepossessing, but in that moment John Faraday knew that he wanted the beautiful Lizzie for his wife and this cottage in which to spend the rest of his days with her. Once they had discovered their future home, for they both knew this would be it, they began making enquiries as to ownership, but at every turn they drew a blank.

John was earning well, so after a very quick engagement he married his darling Lizzie in the spring of 1766. One year later, almost to the day, their marriage had been blessed with their son Jacob John Faraday. Lizzie had then given birth to another child, a girl, when Jake was just one year old, but the child had been stillborn. No more children ever came their way but Lizzie consoled herself that it didn't matter because Jake had been given every one of God's gifts and was the most perfect child. He was kind and thoughtful with a mind as sharp as a razor and beautiful with his father's thick dark hair and lashes and midnight blue eyes. She often teased him saying that he would have every lass between Plymouth and Bristol after him as soon as he was grown, which embarrassed the boy no end.

The Poundsmill smithy said he had heard rumours that the old place had once, long before his lifetime, belonged to a seafaring man who kept himself to himself. Some said he was a smuggler and there was a secret passage from his cottage down to the caves below. Others said he had gone mad living on his own and had walked off into the sea to die, but no one knew anything for a fact.

Time went on and, as no-one could throw any light on the origins of the cottage, the local magistrate said that if they wanted to take the risk, they could renew the boundary fence and if, after 12 years no-one could prove ownership, they could legally lay claim to the land. So with encouragement from Lizzie, John determined that he would renovate the house and make a home to be proud of. They moved in as soon as they were married and John built a good solid barn from timbers donated by Sir Edward. The barn was their temporary home whilst he worked on bringing the old cottage to life. Lizzie set about clearing the land and came across an old iron nameplate inscribed Spinnaker Cottage. The first thing they did, once they found it, was to restore the sign and put it on their new fence for all to see; Spinnaker Cottage, their home.

Chapter 3

The stranger had been under their roof for three days now with Lizzie tending him. His fever had broken but he was very weak and could only manage the smallest portions of soup. However, he was able to sit up with help and, while Lizzie bathed his face he spoke. "You've been real kind to an undeserving man but I must leave here tomorrow."

"I'd like to see you try," said Lizzie. "You are as weak as a kitten. Why, I doubt you could even walk to the window, much less down the stairs."

"But I must go. I've caused thee trouble enough and I don't want to bring any more to your door. If your good man could just tell me where I am I can steer a course away from here and leave you good folk in peace."

"Why, we don't even know your name, we can't send you off without even knowing that or anything about you!"

"Eli Matthews, that's my name and I'm a bad man, nothing but trouble." He fell back onto his pillows exhausted, strands of hair sticking to his brow with the sweat.

"Don't take on now Mr. Matthews." Picking up the bowl Lizzie moved towards the door. "I'll leave you to get some rest."

"But you don't know! You don't know," and with that Eli began to sob deep, heart wrenching, shuddering sobs that wracked his whole body. Lizzie put down the soup bowl and sat on the bed folding her arms around Eli and rocking him as though he were a child.

"There now, you're safe here, sshh, sshh."

When they had finished their daily chores and they were gathered round the supper table Lizzie told of her conversation with Eli. "He'll be a bit stronger tomorrow," said John. "Not strong enough to go but at least he can tell us about himself and how he came to be near deaths-door in our barn. No, he's going nowhere until we get to know all about him. Right, you go and check on Jess and her brood Jake; make sure she's got plenty of water and that you lock the barn door, and I think I'll have another glass of your ale before we turn in, Lizzie. Tomorrow we get to the bottom of our mysterious guest."

Once they had finished breakfast - fresh eggs and bread toasted over the fire, Pa led the way up to Eli's room. Ma was carrying scrambled eggs and milk for their patient, Jake bringing up the rear.

"Good morning to you Eli Matthews. Ma has some food for you and while you partake of it - if you don't mind, we would appreciate learning a little about you and how you came to be is such a poor state in our barn." Eli struggled to sit up and thanked Lizzie for his eggs.

"I don't know what to say or how I can thank 'ee all enough for all your kindnesses. I don't want to appear ungrateful but I really must leave today or tomorrow - believe me, I must go to save any misfortune coming to 'ee." His pale blue eyes, gummed together in the corners, began to fill and his hands shook so that the eggs kept dropping from his spoon.

"Calm down now man, it's because we have great concern for you that we ask! Why don't you start by telling us where you are from and what manner of work you do?" With Lizzie's help Eli finished his eggs, drank some of the milk, and sighing deeply, leant back on his pillows and began to speak.

"I think I need to start at the beginning. My life changed forever when I was seventeen, twenty or so years ago." John, Lizzie and Jake tried not to show their surprise - Eli was near to John's age but looked at least twenty years older. "I killed a man, see - at least 'twas I responsible for his death." Silence in the room, all ears waiting for more.

"I lived on Lord Feeney's country estate just outside of Stoke, quite a ways north from here. Me, Ma and Pa and my three sisters lived in a tied cottage and we worked on the land, at least Ma, Pa, me and Ruth my oldest sister did; the twins were too young but they used to help out with some of the livestock."

"Anyway, one day Lord Feeney's eldest son, Mr. Lawrence called on us and said we weren't pulling our weight; we either had to work harder or pay more rent. It wasn't true o'course and Pa said so. His lordship pretended to think awhile; then he let us know why he had *really* come. He said there was a way to help and he would leave things lie if Ma would go to work at the big house. Well, we all knew what that meant! Ma was a real good looking woman and his lordship was hankering after her. Pa, beside himself, grabbed Mr. Lawrence's leg, shouting that he was a blackguard and a lecher, so Mr. Lawrence ups and starts to use his horsewhip beating Pa across the head, time and time again."

"Ma tried to make him stop, hollering at him all the while so he did no more than whip her too! Before I knew it I had grabbed him and pulled him from his horse and I took the whip and used it on him. He tried to get up and turn it on me and we was tussling, rolling around on the ground trying to get the better of each other. All the commotion unsettled his horse who kicked out catching his lordship on the side of the head and he just fell - dead!" Eli paused to sigh deeply. "So there we were, Ma and Pa covered in blood, my sisters screaming and crying and Mr. Lawrence lying on the ground with his head cracked open just like one of yon eggs there. It all happened in a matter of minutes. I had become a killer in the blink of an eye." Eli closed his eyes, reliving those dreadful moments over again.

"Course we was all terrified but I told Ma and Pa they would be alright and they should just tell the truth - anyone could see they had been hurt quite bad, but of course I knew that if I stayed there was no doubt I would be swinging from a gallows soon enough, so I had to run. Ma threw things in a cloth for me to eat and that is the last time I saw any of my family." Eli's face was etched with sorrow, eyes brimming over. The little family gathered round his bed waiting, now full of compassion for this man, until he was able to go on.

"Well I knew I had to get right away so I resolved to go to sea. I wasn't sure which direction I should go so I headed south. I walked for I think about four days keeping out of sight as much as I could; setting off at dawn till daylight then hiding until dusk and walking till it was too dark to see. After a time I was feeling pretty bad, what with no food and no decent rest. Anyway, I came across a cut - a canal you know - and began to follow it hoping I was still heading south. Come the night time I bedded down under a bridge and that's when I had my first bit of luck in ages. I woke up to someone gently shaking me - and asking where I was headed. Sam Fellows was his name; he was a bargee carrying a cargo of coal."

"I told him I was heading for any port where I could join a ship so he said I had best come with him then as I looked as though I could do with some food in my belly and a rest up; he was a good man was Sam. I remember he kept chuckling to himself that first day and when I asked him why he said he'd stopped under the bridge for a shit."

Looking at Lizzie he continued, "Please excuse me Mam, and he thought he'd wipe his arse on the old rag on the ground that turned out to be me. Of course, when he saw there was a body under the rags he went to relieve himself elsewhere before waking me. He said I should be thankful he'd had a skin full of ale the night before otherwise he wouldn't have needed to stop." Eli paused again, this time a faint smile on his lips.

"Those few days on Sam's barge were some of the best times. He taught me how to steer his barge and how to walk it through tunnels. He taught me the proper names of plants and birds and explained how some of the birds flew away in the winter and some came here from colder places. He just seemed to know so much and to be so at one with all about him. I'd worked on the land ever since I could remember but never saw it as he did; never had the time I suppose." Eli frowned, "We had to work too damned hard; didn't get time for studying such things and we was too hungry to much care about them, anyway."

Another smile. "He was always laughing and joking was Sam and he fed me up fit to burst, loved to watch me tuck in. "That'll stick to yer ribs," he'd say. "I got real fond of him and felt I could trust him so eventually I told him why I had to get away. He just patted me on the back and told me not to worry, he would help find a ship that would take a landlubber on with no questions asked, and he was as good as his word. He said the likes of us poor folk never got a fair chance in life and he was right, that Mr. Lawrence, for all his money and grand clothes, wasn't fit to lick my Pa's boots!

"Once we had reached Birmingham and offloaded Sam's cargo he took me to meet an old mate of his who was headed for London. He handed me over to Old Pete who said there were plenty of ships that would take me on as crew, especially if he put in a word for me. Of course I had no means of paying either of them for their charity; all I could do was make myself useful and help them out where I could. We got through quite a few jars of ale that night I can tell you. Next morning I had to say goodbye to old Sam and I don't mind telling you it made me weep.

"Now lad," he had said, "You're a good 'un and what happened to you could like as not have happened to me or hundreds like us, so get on your way now; Old Pete will see you right. God bless and keep you lad".

Eli's eyes filled up again. "He said he would try to get a message to my folks to let them know I was safe and was going to sea. I often used to think of him later in the bad times just so I could remind myself that there were still good folk in the world." Eli sank further down into his pillows.

"Shall we leave you to rest for a while," said Pa.

"No, no - if I could just have a little more milk." Lizzie held the half full glass to Eli's mouth and, with her arm supporting him to sit up, he finished it.

"Old Pete kept me busy for the next few days and when we got to London's Dockland he found an old shipmate and got me on board a cargo ship, The Dolphin it was called, heading for Boulogne. We set sail next morning and that was the beginning of my life at sea."

"Well, I worked my passage to Boulogne, and left The Dolphin penniless and with a warning to watch my back and to stay away from doxies ringing in my ears. No danger of that. I'd been told in too much detail just what happened to a man who got the pox." Eli looked at Lizzie, "beg your pardon Mrs. Faraday. I didn't know a soul and had no idea what to do next and I don't mind telling you I was pretty scared. As I set off along the quay I heard English voices raised, it sounded like in anger. They was coming from a rough looking old wooden shack, what had a sign swinging above the door with a picture of a maid carrying a flagon in her hand. Half the windows had no glass and the frames was just rotten wood. There was a kind of bamboo curtain over the doorway and the stink of filth, stale fish and ale coming from it nearly made me puke."

"Still, someone in there spoke English and I needed work but just as I was plucking up the courage to go in a fella came hurtling out, knocked me sideways and spilled his guts all over me. I'm getting up and another drunk staggers out and takes a swing at me for downing his mate. I hit him back and before I knew it there was all hell let loose. I found myself in the middle of a whirling mass of fists, bottles being smashed into faces, blood everywhere. I was scared shitless." Eli glanced quickly at Lizzie hoping once again that he had not offended. "I tried to fight my way out of the mess but then something hit me on the side of my head and I knew nothing else until I woke up in a hammock on board I knew not what ship and going I knew not where."

It turned out that I was on The Secret Lady - a buccaneer's ship and I'd been dragged on board when the law had turned up. Some of the crew had got into a fight with some Frenchies and, as I had fought on their side - I didn't know who I was hitting mind you, they decided to take me on board." Eli shrugged. "Although there was no force to make me, I joined the crew, made my mark in the book, and sailed under Cap'n Stills." John, Lizzie and Jake glanced at each other wide eyed - Eli was a Pirate!

"I can see 'tis a shock for thee. It were a shock for me too when I realised that the crew was, shall we say, of a different persuasion than myself, but once they knew I preferred the fairer sex they never bothered me, and I can say no other than it was a happy ship and we had real good times. We was a kind of family; it sort of made up for not having one at home any more. It wasn't like you hear though. Yes we chased down a few ships and robbed 'em but it rarely came to harming anyone. We was just robbers and thieves, not cut-throats. Every man there was equal see, every man got a share of any booty and we was free men. Most of the lads were like me, they had prison or a hangman's noose waiting for them at home and the way most of them told it, they knew they wouldn't get justice so they'd run; their real crime, see, was being just that bit different, and in some cases dirt poor like me. No, Cap'n Stills was a fair man and for a few years all was good." Eli's brow creased "Then Cyrus Mallet joined the crew. Can I leave off for a bit - just need a rest?"

Chapter 4

No-one spoke, Lizzie patted Eli on his good shoulder and the Faraday trio made their way downstairs deep in thought. "I don't know what I thought he would say," said John, "but he's taken the wind out of my sails and no mistake." He was thankful that Eli's references to his shipmates' proclivities seemed to have been lost on his wife and son, who knew nothing of such things. The family ate ham, bread and chutney in virtual silence, washing it down with ale - water for Jake; all of them with myriad questions whirling around in their heads.

After giving Eli an hour Lizzie took him up a bowl of broth. He was awake and drank quickly, mopping up the dregs with the last pieces of bread. She made a mental note that his appetite was returning - a good sign. When he had finished he nodded to Lizzie. She went to the top of the stairs and beckoned the others up.

"Now we come to the hardest part. As I said The Secret Lady was a happy ship and yes, although we was pirates we was honest with each other. There was not a man jack of us I couldn't trust with my life." Eli sighed heavily, "but then we put to shore in Zanzibar and picked up two new crew; we'd lost a couple of old 'uns on the way y'see." Eli pursed his lips and nodded his head. "Cyrus Mallet and Joshua Mills was their names. He was a real wrong 'un was Mallet. I knew it as soon as I set eyes on him, and he was real strange too. Never really got close to anyone, just seemed to bend them to his way of thinking. Like, when we hove into port, all the lads, except the watch, would go off to the taverns, have a good drink and probably find themselves some fun; but he would take himself off, dressed as a parson if you like!"

"First time I saw it I thought he'd taken leave of his senses. He never told anyone where he went or what he did - all I ever heard him say once was that he had been tending to his flock - and the Lord knows what that might mean, but the look on his face when he said it fair chilled me to the marrow, and when he looked at you, really looked at you with those cold ice blue eyes, it made your guts turn over - I avoided him like the plague."

Looking at the ceiling Eli continued on a different tack. "I'd go off with the lads to let my hair down too, they were a good bunch and sometimes we'd laugh fit to bust, but I never went with them doxies, not me, I knew better. No, I just amused myself so to speak." Lizzie could not help blushing when his meaning filtered through. She glanced at Jake but the inference had gone unnoticed.

Sombre once more, Eli continued "Anyway, once Mallet came aboard it didn't take too long before things began to go wrong. He started questioning the Cap'ns honesty, asking was it fair that he kept a bigger portion of spoils than he gave to the crew. He questioned his seamanship too, not in front of him mind, no - just whisperings behind his back. Then things began to go missing, the crew began to argue amongst themselves and work didn't get done properly. Gradually the whispered untruths began to make some of the lads discontented and Mallet gathered a small group round him splitting up our family."

Eli shook his head. "Men I had counted as my friends now began to look at me with distrust and sneer at those of us who were loyal to Cap'n Stills. That was bad but things got a lot worse when the first mate, who had been urging the Cap'n to put Mallet and his mob ashore at the next opportunity, suddenly fell overboard. He wasn't the last either; everyone who came out against Mallet seemed to meet with some kind of misfortune, either falling over the side or from the rigging or eating something that poisoned their guts and saw them off."

Grim faced Eli continued. "Anyway, it came to a head when they started to pick on little Billy. Billy was like the ships mascot. He was a little runt who came no higher than my middle. He was a fully grown man and his legs and arms were real short, but he was a good 'un. He worked hard and was always sweet tempered. William Spiers was his given name but when his parents realised that he wasn't growing properly they sold him to a circus. Cap'n Stills came across him and took pity and that's when he joined the crew. He loved the Cap'n, and we all loved him - least I thought so. He could go aloft quicker than anyone and even with his little short legs was as nimble as they come, and as brave as a lion. He's saved my sorry soul many a time. I was always grateful to have Billy on my side when we got into a skirmish I can tell you."

"It's a shameful thing to say but with all the bad feeling on board, it wasn't long before some of the men, particularly Joshua Mills started walking like apes when Billy was around, making faces and scratching under their arms - bastards! No-one laughed on the ship any more, not in a happy way anyway, but they split their sides taunting Billy. One day it was too much for him and he did no more than run Mills through. Course then there was all hell let loose. Up to then the Cap'n had never had proof of any wrongdoings but this time he caught them at it. He ordered the crew below decks and said he would have the next man he caught hurting Billy flogged, but Mallet and his boys weren't havin' none of that. Mallet said Stills wasn't fit to be Captain and that he, Mallet was the only one on board with any authority. Stills was incensed, and called for a show of hands in his favour." Eli shook his head. "Of the whole crew of fifty odd only ten of us voted for the Cap'n, the others were all too scared to go against that evil bastard; they knew it could mean their end. So we eleven were all put down in the bilges not knowing what was to become of us. We felt the ship alter course and, after the most miserable night, we heard the watch calling Land Ho. We were all taken on deck and made to watch as Cap'n Stills and Billy were taken in a longboat and chucked out onto a small island which weren't much more than a sand bar, with nothing but the clothes they stood up in." Eli spoke quietly, almost to himself. "Mallet left them there to endure a slow lingering death - I have never felt so helpless in all my life, or so full of hatred."

He explained "It's a tradition see, with buccaneers, that if the crew vote to get rid of their captain, they put him ashore, but always with a keg of rum and a pistol to ease their ending, but those poor devils got nothing, nothing at all. Cap'n stills didn't deserve that, nor Billy, God rest their souls. I will never ever forget sailing away from those two men - that bastard!" Eli began to sob, clutching at the bedclothes, his head on his knees.

It took Eli a few minutes to regain enough composure to continue. "The next few weeks were nothing but misery. We nine were made to do the work of the two missing men. We were kept short of food and grog, and the ship I had come to look upon as my home became nothing short of a prison so I - we resolved to jump ship at the very next port. That wasn't to be though as Mallet and his new henchman Cooper set a course for a small group of islands in the Indian Ocean. The rumour was that Mallet had heard of a vast treasure there on the islands, enough to make him the richest man in the world. Anyway, we dropped anchor off the biggest of the group and went ashore in the longboats."

"Some real strange looking savages came down to meet us as we landed, not a stitch on some of 'em, and they was nearly black. I was real scared but they were smiling and seemed happy to see us. They was all excited and jabbered away to each other and showed us into a clearing where stood a man who seemed to be the boss. He welcomed us with open arms - had us all sit on the ground and the women brought us strange fruits to eat and some sort of drink. It wasn't ale but burned as it went down and went straight to your head. The women didn't have a stitch on either - I couldn't believe my eyes. We was enjoying ourselves I can tell thee."

"Then Mallet started asking about treasure; course the chief didn't know what he was on about so then Mallet showed him some pearls he'd brought in his pocket. The old chief shook his head; it was obvious he didn't understand. Just then the chief's wife came out of a hut; she was just about to have a baby by the looks of it." Eli sunk his chin into his chest. "I think the boy should leave, the next bit is not for such young ears."

Jake protested and after some thought John said, "He does a man's work around here and I'm sure he is man enough to stay."

"As you like, then." Eli sucked in his breath and blew it out through pursed lips. "Suddenly, with no warning, Mallet jumps up shouting and grabs the woman round the neck. He shouts again asking where is the treasure, but o'course the poor chief he still doesn't know what the man is talking about, so Mallet does no more than slice the woman open from throat to belly. She screams, the chief screams, the baby falls out - oh God it was alive! A tiny human being mewling - making noises! The woman drops in a pool of blood and the chief launches at Mallet who slices him as well!" Eli shook his head from side to side, eyes shut tight. "As long as I live I will never forget what that devil did, never, never, never." After a lengthy pause, "That was not the end of it either, all the savages went barmy, started running to their huts to get weapons but Mallet and his cronies just shot them down as they ran; they didn't have a prayer poor sods. I thought I would go insane; I just up and ran, the only thought in my head was to get away from those horrors. I could hear the women screaming and when I looked back they were being rounded up - God only knows what tortures they were subjected to."

"I ran to the waters' edge, retching all the way, and grabbed at one of the boats. I was just pushing off when this savage; he was about my age and scared witless, got hold of the other side of the boat to help me push. I don't know how but we got her off the sand, I jumped in and he stayed in the water pushing until he was out of his depth. It was a big boat for us two but I tell you I rowed as though the devil himself were after me and Junti, that was his name, lay in the prow using his arms. We didn't stop until we rounded the bay and were out of sight. I didn't know what to do but Junti, shivering and shocked to the core, pointed to one of the smaller islands, nodding his head. I didn't need much encouragement to do as he wanted, I can tell thee."

John, Lizzie and Jake were stunned into silence. What they had just heard was beyond anything they could have imagined. Lizzie held Eli's head in her hands and kissed his forehead. She put her finger to her lips to silence them all then left the room. Not a word was spoken, everyone trying to reconcile themselves to the unspeakable things that Eli had told of - that they had heard. Lizzie came back with four tots of apple brandy, (an annual Christmas box from Lord Villiers.)

"I think we could all do with this." They supped in silence; small talk would have been an insult to those poor slain creatures - totally out of place.

After a few minutes Eli commenced his tale. "I said his name was Junti, well that was what he called himself. When we made the beach he ran ahead of me beckoning me to follow. About sixty paces in we came to a sort of basin in the ground surrounded by great big trees, palms I've since learned they was called. The basin was full of plants that looked liked reeds bearing huge scarlet flowers. It seemed odd to me, but Junti lay down at the edge of the basin, parted some of the plants and began to drink. He signed for me to do the same so I did, and the water was fresh and sweet."

"I tell thee, I buried my head in that water and scrubbed and scrubbed my face till I made it red raw but I couldn't rid myself of the smell of all that blood! Well, we drank our fill, then Junti began pulling up some of the plants, he filled my arms with them, pulled up more for him and ran back to the boat. We pushed off surrounded by nothing but sea. We had no compass - nothing, but Junti seemed to know where he wanted to go so I followed his lead. He didn't need a compass see, he seemed to watch the flow of the water and check the stars; it was almost as though he were reading a chart. He didn't seem bothered either that we had no food or water. I sort of took strength from him and decided to leave my fate to the gods."

"We were in the boat rowing alternately for three days. I understood after a while why Junti had garnered the rushes. He showed me how to split the outer covering at the base of each plant and suck out the liquid. It tasted good like fresh grass, and not only did it quench our thirst, I didn't get hungry either. We made land in the early hours of the fourth day. Junti steered the boat through a small reef and we pulled the boat onto the white sands of an island that Junti called Umbeebo. We were both near to exhaustion so we scraped nests in the sands under the trees and slept like dead men."

"We stayed on that island for I suppose a month maybe and we got to know each other pretty well. We learnt each others' words for most things that were around and found we understood each other enough to get our meanings across. What Junti kept asking was why? Why had his people been slaughtered when they would share all they had? Eventually I managed to make him understand that Mallet was looking for treasure - jewels, pearls, gold. Junti knew what Mallets pearls were, and when I said the word treasure he seemed to understand. He went to our hidden upturned boat and pulled out some of the reeds - he pointed to them and then to himself."

"Treasure," he said.

"And then I understood - Junti's people had no gold and jewels; their treasure was nature's bounty." Eli closed his eyes and shook his head. "Dear God in heaven, his people had been slaughtered for a bunch of reeds."

Eli took a minute to gather himself together and then continued, "It turned out though that the plants were pretty special. I gradually learned that the red flowers were harvested by Junti's people then dried and used for medicine. They were either made into a paste to put onto wounds or brewed and drunk to quell fevers and the like; according to Junti they cured near everything and that's why they were so precious. Well, we dried what flowers there were and took them with us when we left the island and I was pretty glad of Junti's foresight when I cut my foot pretty deep on rocks pushing our boat over the reef - I've seen men lose a leg with a lesser cut, when it's turned bad. Well, Junti mashed up one of them flowers with sea water and pushed it right into the open gash, and I swear to you that my foot was healed as good as new in a few days. Them flowers was all but magic - they really were treasure!" Eli held out his arm, "I got one tattooed here on my wrist. We both had one done later - we was blood brothers see."

"Like I said, Junti really understood the sea and seemed to follow waterways that I just couldn't reckon, so anyway after a few days we was picked up by a Bermuda Sloop. Junti caused a bit of a stir but the crew found him some clothes and we eventually hove to in London. We found lodgings and work there crewing for merchantmen and clippers, loading or unloading cargo, anything really, and that's where I met Ruby, dear, sweet, kind Ruby."

"She was the best thing that had ever happened in my life and for about three years I can say I was the happiest I had ever been; I even thought I might get married! I had Ruby to come home to and Junti to work with, life was good. He was the kindest, most honest man I had ever met - we looked out for each other - you know? Anyway, one black day we docked and I went home to find my Ruby with her throat cut, and she'd been beaten up pretty bad beforehand too."

Lizzie put a hand to her mouth "Oh Eli, who would do such a thing?"

Eli's face twisted into a bitter mask of hatred "Who do you think - Mallett. He'd left his calling card - a small crucifix - the twisted bastard. Me and Junti knew we had to run then but we hid until dark when I went to see Ruby's sister. She was beside herself with grief, as was I. She said that a priest had been round looking for a black man and a white man who had stolen gold belonging to the church. Someone must have told him that I lived with Ruby and that had sealed her fate, God rest her soul. So that is when Junti and I upped and went our separate ways. Everyone knew us to be friends so it would be too easy for Mallett to track us down if we stayed together. Ruby's sister said she would give her a decent burial - God bless her."

"By now Junti was all but an Englishman, except for the colour of his skin, and he loved London, so he said he would find safer work away from the docks. I moved down to the coast and took work anywhere I could. I never stayed anywhere too long. When I began to feel uneasy I would move on. All no use though; I don't know how but that devil followed my trail like a bloodhound. Five years and I could never shake him off! He'd convinced see that there really is a hoard of treasure and that Junti and I know where it's hidden."

Eli paused to gather his thoughts once again, "Until a couple of weeks ago I was working for the smithy in a village called Fulton. I think it's just a just a few miles east of here. I was supping a pint one evening to slake my thirst when who should walk into the Inn but Mallet himself! I tell thee, I near choked to death on the spot! I upped and ran as though the devil himself were after me - which he was. I ran across country and made for some woods but him and that animal Cooper were never far behind me." Another pause, "They shot me and I fell into the underbrush. I heard them looking for me - just lay there waiting for them to find me and slit my throat, or worse. I suppose I wanted to die there and then." Eli paused, "They killed him you know - Junti. I heard them talking; they tortured and killed him." Eli fell back onto his pillows, more tears flowed. "So when it was clear I left the wood and your lights led me to your door and now you know why I just have to leave before any harm comes to 'ee."

"I'll be the judge of that," said John. "You are under my protection and I'll not have anyone harmed while they are under my roof." Trying to lighten the mood, "Lizzie how about some of that nice fresh gammon with your pickles and bread. I could do with some food and a spot of ale. How about you Eli, could you manage a small platter?"

Eli smiled wanly and shook his head. "Maybe a little more milk if you have enough."

The family trudged downstairs, all helping to assemble the meal in companionable silence, each deep in thought. They had all been shaken to the core to hear Eli's tale. All the while they had carried on their idyllic existence tucked away in their little backwater they had been unaware that such wickedness existed in the world. In their fourteen years at Spinnakers the evils of the outside world had never crossed their doorstep, until now.

Chapter 5

Several days later Pa was chopping up logs in the yard ready for the coming winter and Jake was stacking them inside the barn. John had spent a few hours in the evenings talking with Eli man to man and he was musing on all that they had discussed. The poor fellow had experienced so much and yet he still had a good heart. John decided that he liked and trusted him, despite his chequered and unlawful past. To begin with, he had been worried about Eli's insistence that Mallett would track him down, but as days passed so did his concern.

Jake loved these times working with Pa. It was a beautiful autumnal day and Jess had taken time out from the pups and was watching the proceedings, enjoying the warmth of the sun. Suddenly she sat up and both Jake and Pa followed her gaze to see two figures in the distance. As they approached Jess began to growl and her body tensed visibly. "Go and tend to your pups now Jess, we'll see to these gentlemen." Reluctantly Jess did as she was bid, but sat in the barn doorway eyes fixed on the approaching duo. "Jake, go into the house and get our friend upstairs into the hidey hole. Tell him we have strangers in the yard and he is not to make a sound or come down from the room until he hears your voice and your voice alone. Strip the bed and put back your blankets, and push the washstand in front of the secret door - I want the room to look just like it did before Eli arrived. Hurry now, do as I say and come straight back out here when you've done." Jake, slightly flustered, hurried off to do as he was bid.

When the visitors were within hailing distance John could see that one of them, tall and thin was dressed as a parson, the other shorter and much more muscular, wore ill fitting clothes which were obviously too small, probably stolen from someone's washing line. Eli's description of the pair had been very accurate. Mallett, tall and willow thin, with pale skin, white hair down to his collar and the palest cold blue eyes that seemed to look down into your soul and which sent a chill running the length of your spine. Cooper muscular but running to fat, a good few inches shorter and the complete opposite to his companion, with a swarthy complexion, black hair, thick black eyebrows and one black eye, hard as a marble.

"Good day gentlemen, what brings you to these parts? It is very rare for us to get visitors, have you lost your way?"

"Good day to you Sir. No, we are not lost. My name is Father Westering and this is James Farrow. My parish is over near Wafham but we are here on a rather delicate matter. We were escorting Mr. Farrow's brother from his home just outside of Fulton to a safe house attached to my church. He needs care now you see as the unfortunate man has lost his mind. Sadly he managed to run away from us and now we are very much concerned for his safety; in short, he is a lunatic and is wandering abroad without adequate clothing or means of any kind and we fear for his life with the winter nearly upon us." John feigned a look of concern. "He is about the same height and age as James here but now considerably slimmer and, because of his condition and his prematurely white hair, looks rather older than his years. The Inn keeper in the village said he thought he saw someone of that description heading in this direction so we are searching as best we can in the hope of finding him."

"I'm sorry for your misfortune gentlemen but we've seen no-one. As I said, it is so rare for us to see strangers around here that we would surely not miss him, and Jess there always lets us know of anyone approaching. Please let us know where we can find you though just in case he should show up." Jake appeared in the doorway as they spoke and gave his father a nod. John put down his axe, "I'm failing in my hospitality gentlemen, do come inside now, you must at least have a drink of ale before you start back to the village." Feigning surprise at Jake's appearance, "Ah, there you are lad, these gentlemen have walked all the way up from Poundsmill and are in need of a drink I'll be bound. Pour us some ale and they can rest their legs for a while."

"Yes Pa."

As they all entered the parlour John explained to him, "These gentlemen are searching for Mr. Farrow's brother who may be acting in a strange way so if you see anyone around son don't you go near, just find me straightway. Do you hear? You never know how lunatics will act."

"Yes Pa." Jake tried to look suitably scared as he poured the ale then went to check on Jess.

When they had supped up the two visitors bade farewell and said they would be at the Inn in Poundsmill for a day or two. They thanked John for his hospitality and started off down the track leading to the lane. Lizzie watched them disappear over the horizon, "Thank goodness they've gone John; they gave me the creeps and no mistake."

"They'll be back in a while on some pretence or other just you wait and see. I'm guessing they'll want to take a look upstairs so don't be alarmed if I arrange it and ask them to help me with that linen chest I made for Mrs. Walters. Jake, give me a hand to get it into the parlour in readiness." They carried the chest from the barn into the parlour - it was a beautiful piece and Jake, not for the first time, felt proud of his father's skills.

"Now, are you sure there's no sign of Eli having been in your room?"

"Yes Pa. Shall I go and tell him they were here?"

"Yes, and warn him to stay put as I think they will be back and we may be bringing them upstairs so that they have an excuse to look round, and be sure to tell him again that he is not to make a sound until he hears you telling him it is all clear once and for all."

Jake dashed up the stairs calling out to Eli. He pulled back the washstand and climbed the short staircase to the hidey hole. Eli was sitting on a small truckle bed, fear etched into every line of his face. Jake explained what Pa thought may happen, told Eli not to worry and slipped back into his room pushing the concealed door into place and replacing the washstand. He checked his room once more, saw no sign of Eli's occupation and went back out to his father who nodded towards two figures in the distance.

"There you are Jake, what did I tell you?" Jake screwed up his eyes and sure enough saw two figures approaching, one clad in a black cassock. John, leaning on his axe waved as they approached.

"We are so sorry to bother you again but poor James has lost a rather expensive kerchief and thinks he may possibly have dropped it here. I wonder if we might bother you to check under your parlour table."

"Of course," said John with a smile. "In fact, could I ask a favour of you while you are here? I wondered if one of you could help me with my wife's new linen chest. She wants it moved from the parlour into the lad's bedroom; (eyes raised to the ceiling) I could carry it myself but if there are two of us to take the weight it won't get knocked and therefore I won't get scolded."

"Better than that my dear chap, James and I will do the

lifting and you can just direct us to the location."

"Done," said John "and I say another ale will be in order before you go, what do you think to that?"

The chest was duly transported into Jake's room, Pa making sure that the door to his room was wide open too. He saw two sets of eyes searching every nook and cranny and knew that he had been right, they had been determined to check the house somehow or other - hopefully his ruse had worked.

"Now, let's look for that kerchief of yours Mr. Farrow and I'll get Jake to take a look round the yard while we take a drink, just in case it fell from your pocket outside."

"Thank you so much Mr. Er..."

"Faraday, John Faraday and it's me who should be thanking you. Lizzie here has been on at me to sort that chest out for the past few days and now thank goodness it's done, so I am indebted to both you gentlemen." John poured three glasses of ale which were consumed in a strained silence.

Jake called in through the door, "No kerchief around Pa, I've looked all over the yard, it's not here."

Mallett stood, "well we won't take up more of your time Mr. Faraday, er... John, we will just have to purchase another kerchief for you James; it is such a shame though - it was good quality silk."

As the Faradays watched their visitors leave for a second time Pa called out, "We'll be sure to keep our eyes out for your brother Mr. Farrow." The two men turned and waved in acknowledgement no doubt cursing the fact that they had drawn a blank.

Jake said, "How did you know they would come back Pa?"

"Because my dear lad I've been on this earth for some

years now and I know a bad lot when I see it and that man
is no more a parson than I am King George. He's crafty to
be sure but your old Pa isn't quite as simple as he makes
out." Jake laughed and hugged his dad, looking up into the
strong handsome face that he loved so much.

Jake and Lizzie went back into the house to give Eli the
all clear. Then Lizzie set about preparing their supper and
Jake went about his chores feeling quite cheerful. He was
full of hero worship for his Pa and all was well with the
world. Ma and Pa were the best people ever, Eli was safe
and Jess had four beautiful pups and, best of all, Pa had
promised him a jug of ale for being such a 'trouper'!

John stayed outside until well after dark. He was uneasy
and unable to forget Eli's words of warning. He looked into
the barn to wish Jess goodnight and fondled her pups who
were all snoozing peacefully, little round tummies moving
up and down with each breath drawn and exhaled. "Well
done Jess. You knew those two were bad ones didn't you.
I'm relying on you now to let us know if they come back.
God bless you girl, sleep well, I'll have one ear cocked for
your signal." Jess nuzzled his hand and gave it a gentle lick,
she knew they were all in her care and she would always
do her duty. John secured the barn door and went in to
supper. He paused before opening the door, putting on a
broad smile before he entered and, rubbing his hands
together, "Now my beautiful wife, what delights have we
for supper tonight."

Early next morning, before the sun was truly up, Jake
crept out to check on Jess. Her tail thumped hard on the
ground at his approach and the pace quickened as he knelt
down to fondle her pups. He was full of 'bonhomie' and
felt really quite grown up. Sitting round the fire with Ma
and Pa drinking ale last night he had somehow left his

childhood behind and was so proud that his Pa looked upon him as a young man - someone he could rely on. He suddenly wanted to 'do his bit', so he put his idea to his old friend.

"Those men that came yesterday, I know you didn't like them Jess. I was thinking I could run into Poundsmill to see what I can find out; make sure they've gone right away. If they haven't I could keep a watch and let Pa know if they start back here. I could do my chores and then say I was going chestnutting over at Cobbitts wood, what do you think?" Jess wagged her tail as he laid his hand on her head and looked directly into her eyes. Jake took this as a sign that she approved of his mission, ruffled her head again and went in to stoke up the fire for breakfast. He whistled through his chores and after bolting down his food he set off for Poundsmill, feeling a little guilty about lying, but proud inside that he had taken on his share of responsibility to keep his family safe.

He reached the village in record time and began his search, walking the streets slowly, careful to see those two blackguards before being seen himself. There was no-one around, the whole place seemed deserted; the only people he saw were in a boat pulling in to the quay. He noticed a big ship, much bigger than the local fishing smacks, out to sea, wow, wait until he told Pa. The village, having only three short streets had not taken long to reconnoitre so Jake decided to sit in the little garden at the rear of the Jugged Hare Inn. He took out a small flask of water from the hessian bag he had taken to 'collect chestnuts' and had just taken a swig when he heard quite a commotion. He stoppered his flask and scurried round to the front of the inn - it was a quiet life and any excitement was welcome.

He saw two men; one was a sailor, wrestling with

someone who was shouting at them to leave him alone. As Jake watched, they did no more than crack him over the head with a stick and hand him over to two others who carried him to their boat. One of the men, the sailor who had wielded the stick called out to him, "Hey you boy, come here." Suddenly he didn't feel grown up any more and decided to run, he turned for home only to crash headlong into the second sailor, who had manoeuvred to cut off his retreat. His face crumpled against the rough cloth of the man's shirt, and he was conscious of the smell of sweat and tar. "Leave me alone, I haven't done anything. I'm just going home – now let go of me!"

"Ho, we got a right little tiger 'ere and no mistake. How old are you son?"

Like a fool Jake, wanting to appear more important than he was so that they would leave him alone, piped up, "I'm fifteen and my Pa is waiting for me – he'll be along any minute and then you'll be in trouble."

It was obvious to the two men that the boy was nowhere near fifteen, but as they were desperate for recruits, and the Captain had ordered a hot press, they chose to accept the lad at his word. They laughed mimicking Jake's falsetto voice. "Oh help! His Pa will be along any minute. Oh save us – help! Pa's coming - we're quaking in our boots!"

Jake lashed out at the man holding his shirt, kicking him on the shin. His captor's tone changed. "Right you little bastard. You have now volunteered to join us in His Majesty's navy – ain't we the lucky ones."

Horrified, Jake struggled and kicked as he was dragged inexorably toward the waiting long boat. He heard a voice, "I'm sick of this little runt – sort him out Bob." He was not even aware of the blow to his head; he fell to the ground unconscious...........

"Why are we going back"? "Because, you cretin, he's there and I know it." Mallett and Cooper trudged along the hilly coastal path back towards Spinnakers. After their last visit they had booked in to the Jugged Hare in the village and had been in their room when His Majesty's raiding party had descended on the village. It was unlikely that a man of the cloth would be pressed but a muscular specimen like Cooper would have been a prize catch so they had left via a window and crept away from the melee, slept out overnight and continued on to the next Hamlet to find much needed hot food and a warm bed. Now here they were toiling their way back under a lowering sky which was threatening rain any minute. Cooper sullenly asked, "What's the plan then? Do we kill 'em if he's not there?"

Mallett rounded on him, a rectus smile on his face that silenced Cooper who realised he had gone too far. To question Mallett's reasoning was living dangerously indeed. "We will watch the place you mindless oaf - see how the land lies. We want to catch them unawares - have the upper hand." Cooper nodded his ascent and wondered why he had not thought of that.

Chapter 6

Jake had taken the sunshine. Lizzie was torn between anguish and anger. Angry with Jake for lying to them and full of anguish since they had learnt he had been taken by a press gang in Poundsmill. Why had he lied? What was he doing there? It had been three days now since he had gone and his absence had wrought such a change to the house. The golden sandstone block walls that had once radiated sunlight and warmth now seemed hard, cold and bleak. The house was silent - no Lizzie singing and talking to the livestock, no laughter, no friendly banter full of innuendo between her and John, just cold grey silence. Lizzie baked bread from necessity but the missing ingredient of her love affected the outcome. Where they used to salivate over the ambrosia of thick freshly baked slices lathered in butter, they now chewed half heartedly on bread left too long in the oven which seemed to turn to ashes in their mouths.

John carried out his chores mechanically, no longer interested in the beauty of his craft - his latest commission abandoned in the barn until who knows when. Lizzie would sit cutting her rags into strips for rug making, no longer interested in co-coordinating colours, staring for long moments at a time, into thin air. The multi coloured rugs in the making of which she had taken so much pleasure, and which she had thought made the parlour look homely and warm, now looked startlingly harsh and garish, totally out of place in such a sombre house. She was dragged back to the present when John came in with an arm full of logs for the fire. "I can't stand this Lizzie. I'm going back into Poundsmill to see if I can learn more. If I don't do something I'll go crazy and if I go now I can be back before dark. Will you be alright to bed everyone down?" Lizzie nodded mechanically.

"Yes, you go I'll be fine. I'll put that ham hock on for supper tonight; the Lord knows John, you could certainly do with some decent food inside you."

Lizzie sat staring into space long after John had left and it was only hearing Eli coughing that roused her. She took him up a pot of broth and a chunk of dry bread letting him know that she would be outside catching up on chores for a while. Eli drank the broth, dunking the bread to soften it. How had it come to this? These people had done nothing but good for him and now they suffered so - his life was cursed for sure. He was a Jonah and now he had brought pain and despair right to the doorstep of these dear good folk.

....

The two shipmates had been watching, hidden in the gorses for some time. "There's no-one around at all, can't we just go in and see for ourselves?"

"Sshh look, here comes the wench, she's a pretty little body and no mistake." Mallett felt himself becoming aroused. "I think before the days up Cooper, we'll try her out. I bet she'll fight like a wild cat."

Cooper's porcine eyes glinted, sharing the lust that they both felt. "It's been a long time," snorting, "I'll show her what a real man can do for her; that I will."

"There's no sign of young Master Faraday but he must be around somewhere. You make your way to the barn and stay there until you hear from me. I'm going to circle around. I may be able to take him by surprise then that only leaves us the woman to deal with. I sense Eli is around but he'll shit himself once he sees us; he'll be no bother the spineless bastard. Now, get to that barn and stay there until

I say otherwise." Mallett settled down to watch and wait. He saw Cooper steal into the barn and pull the door to behind him.

As the intruder crept in Jess raised her head and began to growl; her pups were all suckling and she was vulnerable. Cooper, moving swiftly for such a big man, grabbed a rope and slipped it under her collar, tethering her to a post and muzzling her. He was about to slit her throat to keep her silent but then his sadistic nature took over, he would finish her off in a while but first he would have fun with the pups, and make her watch.

Eli lay back on his pillow, the silence in the house was deafening and from nowhere the old familiar feeling of dread descended on him. He charted Lizzie's progress from the familiar sounds of her sweeping the yard and filling water pails, but the usual hubbub of animals living out their daily lives was missing; the silence was oppressive. Something was wrong. He pushed back the blankets and pushed himself up standing gingerly; apart from getting up to relieve himself in a pail in the corner of the room he had not been out of bed. He felt a little light headed but picked up the woollen socks and a pair of John's old trousers that Lizzie had altered to accommodate him. He sat on the bed and pulled on the socks with his one good arm. He put his legs into the trousers then, covered in beads of sweat from the effort, lay on the bed lifting his hips so that he could pull them up, stuffing his night shirt into the waist - there was no way he was up to putting on a shirt. He went to the window and opened it ajar just in time to see Lizzie enter the barn and hear her cry out. "Oh no, nooo," then she screamed.

Lizzie had swung the barn door wide and entered for the first time that day a smile touching her lips in anticipation of seeing Jess and her pups. She loved to watch them together. Jess was such a good mother. The sight that confronted her though could not have been further from the scene of domestic bliss that she had anticipated. She saw Jess tethered, distraught and straining to break free, and the revolting man Cooper, hands covered in blood. Three dead pups had been disembowelled and were hanging on hooks above Jess' head dripping blood and gore around her and her remaining pup, their little limbs drawn up to their chests, mouths still open as they had cried out in their last agonising moments of life. Lizzie screamed out involuntarily, she thought she might faint from the horror of it. Before she knew any more Cooper had grabbed her shoulders with his blood drenched hands and pushed her to the ground. Then he was on top of her, pushing up her dress, pressing on her throat, his rancid breath and unshaven pock marked face inches from hers, his one hard black eye staring straight into hers, fat lips drawn back over brown teeth in a lascivious, mocking grin. "Come on now girl, I'm gonna show you what a real man can do for you." She screamed out for John, this could not be happening, Oh dear God no.

Eli made his way down the stairs, 'a weapon, I need a weapon.' Spotting Lizzie's scissors lying where she had left them on the table, he grabbed them up slipping them into his waistband and in stockinged feet, hurried as best he could across the yard to the barn. The grizzly scene that met him as he peered round the open door sickened him to his very soul. Lizzie's cries brought him out of his shock, his attention returned to take in the rest of the tableau. She was on the ground, eyes as big as saucers, with Cooper astride her. He had one hand round her throat, his other hand fumbling with his belt. Eli's instincts were to throw himself on Cooper but he knew that in his weakened state he could not risk a close encounter with such a bear of a man using just scissors - the nearest tool to hand was a pitchfork.

He grasped it in his good hand and eased up to the pair on Cooper's blind side. Even with two good eyes Cooper would not have been aware of Eli's presence - he was far too engrossed with the job in hand, grunting like the filthy beast he was. Eli planted his feet either side of Cooper's back, raised the pitchfork as high as he was able and plunged it into the heaving back with all the strength he could muster. Cooper jack-knifed onto his feet, completely taken by surprise, hands scrabbling to reach his back. Staggering he turned to see Eli. His face registered recognition, realisation, then fear as Eli stepped forward and raising his good arm once again, plunged the scissors into the side of Cooper's neck severing his carotid artery, pole-axing him. Struggling to fend off the blackness that was threatening to overcome him he crouched down and falteringly reached for Lizzie. She came to him and clung, shaking, sobbing and ashen faced. Just as Eli was about to offer a few words of comfort they heard Mallett call out, stunning them into silence.

Mallett, who had concealed himself in bushes at the front of the house, relieved himself with a smile on his face. He had heard the screams and knew Cooper was the cause of them. The thought of it was arousing him again and he wondered if it was worth bothering with his flies, maybe he would have his turn now. Just as he stood to stretch, he saw John in the distance walking slowly, head bowed as though he had all the troubles of the world on his shoulders. A cruel smile played around his thin twisted lips. Never mind, it wouldn't be long before the poor man would be put out of his misery. He began to button his flies - but before that perhaps he would make him watch.

....

John trudged toward home, the grey weather matching his mood; the burgeoning hedgerows only served to accentuate his sense of loss. He had been homesick when he had first left his parents, until he me Lizzie that is, but that feeling held no comparison to the heartfelt sickness of losing Jake; it was almost more than he had the strength to bear. His heart was hammering in his chest and he was struggling to breath as he remembered how they had all three collected sloes and blackberries and how he and Lizzie had laughed so at Jake's puckered face when he had surreptitiously popped a sloe into his mouth; how they had all sat round the fire licking their lips and fingers after indulging in great thick slices of Lizzie's bread smeared liberally with bramble jelly. So often they had walked this path with himself and Lizzie pointing out different birds and plants to their son, explaining country crafts and the variance of the seasons so that by the time he was only knee-high to a grasshopper he was quite the expert. He loved mother-nature and all her creatures; he was such a compassionate little soul.

John had learned that Poundsmill had been raided by a press gang from a Man of War. Big Eddy, the landlord of the Jugged Hare confirmed that he had seen Jake being thrown into a longboat along with a couple of other unlucky souls. Apparently the Captain of the vessel, 'The Huron,' was a hard man and some of his crew had jumped ship, hence a need for replacements. Replaying this again and again in his head John was distraught and without being aware of it he cried out loud "What am I going to tell

Lizzie?"

"You can tell her that you have visitors."

John had been so lost in his own misery that Mallett's appearance took him completely by surprise. He felt a sharp prick in the small of his back, then, "Hello my friend, I have a knife at your back so just keep walking. I know you have been hiding that scum Eli the little snake, and you WILL tell me where he is; you'll soon learn that you don't cross Cyrus Mallett and get away with it." John, too slow to react effectively had no choice but to walk on towards the house feeling now that his world was indeed completely falling apart. "Not the house, we are going to the barn. We have a little surprise for you." As they approached Mallett shouted "Cooper pull up your pants and come out here."

Hearing this, Eli and Lizzie stood transfixed, caught like rabbits in a snare.

"It's very quiet in there - if you've damaged her you animal I'll damage you - I told you to leave her alive and to leave something for me. I may have an audience, and I'm sure he will enjoy watching his little woman perform."

John, understanding the meaning of this snapped from his torpor - dear God they had his Lizzie. Overcome with fury, and heedless of any consequences, he raised a fist to smash into Mallet's face but his reaction had been anticipated, and with a strength that belied his slim frame Mallett slammed John's hand against the barn door impaling it with his stiletto. John roared out in pain and sheer frustration at not being able to protect his darling wife, his fear for her safety uppermost in his mind.

Her husband's anguished cry catapulted Lizzie into action. From being frozen with shock and fear she became incandescent with fury. Roaring like some crazed animal she stood on Cooper's back and with a strength fuelled by pure adrenalin drew up the bloody pitchfork thrusting it in front of her as she ran from the barn, a tigress protecting her own.

Mallett heard the noise, saw the woman and felt the blow. He had been so taken aback at the speed of this unexpected turn of events that he had not noticed his attacker was wielding a weapon until he looked down to see that he was impaled on its rusting prongs. He fell to the ground with the force of the blow unable to quite comprehend what had just happened. The rage in those eyes seemed to hold his; he was transfixed by the life force behind them. He watched, helpless, as the fork was raised above him once again - and realised with extraordinary clarity that he was going to die. He had met his Nemesis, not as expected in the form of a hangman's rope or a musket ball or dagger, but in the form of a diminutive, deranged, and he noticed irrationally, beautiful woman.

Lizzie plunged the fork into her prey again and again - his eyes never left hers but now they were unseeing, his expression in death one of complete disbelief. As suddenly as it had come, the fury left her and she dropped to her knees sobbing, exhausted.

Eli, who had witnessed all open mouthed, found his voice, "I swear, in all my life I've never seen anything like that, my! What a woman! I think she thought you were done for John." Nodding towards Mallet. "He grabbed a tiger by the tail for sure - and Christ knows he paid the price." Eli went to John and grabbed the stiletto handle protruding from his hand "Hold on friend, I'll have to work it out and it's going to hurt." With that he did - and it did.

Chapter 7

Lizzie was still on her knees cradling her face in blood spattered hands. "Give her a hand John and get her inside." Eli still holding the stiletto went into the barn to cut Jess free. He gathered up her tiny mutilated pups in a bundle of straw and laid them next to her as she nuzzled the last of her brood. "There you are girl, I'll leave you with your little ones for a while; you need to know that they are gone; you need to grieve."

He left the barn to join John and Lizzie who had not moved. Gathered in the yard they were a sorry party, all three hardly able to believe what had just taken place. They huddled together in the rain each leaning on the other thereby gaining enough strength to stay on their feet. Eventually Eli took charge. "Let's get you two into the house and into some dry clothes - we'll have to think on this tomorrow but that pile of shit can stay there until then - it's getting dark and we won't be getting any visitors I'll be bound." Lizzie fell to her knees once more, vomiting. Gently they helped her up and walked traumatised, back to the house. The rain began to fall heavily, Mallets blood and Lizzie's vomit pooling together in the puddle that was fast forming around the dead pirate.

The parlour which had once been their cocoon and such a warm safe haven was now just a cold grey stone room with no comfort to be had in it. Eli sat John and Lizzie down and poured two large measures of apple brandy, putting a wooden cup to the lips of each in turn and forcing them to drink. The pair sat like automatons, John silent, Lizzie bottom lip chattering, rocking slowly, keening, almost as though she had lost her mind. Unable to use the bellows, Eli wafted the fire with an old blanket until it sprang into life then swung over it the pot of left-over broth to heat through, should anyone have the stomach for it. He then poured water into an old jug which he stood directly onto the embers. Once the fire was glowing to his satisfaction he crossed the yard picking his way around Mallets' corpse and went in to Jess. He picked up her one live pup and led her into the house where they could all be together in shared sorrow. He closed and locked the door leaving the rain to wash away the horrors of the day.

He laid a rug in front of the fire and settled Jess and her pup in front of it as best he could and then he turned to John. "Come on lad we've got to see to that hand." He uncurled John's fist and laid the wounded hand flat onto a cloth fetched from Lizzie's linen box. He then poured a little of the heated water onto it to wash away the old blood. "This is going to hurt like hell lad but it's got to be done." He poured two large measures of apple brandy, giving one to John telling him to take another swig and as John did so, he poured the other into the wound as he had seen the sawbones do at sea. John cried out and banged his good fist on the table. "That's good lad, you've come back to your senses; at least I know you are still with us." He bound the hand as best he could with a fresh cloth. "Now, you and yon tigress of yours need to get out of those damp clothes and get yourselves to bed." John nodded, got to his feet and helped Lizzie, lifting her under one arm. She looked at John, then down at his hand

"You need some salve on that," was all she said, and with John still supporting his wife, they slowly climbed the stairs.

"Lizzie. Did he?"

"No John he didn't; never got the chance thanks to Eli."

Eli helped himself to another large drink and pouring

down half in one gulp to numb the gnawing pain in his shoulder which, since their ordeal in the barn until now, he had been unaware of. He sat with his head in his hand and gave vent to the kaleidoscope of emotions that had assailed him over the last few weeks. His sobs wracked his body and hurt like hell but he just could not stop. These poor folk, the poor lost lad, poor Jess - he had blighted their lives forever, what had his life turned out to be - why! He was just a pariah; a bringer of misery. He thought of the grizzly task that awaited them on the morrow and prayed that they would all have the resilience to see it through. He was at last free of the devil and his disciple who had haunted him all these years, but at what cost? He drank a good deal more brandy then staggered over to John's rocking chair. Lizzie had made cushions filled with down and he sank gratefully into them, covered himself with a blanket and fell into a deep, soporific sleep in the glow of the fire.

He awoke in the grey dawn as the cock crowed. His shoulder and head were on fire, and his tongue was stuck to the roof of his mouth. It took a few seconds for the horrors of yesterday to come flooding back, but it had happened, and it was real.

He ached from top to toe but he persevered with making up the fire and putting on a pot for hot water. A very subdued Jess lay at his feet, curled round her one remaining offspring. He reached down to caress her; he had come to love that dog as much as any human and he wished it had been possible to inflict more pain on that bastard Cooper who unfortunately was beyond feeling anything now. He sat and sipped a hot toddy whiling away an hour but it was getting light and he had to get John and Lizzie to help get rid of the carrion that lay outside. He climbed the stairs to their room but when he looked in at them he nearly lost his resolve; the pair looked so young, too young for such a task. They were still fully clothed, **Lizzie wrapped in John's arms, both deeply asleep. He didn't** want to wake them but having just one good arm there was just no other choice.

There was still a steady drizzle as they ventured into the yard. The sodden misshapen mess that had been Cyrus Mallett lay as it had been left. John fetched his handcart from behind the chicken run and, each man pulling with his good arm managed to drag the carcass onto the boards. Next they tackled the far greater bulk of Cooper, who they managed to get to the cart, but try as they may they just did not have the strength between them to get him aboard. Very reluctantly they called on Lizzie to help. She, a wan tiny figure, still in her bloodied clothes, who tugged at both their heartstrings, came without complaint.

They tied a rope under Coopers arms and asked Lizzie to pull on it from the other end of the cart whilst they got a hand on either side of his body but it was looking to be an impossible task until Lizzie, looking down at this hulking disgusting excuse for a human being, his filthy hair, his great fat lips in his pock marked unshaven face, remembered the stench of his body, the hot fetid breath on her face and was filled with a rejuvenating hatred and revulsion. "When I count to three you lift and I'll pull. She duly counted, and on three, releasing all the pent up anger and loathing she felt towards this piece of human flotsam, let out a roar and pulled with superhuman strength, until the hated cadaver lay alongside the other, the men hardly having to help at all. Eli covered the corpses with hay and they went inside to garner their strength for the disposal.

They sat around the table drinking hot toddies in silence until Eli stood. "Are you ready John?"

"Aye, best get it done and finished with." As they went through the door John turned to Lizzie "We'll be back soon. Stay here with Jess - look after each other. I love you Lizzie!" When they had gone Lizzie put two cushions on the floor next to Jess, and settled on them curling her body around the dog and her pup, a protective arm across them. There they lay gaining comfort from each other; two mothers bereft of their young.

Outside the two men lifted one handle of the cart each, Eli with his right, John with his left, so that they each walked alongside the cart rather than between the handles, and they started out towards the same coastal path trodden by the two dead men only the day before. John had explained to Eli that several hundred yards or so from their smallholding there was a small inlet where they could dump the bodies and the tide would carry them out to sea. As the path was rarely used and there would be a full tide about noon that day, the chances of anyone finding them out in their crime were, God willing, pretty slim.

It was a difficult and anxious journey. The uneven ground under foot and their poor state of health slowed them a great deal. One kept his eyes on the horizon fearing that by some quirk of fate some hapless soul would choose to use the path that very day and they would be undone. The other watching the sea, fearing that they would be too late to catch the tide. Eventually, sinews stretched almost beyond bearing and soaked in sweat, they reached their goal. They turned the cart end on to the path and, with one last effort hoisted it up so that their burden slithered and fell into the abyss below. John peered over the cliff and was much relieved to see the surf already lapping over the bodies; the dead would soon be in Davy Jones' locker or better still, the hell that they deserved, and the living could all breathe easy once more.

John slumped on the ground next to Eli. "We'd better not stay here friend. Let's walk back a little way then we can rest a while. After all we have done, it would be foolish to give anyone cause to ponder on our actions." He stood and helped Eli up with his good hand. No more was said as they turned the cart and started for home. Two men, close in age, stature and temperament, but much altered by the circumstances of their births which had governed the lives meted out to them. John, head held high, handsome, straight backed, strong and true. Eli aged beyond his years, shoulders drooping from the burden of a life of hardship, head bowed habitually, averting any threat of confrontation or danger. None the less, fate had brought them together and their ordeal had cemented their friendship. They were now two sides of the same coin, brothers under the skin.

Chapter 8

Jake woke to the foul smell of vomit and bilge water and immediately the memory of the press gang and his capture flooded back. He knew he was somewhere down in the bowels of a ship and sensed from the movement and creaking of the timbers that he was at sea. A sense of panicked desperation and desolation engulfed him, he drew his knees up to his chest and, unable to stop himself, he began to sob, deep wracking sobs that shook his whole body. What a fool he had been to sneak off; his parents would be frantic with worry and would probably never know what had happened to him.

He felt something push against his foot "Here leave it out mate. It's bad enough being stuck in this stinking 'ole without you giving me ear ache." In the gloom, through his tear filled eyes Jake could only just make out the owner of the voice as a dark shape sitting alongside him.

"But I need to go home. I didn't tell Ma and Pa where I was going and they will be worried out of their minds by now. I've got to tell someone that I need to go home."

From further away another voice, older and harsh "Too late son, we've all been pressed into His Majesty's navy and there is bugger all we can do about it. God's teeth, if I ever escape from this hell hole of a ship I'll never, ever sup ale in a tavern again!"

The first voice again, "That'll be the day you old sot. When they dragged you out you was drunk as a skunk and I 'spect it's you we've got to thank for that bloody stink in 'ere, pewkin' up yer guts all over the place, I hope they chuck you over the side when they see what a useless bag o' shit they've dragged on board, and anyway the only way the likes of us will get out of this lot is in a box!" Silence -

enough said! At this, Jake couldn't help it and began crying again.

Someone shuffled closer to him "Anyway young 'un, they call me India, what's your 'andle?"

"'Andle?"

"Your name mush, your name".

"Oh, it's Jacob and you don't sound very old yourself."

"Well I may not be old chronically but I've done a lot of living I can tell yer, 'cept I've cocked up this time. I didn't think things through and now I've got to face the conserquences. "

"What's the conserquences?"

"Well, them's what happens because of something you've done. Like, I nicked a few eggs to sell on me way down 'ere from London - I 'ad to leave in an 'urry - and if I'd thought things through I could have said to myself, stay low till market day tomorrer when I could have wandered around unnoticed, sold me eggs and probably nicked a few bits besides in the crush; but I didn't! I went into the tavern to sell them eggs and stuck out like a sore thumb 'cos the place was nearly empty, and the conserquence was – them Crimpers trapping me so I ended up 'ere. Like you; you went to the tavern without telling your Ma and Pa," In the dark India tapped his head. "Didn't think it through and the conserquence is?"

Jake extended his arms in the dark, palms up, "This?"

"That's it Jakey boy, you should always think things out and consider the conserquences."

It was a strange conversation to be having in the circumstances but Jake was curious. "How do you know all this, about conserquences and such?"

India sighed, "Well, me Ma died when I was about two and Miss Bella looked after me. She croaked about six

weeks ago, poor old girl; that's why I 'ad to leave London
sharpish. I 'ad to look after myself, and got caught nicking a
pork pie. I should've taken a couple of small ones that
would fit under me jerkin see that wouldn't 'av been
missed, but - didn't think things through again - I was
greedy and took a big one. The baker missed it straight
away and saw me leggin it. He knew who I was so I
couldn't go back to me lodgings and I 'ad to sling the pie
too in case I was caught - and it was slowing me down. The
conserquence was that I 'ad to leave London in a hurry, and
I went bloody 'ungry too."

"Anyway, Miss Bella told me lots of things; she taught
me letters and numbers too! As a girl she had been quite the
young lady at it see; getting edercated at home and all. Her
dad was in the Grenadier Guards and her two older
brothers was away at school. But all good things come to an
end as they say, and her Papa (as she called him) was
killed. He left them well provided for but 'er old lady
ended up meeting another soldier who promised they
could all to stay together as a family if they was wed, but as
soon as her Ma married the lyin' bastard he sent the boys
off to the army and arranged for Bella to work as a
governess in Knightsbridge."

India was a born story teller and enjoyed having a
captive audience despite the miserable circumstances. "She
was fifteen then but her employer started the old malarkey
trying to force himself on 'er so she ran away. She 'ad
nowhere to go and 'ardly any money and couldn't get
another position, as she called it, as a governess without
having what she called a reference. So, 'er money run out
and by that time she'd got into the habit of drinkin' gin to
keep herself warm. To cut a long story short, Jakey boy, she
became a working girl."

"But you just said she couldn't get work."

"No Jake, a working girl, a woman of the streets, a doxy!" Although India couldn't see Jake's face he knew that the boy just didn't get it. "Gor blimey Jakey, don't you turnip growers know anything? I think we'll have to talk about this when you are a little older."

"But you're about the same age as me aren't you?"

India raised his eyes to the timbers above and shook his head "In years Jakey boy, in years." Anyway see, the conserquence of Bella's Mama getting married was that she lost 'er kids, and Bella and 'er brothers lost everything."

A gruff disembodied voice "For Gord's sake shut up you two. No-one's interested in your bloody life stories and I want to get some sleep."

Even in this cold stinking marine prison Jake did feel very sleepy and his head throbbed, it hurt more than it had when their goat Billy had kicked him. He lay on half of the rough stinking blanket that had been thrown down as bedding and pulled the other half over him. Instinctively he reached out to touch India, and found the hand that was seeking his. The boys dozed off fingers entwined, both happy in the knowledge that their coming ordeal would not now have to be faced alone.

Jake woke with a sharp nudge in his back. He struggled out from the blackness of his surprisingly deep sleep and saw light streaming in from a hatchway above, a short staircase leading down from it. "Come on lads, Cap'n wants to see what sort of fish we've caught." The owner of the voice was a kindly looking young man, Jake guessed maybe three or four years older than himself. His blond hair was pulled back and tied like a horse's tail and he had on white breeches and a blue jacket. He moved around Jake and nudged India who was beginning to stir.

"All right, all right, I ain't deaf and ain't no fish either. You'd better check on that old sot over there. He was snoring like a good 'un last night and then he just stopped, maybe he's snuffed it."

As he spoke the mound under the blanket opposite moved "I ain't snuffed it - I need a drink!"

"My name is Midshipman Henson and I'll take you for something to eat and water to drink as soon as we have dealt with the formalities of registration and such."

The drunkard, climbing out from beneath his blanket was enraged. "Water, water! I ain't drunk water since I was ten years old!"

The trio climbed the staircase and were able to scrutinize each other for the first time. The older man was gaunt and rough looking. He looked very much like men Jake had seen before staggering from the Inn; malnourished, haggard, unkempt and unshaven and his jerkin and trousers were stained with last night's vomit. But it was India who fascinated Jake. He was shorter than himself, quite a bit thinner, with a head of thick black hair that curled round his oval face. He had a small nose, full well shaped lips and large expressive liquid brown eyes with which he could speak volumes without ever uttering a word; he was almost girlishly pretty. But the most amazing thing about India was the colour of his skin, he was brown! Jake reached out to touch his face.

"It's alright mate," said India, "it won't rub off."

The hatch opened out to a store room packed with great coils of thick rope, trunks, boxes of tools and all manner of things that Jake had never seen before. From there they mounted a narrow stairway that led up to a cavernous, long room with a row of huge cannons spaced evenly along either side and beside each was a pile of metal shot balls.

Hammocks and lamps hung between the guns and there were wooden tables and benches at odd intervals along the length of the room on which stood various wooden pales and mugs. Both boys were overwhelmed by the sheer size and smell of their surroundings.

"This is the lower gun deck," said Henson, "follow me - look sharp now." They climbed another flight of steep, narrow wooden steps which led to another huge area replicating the one below. One more flight and they followed Henson along a passage until they came to a well polished mahogany door upon which Henson knocked.

"Come." The voice, Jake soon discovered, belonged to Lieutenant Bridger. Henson opened the door and ushered the three pressees in. "Leave the door but wait outside."

"Yes Sir."

Lieutenant Bridger sat at a long table facing the three new recruits. He took a moment to study them then stood and walked around to the front of the table. He placed his hand on a large, leather bound book; next to it a pewter ink and quill stand. He stood about the same height as Jake's Pa and looked very stern. He had on black shoes that had a shine to them, white stockings and white breeches, but it was the navy frock coat with its shiny brass buttons and gold piping and embroidery that fascinated Jake; he had never seen such finery.

"Come and stand here." He pointed to the edge of a patterned rug two feet from the desk. "You first," addressing their adult shipmate. He wrinkled his nose and was unable to disguise his displeasure at having to be in such close proximity to the man. "What is your full given name?"

"William Baxter."

"William Baxter - SIR." The lieutenant roared. "When

addressing any officer aboard this ship you will call them Sir, is that clear?"

"Yes."

The lieutenant tapped the book with his knuckles and roared once again, "Yes - SIR." Picking up the quill he entered Baxter's name then told him to make his mark in the column alongside it. Once he had done so the lieutenant ordered him outside to wait with Midshipman Henson.

He then addressed Jake, "your full name lad."

"Jacob John Faraday," then just in time, "Sir." Bridger nodded his satisfaction and taking up the quill again entered Jake's name and told him, in a much more kindly manner than used for Baxter, to make his mark. Jake looked at the all the names above his and at the marks their owners had made - there were lots of crosses and some squiggles. He took the proffered quill and drew his initials JJF, as his Ma had shown him, and then a cross.

Looking at India, "Now you boy. What is your full name?"

"India, Sir."

"I said your full name - what was your father's name."

"I dunno; I never knew 'im."

"Well what about your mother, what was her surname."

"Oh, her name was Molly er Brown, I think - so I 'spose my full name is India Brown." India grinned from ear to ear. Pushing up his sleeve to expose his arm he said "Heh, that's funny 'innit - India Brown - er -Sir."

It took a second or two for the lieutenant to see the joke, a fleeting smile passing his lips. Raising his eyebrows and sighing resignedly he entered the name and handed the quill to India. "Make your mark."

"I can write my name as it 'appens - Sir," and with a flourish he did just that. Bridger looked at the finished result "And with a good hand too - well done."

While India engaged the lieutenant's time, Jake took the chance to take in his surroundings. With a budding carpenter's eye he took in the sheen and beautiful curves of the oval mahogany table they stood around. The curved legs ended with beautifully carved ball and claw feet. The delicate legs on the matching chairs looked somehow out of place on a warship; the seats were padded and covered with a dark blue cloth, all seeming to Jake more suited to some genteel parlour where ladies could sit and sew. He made a mental note to tell Pa all about these beautiful pieces.

There was a small chest of drawers with a little brass rail around the top upon which stood a beautiful cut glass decanter encircled by a row of matching upturned stem glasses. The walls of the room were painted cream and the dark blue and gold patterned rug under their feet, which complemented the seat covering, felt so soft in comparison to the bare boards everywhere else. The whole room, contrasted starkly from the gun deck and rough wooden furniture he had seen elsewhere and Jake wondered at the differences.

He was dragged back to the present by the lieutenant's voice. "Midshipman Henson; bring that man back in here, but not too close." Then, addressing all three he carried on. "You have now the honour gentlemen of serving on HMS Huron. She is a third class ship of the line and carries seventy four guns, twenty eight thirty six pounders on the lower gun deck, thirty eighteen pounders on the upper gun deck and sixteen 9 pounders on the upper decks. There are five hundred and seventy souls aboard; all officers of course being of the highest rank and thereafter the crew are of varying and descending importance, and you gentlemen are at the very bottom of the pile.

"Your Captain, Mr. Hector Coutts, runs a very tight ship with strict discipline and he will brook no insubordination. We are very fortunate that our lives are in his hands as he is a seaman of the highest excellence. I have already said that all officers must be addressed as 'Sir,' and woe betide anyone who forgets. We are on our way to join our main fleet in the West Indies. It seems the French and Spanish have joined forces and have it in mind to steal Jamaica from us. We will endeavour to make the best headway we can - the Captain does not want to miss out on giving the French the hiding they deserve for their treachery."

Most of what the lieutenant had said went over the heads of the three newcomers. The only things they all picked up on were that the Captain may be someone to be feared and they were on a warship that seemingly was on its way to fight!

While the three reluctant new recruits were undergoing their indoctrination, Captain Hector Coutts was ensconced in his cabin drumming his fingers on his desk, absorbed in charting the quickest course to Dominica, checking and re-checking his workings. He was not interested in his crew. To him they were just cogs in the wheel necessary to keep his beloved ship in good working order. Neither did he have an interest in his officers. As far as he was concerned they were all popinjays whose rich families had bought their commissions – not a real sailor amongst them, with the one exception of his first officer, John Pointer, for whom he had a sneaking admiration.

He and Pointer had risen through the ranks on their own merit. Worked and studied hard, towed the line, eventually reaping what he considered to be their well deserved rewards. In truth all the officers on board were capable and conscientious but he was blinded to their merits by his deep seated feeling of inferiority which stemmed from his humble beginnings. Arching in his chair to ease his back, he stretched his arms above his head. "Sod 'em all." He spoke to the ceiling. "I am the Captain, me! My ship! My command! Not bad for a guttersnip, eh boys?"

Chapter 9

Eight bells sounded prompting Bridger to call out, "Henson, take these three to their mess deck for victuals then instruct them in their duties and introduce them to the ship; she will be their home for goodness knows how long now and they need to get acquainted." India looked at Jake, eyes as round and large as saucers

"Not for me it won't. I'm off first chance I get."

Jake and India were shown to a rough wooden table where sat ten boys around their own age. Baxter joined a table of adults. The boys all stared openly at the two friends; India receiving special attention. Not wanting to offend, the newcomers gave a cursory nod to their new shipmates and cast their eyes down to the table. They each received a mug of cocoa, a bowl of some sort of cold porridge and a small pile of ships biscuits. The new boys were both ravenous but found that the only way to eat these was to soak them in the cocoa until they became soft enough to bite into.

Several of the boys sniggered until one of their number leant over to pick up India's remaining biscuit. "'Afore you dunk 'em, best to tap 'em." He banged the edge of the hard square and several small black beetles fell onto the table. "Best to shake 'em out or the poor little buggers drown." The look of horror on the two boy's faces sent everyone into fits of laughter, breaking any remaining tension that remained.

All too soon the meal ended and everyone got to their feet, several patting the new boys on the back and welcoming them with a sardonic, "Welcome to His Majesty's Navy, boys."

Midshipman Henson returned with Baxter and they

followed him to the top deck revelling in the fresh air and the occasional sea spray on their faces. The sheer size of the ship was a revelation to the boys. They had to crane back their necks to get a full view of the three masts which seemed to reach up to the heavens, and they marvelled at the tiny figures shinning along the cross beams and climbing up and down the mass of enormous rope webbing. The ship was in full sail and even for the three land lubbers the acres of white canvass billowing out, taught and fully stretched in the wind, was a magnificent sight. With the ship buffeting through the choppy sea, they had great difficulty in walking without hanging onto each other, and all three marvelled at the rest of the crew who moved around the deck, which was a bewildering hive of activity, with such ease. Henson smiled, "Don't worry you'll soon get your sea legs."

They followed the young Midshipman to the bow of the ship where there were several low benches just below the bowsprit with circular holes in them. "These gentlemen are the ship's latrines, known as the heads, and this is where you will relieve yourselves."

India exclaimed "What? We have to take a shit out 'ere, in the open, in front of everyone?"

"Exactly that," said Henson "and it is very important that they be kept clean so if you make a mess and need to clean up after yourself you haul this bucket (which was attached to a rope) over the side and swab down, is that clear?"

"Bugger that," said India swaying around on the moving deck, "I'd 'av a job to park me arse on that 'ole now as it is - what we supposed to do when it's really rough or pissing down?"

Henson with a hint of a smile, "get wet and hold on

tight!" He turned sharply on his heel and spoke over his shoulder. "This is important gentlemen. Anyone fouling in or around the ship will be severely punished of that you can be sure."

India could not help himself. "Christ almighty, what a shit 'ole - bugs in yer grub and a public shitter."

They made their way along the length of the top deck, weaving around some of the crew who were holystoning the deck to eliminate splinters. Midshipman Henson stopped now and again to explain the various duties that were being carried out, why they were necessary and how they were rotated. He explained how time was kept on board by means of hour-glasses and half-glasses, and how the ships bells denoted the time and end of each watch to the crew.

He showed them the store rooms where all the paraphernalia needed to maintain the marine world that they now occupied was kept, and explained that, in battle, their duty would be to carry gunpowder from the magazine room to the gunners that they would eventually be assigned to. Also they would be expected to make sure there were ample water buckets or ale to slake the thirst of battle and to quench any small fires that may flare up. 'Theirs', he said, was a vital role, as without powder the guns would be silent and the ship and everyone on board would be powerless and without any means of defence. He explained that a watch was maintained twenty four hours of the day, with every man aboard taking his turn, each having a duty to his shipmates to do his bit.

All through the induction Jake could not take his eyes of the riggers scurrying up and down rope ladders, trimming sails, climbing over the great wooden spars with seemingly consummate ease, never faltering in their stride. Henson followed Jake's gaze. "We in the King's navy pride ourselves on our seamanship and there are no finer sailors than those men aloft. It takes years to become a rigger, and they are some of the very best - top of the tree. Who knows, in a few years you could be one of them." India's expression left Jake in no doubt that, like himself, he found the prospect terrifying.

"Now, we need to get you some bedding and some clothes, follow me." They made their way below to the purser's office on the orlop deck. "Good day Mr. Llewellyn, three more recruits present for provisions if you please." The purser, not known for his charm, barely acknowledged the Midshipman. Ill humouredly, he doled out to the three unfortunates one hammock, one thin mattress, one blanket and one set of regulation naval wear (a loose jacket and short loose pants.) He regarded them with porcine eyes sunken into a fat, slightly bloated face; he reminded Jake of their old brood sow, Rosy, although she was a far more pleasant character and, he thought, rather more attractive.

"The hammocks are provided but you owe for everything else and it will be taken from your pay. Once you have paid off half the debt you may purchase a second set of slops (clothes), is that clear?" All three nodded, not being clear at all but the purser's expression left them in no doubt that he would brook no other response. "You can stow your own rags here." Looking at Baxter and wrinkling his nose in a theatrical manner, "you can throw yours over the side." Addressing all three, "you can collect any money due to you when we dock, that is if we are not all dead by then, in which case you won't need it." He pushed a ledger to the edge of his small wooden counter, "Sign here." They duly made their mark, India signing with a flourish. "Change here; then bugger off."

They buggered off just as the bells sounded noon and Henson appeared to take them, once again, to the mess. He collared the 'weevil' boy. "Walden I am putting these lads in your care. They are to join your mess until you hear to the contrary so I want you to show them the ropes and the like. When you've finished here they are assigned to you. What rota are you on today?"

"Rope splicing Sir."

"How appropriate! Very well, set them to it and don't allow any slacking."

"Aye sir."

Henson turned on his heel, "Baxter, get to your food now, you'll be on the bilge pump this afternoon." With that he left, presumably to satisfy his own appetite.

Walden spoke. "Right, my name is Ruben and," pointing, "this is your mess table and this is how it works. With you two there are twelve of us now and we take turns in doing the cooking each day. Can you cook?" Both boys had been around kitchens all their lives so had a modicum of skill, so both nodded to the affirmative. "Well, I'm number ten and it's my shout tomorrow so you can both come with me to the stores and then to the galley to watch." Looking around at the others, "we don't want you giving us the shits." Smiles all round, they sat down to enjoy, as much as was possible, the salt pork stew provided by number nine, together with yet more hard tack and some sort of vinegary cabbage. The mealtime passed quickly, both newcomers being assailed by questions about where they came from, how they came to be pressed and so on. India, who had the knack of telling a yarn, held them enthralled with the details of his heroic resistance to capture. Jake kept silent not wanting to steal his thunder over a mere detail like the truth.

After a long and exhausting day and with fingers sore from twisting and splicing ropes the boys were allowed to go to their cabin. There were around thirty youngsters sharing and India and Jake hung their hammocks from pegs numbers 29 and 30. India threw in his thin, lumpy mattress, swung into his and patted it. "That's cheery 'innit?" he said. "I was asking why we ain't got beds and one of the old boys said these take up less room and they double up as a shroud, so when you croak it, they sew you up in it, then tip you over the side." He suddenly became very serious and shuddered, "Jakey boy, if anything 'appens to me, don't let 'em sew me up, promise? I couldn't stand it. Tell 'em to save my 'ammock for the new boy." He grabbed Jake's wrist, "promise me, won't yer?" Jake, not quite sure of this previously unseen serious side to India nodded his head, "Ok."

That night they learnt much more about each other, sharing stories of their so very different childhoods. India had been born in a brothel and his mother had died when he was around two. According to Miss Bella, (the madam) his father had been a regular visitor and called whenever he was in port. He and India's mother it seemed had felt a great deal for each other but circumstances prevented them from having a more conventional relationship. "I wish I'd known either of 'em. I can't really remember me mum and of course I never met 'im. Miss Bella was me mum really I suppose," sighing "I don't 'alf miss 'er."

Jake realised with a jolt that he had not thought of home once that day. "All I know about my dad - this is what Miss Bella told me - is that he came from a long way away and all his family had been killed by cut-throats. She said he had seemed nice enough - she remembered he had a flower tattooed on his wrist, he said it was a special one from his homeland. He drew a picture of it for me mum and Miss Bella kept it for me, it was lovely, a beautiful red flower. I was always looking out for one at the markets but never saw nothing like it. The picture was the only thing I ever 'ad of me own, but I 'ad to leave it behind when I legged it."

Jake's mind did cartwheels. It was just too much to take in. His mind flew to Eli propped in up bed; he distinctly remembered Eli saying that his friend Junti had a flower tattooed on his wrist to remind him of his home. Was it possible that India's man and Junti were one and the same? That India was Junti's son! Surely, that would be just too much of a coincidence. He decided to put any further discussion on the matter to one side to give him time to ponder on it. "Why were you called India?"

"Like I said before, Miss Bella's old man was a soldier and he used to tell her tales about where he'd been and what he'd seen. She had kept some of the pictures he'd brought back from somewhere called India. Well, Miss Bella said me mum loved looking at 'em because the men was so handsome and the women was beautiful and covered in jewels - Mum thought it must be the best place ever; so when I come out brown, that's what she called me - India."

"Will you two shut up? It's bloody hard enough sleeping in this shopping bag without your constant jabbering."

Jake looked at India, who rolled his eyes to the heavens, shrugged and laid down in his hammock, bum in the air. He so wanted to go home; he had so much to tell and now in the empty quiet he missed his family so. Eyes wet with tears and trying hard to stifle his sobs he drifted off, memories of Ma, Pa, Jess and her pups following him into his dreams.

Chapter 10

Over the next few weeks the boys became familiar with the ship's routine. Each day of the week specific tasks were carried out but all were also tasked with various jobs from serving officers in the wardroom and gunroom. There was also helping the warrant officers with their various trades or carrying out menial duties such as cleaning the manger where the ship's livestock was kept, or cleaning out the heads. In short they were treated like dogs and at the beck and call of everyone. They began to recognize various officers and crew by name, some popular, some not, although most of the adults on board ignored them, just shouting orders as and when necessary. There was a strict pecking order with officers top of the pile, then riggers or topmen, then able seamen and lastly the group called waisters, of which Jake was one, comprising of non skilled workers and pressees. The skills needed for sailing the ship and all that it entailed were the responsibility of the first three sections with the last quarter taking most of the watch and doing the more domestic, menial jobs in the waist of the ship – hence their title – waisters.

The duties were hard and tedious and frequently interspersed with orders to 'rig for action' which meant stowing away every piece of unnecessary equipment and running out the guns. These moves were rehearsed over and over so that, when the fighting began, every man would know exactly what was expected of him and there would be no weak links in the chain. Jake and the other powder monkeys were tested and drilled and sent time and again to the powder magazine to carry back bags of gunpowder to their allotted gunner. Jake remembered Henson's words and began to feel a certain pride in having a specific role and doing it well. Although reluctantly; he was one of a ships company, each doing their bit for the good of the ship, fitting together like some gigantic jigsaw puzzle. It was, he had been told, this ceaseless training and meticulous attention to detail that enabled the British Navy to rule the waves.

Jake had been assigned to gun number thirteen. The lead gunner Sol Benson was a taciturn man who took a great deal of pride in the expertise shown by his crew. There were six on the gun altogether; Mel Cartwright, Ginger McCall, Bill Holder, Jonjo O'Hara, Slim Sullivan and Jake, the powder boy, making seven. During the seemingly endless drills they had gelled together and Sol had been impressed with Jake's voracious appetite for knowledge, constantly asking questions covering every aspect of the ship from its fire power to the navigation and manoeuvring of such a titan.

Most of the gun crews were regular servicemen and, despite some of the hardships, loved the life at sea on a man of war and the excitement of battle. Jake learned from some of his group, when the rum ration made them a little more garrulous, that Sol had been pressed as a lad but had grown to love the life and had advanced himself to become a non-commissioned officer. He had some years hence amassed a reasonable amount of prize money and had intended to leave the navy, marry and open a boarding house, but had been persuaded by his prospective father-in-law to invest his savings in flawed investments and subsequently the wealth he had accrued soon disappeared, as did his would-be bride! Being once again penniless he had rejoined the navy and made it his life. Jake began to feel, not for the first time since his enforced slavery, that he and his parents had, at least up to his pressing, had the very best of a charmed life. He concluded that, if he had to be enslaved, it could be a lot worse. He liked Sol and all the others and began to think of them with not a small amount of affection.

The only break from the rigid timetable came on Sundays when a church service was held in the morning and all those not on watch had the afternoon to themselves. It was during these times that all the boys would gather and talk. They were a very diverse bunch and conversations covered a wide range of topics, from food to families and home, but the subject that took up most of the time were the other crew members. Jake had already befriended a few, his gunner, Sol Saunders and Pete, the officers cook, who would sometimes slip him a piece of roast lamb left over from the Captain's table, and old Joe who cared for the animals in the manger. The person most often talked about though was the Bosun's mate, Charlie Croucher and his seemingly constant companion and lackey, a simpleton named Billy Lloyd.

Charlie Croucher was disliked by most of the crew and hated by the boys. Very early on Walden had warned Jake and India to stay well away from him as he was dangerous and had an appetite for boys, especially good lookers like Jake and India. "What do you mean?" said Jake, not understanding.

"You mean he's a brown adder don't yer," said India. Walden nodded. Seeing the confused look on Jake's face India said "Blimey Jakey boy, don't you know nothing! What he means is that he'll be after your arse."

Exasperated that Jake obviously still did not understand, he said "You're a right turnip head ain't yer. Look, you got animals at 'ome ain't yer? Jake nodded "Well you must've seen em 'at it' ain't yer?" The penny dropped

"Oh, you mean mating, yes of course. We loan a bull to cover our cows so that we can have milk and we rent Mr. Jarvis's ram to service our sheep and ..."

"OK, ok," said India "suppose Croucher was a bull. Well, he wouldn't want to mate with your cow he would want to mate with another bull. Get it?" Jake looked perplexed,

"But that's not right, and anyway there is nowhere on a bull to."

"Exactly, so he'd stick it up the other bulls arse! Get it now?" Jake was appalled

"You mean, Croucher likes to mate with other men and he..."

Walden interjected "Yes, but better still he likes to mate, as you put it, with boys and yes he sticks it up their arse."

From then on in Jake's eyes, Croucher was the devil incarnate. He was a big hirsute man with black hair plastered down with grease and held in a pigtail. Sometimes Jake would look up to catch him staring with a crooked grin that showed the wide gap in his front teeth where a tooth had been broken. His black eyes like pebbles, hard as flint roved over Jake filling him with revulsion for the man. He, along with everyone else avoided Croucher and Billy Lloyd like the plague, avoiding making eye contact with either of them at all costs. Gradually as the weeks went by he became a little more relaxed about things. After all, there were plenty of shipmates who knew what Croucher was and hated him for it, so nothing bad could really happen.

On these Sunday afternoons Jake loved nothing more than to slip along to the manger below decks and chat to old Joe who cared for the cows, pigs and fowl in his charge. Being amongst the livestock was to Jake almost home from home and Joe always had some yarn to spin about the goings on in the navy which he had been sold into as a boy. As they travelled further south the temperature began to climb and it was on one Sunday, with a gentle balmy breeze just titillating the sales so that the ship slid smoothly through the silky waters, that Jake slipped away virtually unnoticed by his mess mates who were all enthralled by yet another of India's adventures in London's docklands, and made his way down to see his old friend. Everyone called him old Joe more because of his long service in the navy than his chronological age. He was a small man with tiny gnarled hands and one tiny foot, the other having been replaced by a wooden prosthesis from the knee down. He was glad of Jake's company and at having someone to share his memories with; he had grown very fond of this quiet gentle boy. They would sit cocooned in their own little world; Jake enraptured by Joe's often elaborately embroidered tales of battles fought and treasures taken.

Joe welcomed him warmly. He sat propped against the ships bulwark, legs outstretched in front. "Welcome lad, come and sit alongside me." He was in very good spirits, probably down to the extra rum ration sometimes allowed on Sundays. Jake settled down and they soon fell into their usual questions and answers routine; the youngster drinking in any and every ounce of Joe's knowledge of seamanship; the old man revelling in having his ego massaged and welcoming the opportunity to display his considerable knowledge of the craft.

During an interval in his tales, with Joe gazing off into the distance viewing a memory, Jake plucked up the courage and asked, after many weeks of wanting to, how Joe had lost his leg. Joe puffed out his chest and began, "Well son, it was twenty years or so ago now and we was attacking Havana; the Spanish held it then. I was serving under Cap'n Robson on HMS Monarch. I was a gunner and I reckon we 'ad the best run ship in the fleet. Cap'n Robson was a stickler for training he was, but by heaven it paid off. We was that good that we could get off two or sometimes three salvos to one from them Spanish, and Frenchies for that matter."

He shook his head slowly and smiled to himself. "Anyway, it was hell on earth on that gun deck. You couldn't hear a thing once the guns started up, that's where the constant drilling came into it see, and everyone knew their job – no point talking, just used signs. He sighed. "It was real hot that day and we took a couple of hits early on; it was like a charnel house, blood and guts everywhere - and the stink that goes with it, but me and us that were still alive didn't let that stop us - you just don't think of nothing else, just do your job.

Well, we took another hit and the breeching tackle securing my cannon was shot through. Course it swung round loose and afore I could get out the way it took me leg clean off, just like that." Joe stopped, considering his next words. "It didn't hurt. I just sat on the floor amongst all the blood and guts looking at my foot poking out from under the gun. One of the older bucket boys tied me leg with his belt and I don't remember much else. I had a lot of pain and a fever but the old sawbones knew what he was about and got me through it." His face creased into a broad grin and he shook a clenched fist "But we beat them Spanish, took Havana off em and sent em off with their tail between their legs and no mistake."

"Cap'n Robson he was a good 'un he was. Canny to! We took quite a bit of prize money on the old Monarch. I had enough to get by if I'd wanted to stay on land but I'd no family and I love the sea so I stayed in the service. Course I couldn't run out a gun no more so I've worked in the galley and the stores and such since then. Yes, he was a good 'un was Cap'n Robson, not like Coutts here." Joe pursed his lips and slowly shook his head. "There's something amiss with that man, young 'un, I don't think he's sound. Oh, he's a good sailor I'll give him that; knows what he's about when it comes to handling a ship, but he doesn't know men." He leant toward Jake so that their faces were nearly touching, "there's something bad aboard lad so you listen to me. You keep your head down, do you hear, and tell that mouthy young friend of yours, Indigo, to do the same, it don't pay to be noticed on this ship." Joe laid a hand on Jake's shoulder, he seemed agitated, and then he began to cough. He coughed seemingly uncontrollably, spitting into an old cloth and Jake was dismayed to see that there were bloody flecks in the spittle.

Seeing Jake's concern Joe spat one last time and, as his coughing eased, "Jake my boy. Like I said, we all took a fair bit of prize money serving under Cap'n Robson but I know I'm not going to be around long enough now to spend it and I ain't got any family so I'm handing it all over to you. Only thing I ask is that you make sure I get buried well, 'specially if we make land afore I go. Now, I took it on myself to get the purser to write down my wishes. There's more than enough to buy you out of the service and set yourself up as a fine young gentleman, and that thought makes me a happy man."

He held up his hand before Jake could speak. "No more to be said young 'un, we'll just carry on as though nothing has happened, and that's the end of it." He reached across and ruffled Jake's hair. "This won't last forever lad, in a year or so, maybe less, you'll be back with your folks and

I'd be glad if you make a mention of me and tell them that I said they should be proud of their boy." Jake welled up and leant against Joe who in turn wrapped an arm around his shoulders. There they sat in silence, no words necessary, both content in their genuine fondness for each other.

Eventually Joe began to nod, snoring softly. Jake disturbed him as he got up to leave and he waved loosely without opening his eyes. "Bye lad. Remember what I said - our secret now." Jake smiled and made for the wooden staircase but stopped with one foot still on the first step. Panic overtook him as he recognised the approaching voices as those of Croucher and Lloyd. He desperately wanted to hide, the thought of being trapped down here with those two scared him more than he liked to admit.

He slipped behind the staircase hiding amongst stored sacks of hay. The two men descended the stairs their feet inches from his face. "He's out of it the old sot. Just as well it will make things a lot easier for us." Jake's chest was hammering so hard that he felt the two thugs must surely be able to hear it! He breathed through his nose as quietly as he could, clamping his teeth together. There was a tiny gap between two of the sacks but Jake could see nothing but the wooden floor straight ahead of him.

He heard Joe call out, "What the" and suddenly, Joe's foot and stump appeared in his line of vision, he must have been pulled down flat. Joe's voice rang out, "What the fuck are you doing, let me up now. What in the Lord's name are you doing - no, no!" Joe's cries became muffled and Jake watched mesmerised as the old man's foot and wooden peg drummed and scraped on the floor then became very still. "Sit him back up and let's get out of here. Llewellyn's scrapped that bloody will he made so there'll be no-one knowing about the old bastard's stash except us. We'll be rich by the time we leave this tub. I've told our purser friend not to think of double crossing us, not if he wants to live that is."

"Christ Charlie, you're a bloody marvel."

"I know," said Charlie. "I know."

Jake sat, eyes transfixed on the scuff marks made as Joe had fought for his life, hardly able to believe the truth of what he had just witnessed. After some time, when the strength had returned to his own legs, he ventured out from his hiding place and, gathering his courage, went over to Joe who was slumped in a sitting position almost as Jake had left him, but now he was lifeless. The enormity of Croucher's crime and the nonchalant way in which it had been carried out sent Jake into shock. He staggered up the stairs and made for his quarters; India he must find India.

Chapter 11

India was really worried for his friend. Nearly two hours had passed since Jake had stumbled up to him, sweating, shaking, almost incoherent. He had traded some of the Captains roast pork for a noggin of rum and made Jake drink a fair bit of it in one go. Now he sat by his side waiting patiently to find out what was troubling his friend. Jake, relaxed by the rum, climbed from his hammock and beckoned India to follow him topside.

When they were alone he told India everything that had happened, still almost unable to believe it himself. "I need to tell the Captain. They murdered Joe and they are going to steal his money."

"Don't be an idiot. If Croucher finds out what you know, you're dead."

"But Joe is dead! They murdered him. They'll be hung. They deserve to be hung."

"Wise up turnip, that ain't the way it works. There's no proof is there? You said yourself he was ill and he looked as though he'd gone in his sleep, and who's gonna believe a runt like you over Croucher? No, keep yer mouth shut and forget it ever 'appened. Ok, so you won't get his money now but at least you'll stay alive."

Jake slept fitfully that night. Every time he closed his eyes he saw Joe's lifeless legs, sometimes they moved and he woke with a start only for the whole scene to flood back into his consciousness. He knew that everything India had said made sense but, thanks to his regular Sunday morning attendances at church he knew right from wrong; it had been drummed into him almost since birth. A grievous wrong had been done and it should be righted. Jake resolved that as soon as breakfast was finished he would seek out Mr. Bridger, explain what had happened, and ask him to tell Captain Coutts. The Captain was a remote and rather frightening figure to Jake; Mr. Bridger was more approachable and, Jake reasoned, he was obviously an officer and a gentleman and would see that Croucher got the punishment he deserved.

"Come." Jake opened the door to the wardroom with shaking hands. "What on earth are you doing here boy?"

"I have something to tell the Captain Sir, it can't wait, it's just awful."

Bridger frowned and waved Jake into the room. Jake's heart was hammering so loudly that his quavering voice sounded more high pitched than usual. His mouth was dry but eventually he related all that had happened, the relief of unburdening himself making him feel a little light headed. Bridger said nothing for quite some time, seemingly mulling over Jake's story.

"This is a very serious accusation boy. Joe is indeed dead," standing and looking down at Jake. "But your tale could be fanciful," he pursed his lips. "Leave this with me; I'll speak to the Captain but in the meantime not a word of this to anyone. Do you hear - no-one?"

"Yes Sir, thank you Sir."

In the close confines of his cabin Bridger paced up and down, hands behind his back, a worried frown creasing his brow. The door opened and Croucher slid in closing it firmly behind him. The lieutenant spat out "You bloody fool! I told you to be careful. I wish to God I'd never let you talk me into any of this; do you realise we could all be swinging from a noose any time now!" Croucher took the two paces needed to reach Bridger, grabbed him in his strong embrace and kissed him passionately silencing the lieutenant.

"Whoa now. What's got into you? I'm always careful you know that." He reached down caressing his lover's loins gratified at the instant response to his touch.

Bridger, speaking more quietly now, "One of the boys knows you killed Joe."

"Impossible."

"No, he was hiding in hay sacks behind the stairs and heard everything. He knows about the purser, the money, everything. He came asking me to tell the Captain."

Croucher was taken aback for a moment. "Which boy, who else has he told?"

"Jacob Faraday. I told him not to mention it to anyone else until the Captain has made a decision, and I don't think he will - he's too scared."

"Right, leave things to me. I'll have to get rid of Lloyd sooner than I wanted to now - can't have any loose ends. It's a shame, he's a comely lad and he keeps my mind off you." He took Bridger's face in his hands "Now don't worry, it will all be worth it. Lloyd and our friend Llewellyn will get what they deserve when they have served their purpose and we can retire together in comfort for the rest of our lives, just leave things to me." He swung Bridger round pushing him against the door. The lieutenant melted into his arms letting him unbuckle his breeches, thrusting his body forward. They made passionate love, Croucher strong and dominant, a wolfish grin as he gathered his helpless lamb to him. Bridger was putty in his hands and they both knew it.

Wilf Harris sat on the head, hands clutching his knees, gritting his teeth against the pain. He had put off going as long as he could but now he just had no choice, haemorrhoids or no. His affliction was always a source of humour to his shipmates and he cursed them, wishing that one day one or all of them would suffer the same fate. At last he had done the deed but there was no relief from the pain which had been exacerbated by the bodily function, as he knew it would. He had filled the wooden slop pail with sea water and now, shuffling into a well hidden corner, he sank his behind into the cold salty liquid sighing at the relief given. He was sitting, enjoying his moment, when he became aware of raised voices nearby.

They seemed to be coming from Lieutenant Bridger's cabin. He cocked his head to listen harder but couldn't make out anything clearly. He stood to pull up his pants but shot back down into a crouching position, wincing, as the cabin door opened and Charlie Croucher slid out peering all around before leaving. It was clear from his demeanour that he did not want to be seen. Harris, always a gossip, could not wait to get back to tell his mates what he had seen. Sol, Mel and the rest of the crew listened with interest. Why would an officer be arguing with a Bosun's mate and why would it be necessary for him to slink away not wanting to be seen. Given Croucher's proclivities, they could not help but surmise that the unthinkable might possibly be fact.

Over the next few days Jake was watchful, waiting for something to happen, perhaps to be summoned by the Captain. But day followed day and he began to wonder if he had made a serious mistake. All through poor old Joe's burial service Jake had tried to catch Lt Bridger's eye but he seemed to be avoiding him and once, when they accidentally collided, the lieutenant looked straight through him and ordered him to take a double watch as punishment for being disrespectful. Jake kept his own council as he dared not tell India what he had done. He began to feel very uneasy, his old friend had been murdered and yet no-one seemed to be taking action, it began to dawn on him that Lt Bridger was not what he seemed to be - he had lied to Jake. He had ignored his story and now seemed to have turned against him - but why!

It was Sunday again, a warm beautiful day, but Jake was so very sad. He missed his friend Joe and burned inside with anger at the injustice that had been done. He sat alone at the stern of the ship, not wanting company, alternating between wallowing in sorrow and fuming with anger at his helplessness. The sun began to fade and Jake made his way reluctantly back to his cabin, not relishing the continual banter of the other boys, nor for once, India's eternally effervescent presence.

All the boys had noticed a difference in Jake since Joe's death and put it down to his grief. Walden greeted him. "Jake! It's been real quiet here without you and Indy; we've had to put up with talking to each other."

"Where is India? I haven't seen him since mess. I thought he'd come back with you." Jake climbed into his hammock and made it clear that he was not interested in small talk.

He closed his eyes but opened them with a start when he heard Walden exclaim. "Christ, what the hell has happened to you?" Jake sat up and followed Walden's gaze to see India head down, leaning in the doorway supporting himself with one hand grasping either side of the frame. He looked up to show his badly swollen face. His lips were split, his nose had been bleeding. His eyes were sunken into his face, dark circles underlying them. He was ashen under his dark skin and beads of perspiration were mixing with dried blood and hanging in a drooling mess from his chin.

Jake shot down from his hammock and ran to help his

friend. He slid under one arm and called Walden to support India's other side and between them they lifted him into his hammock. Jake gently brushed the hair from India's forehead and noticed that it was cold and clammy. "Can someone get a bucket of water and a cloth?" One of the lads appeared almost instantly with both and Jake began gingerly to clean the poor bruised face. He spoke softly crooning as his mother had often done to him on his sick bed, but there was no response from India, he just stared at Jake with the frightened, pained eyes of a wounded animal, tears welling and falling silently. Jake instinctively knew what had happened. He leant close to India's ear and whispered, "Was it Croucher?" India's eyes closed, his long dark lashes sodden, tears still coursing down his face.

Jake was incandescent with rage. "I'm going to get the doc." He stormed through the ship, racing through the gun decks on his way down to the surgeon's quarters.

"Whoa there," Sol grabbed his arm, "where are you tearing off to son?"

"Let me go! India's been hurt! His face is all broken and his clothes are all bloody. I've got to find Mr. Cameron."

"A few minutes won't hurt son, I'll come with you if you like but just tell me what's happened."

Jake, gulping down air and trying to control his temper let it all out. "It's Joe see, he didn't just die, Croucher and Billy Lloyd, they killed him."

"That's quite a thing to accuse a body of, boy; why would you say that?"

"Because I was there with Joe but I hid when I heard them coming down the stairs. I hate Croucher; he is a dreadful sinner you know. I hid under the stairs in the hay bales and they smothered Joe, I heard him cry out but I was too scared to help him; they just smothered him and left him dead. They want his money. I heard them say that the purser had torn up his will and they would take his money and they've done it before! He was going to leave it to me see. I told Lt Bridger and he promised me he would tell the Captain and it would all be sorted out but he didn't and now India has been beaten by Croucher and he needs help."

Sol's brow furrowed as he listened to Jake's tirade. "You must believe me, I don't lie, I don't know what to do - I must help India because it's my fault he's hurt, I told him see, I told him and he said we should keep it to ourselves but I went and told Bridger and now India is real hurt, and it's all my fault." Jake, could not hold back the tears and began sobbing uncontrollably. Sol glanced around at his ship mates. It all began to make sense. Several members of the crew had met an untimely death or simply disappeared, indeed that was why young Jake and the others had been pressed. He signalled them to say nothing.

"Right lad, I said I'd come with you, we'll get Mr. Cameron to take a look but let me do the talking." Jake looked up at Sol through tear filled eyes. "Do you trust me lad?" Jake nodded. Sol put a hand on his shoulder "Get those tears under control boy, and we'll go."

They found Ian Cameron in the process of extracting a tooth. After a few seconds of grunting and groaning issuing from the poor soul trapped under one of his knees, the surgeon stood and waved the offending brown nugget clasped in his pliers in his patients face; a bicuspid that had once been strong and creamy white, now just a brown shard. "That's good, give your mouth a good rinse with rum and don't eat anything on that side for a day or two." He patted the poor, white faced, crewman on the knee then

turned to Sol and Jake. "Sol, how are you? Not needing my
services I hope."

"No but we have a lad up with the boys and Jake here
says he's hurt quite bad. We were hoping that you could
come along and see to him now."

Ian Cameron was a tall willowy man who had
developed a stoop, probably from spending most of his
working life in the cramped conditions aboard ship. Jake
thought that at one time he must have been a handsome
man. He had neat, regular features and clear blue eyes, the
vestiges of his youth just about discernible. The eyes were
the only colour in his gaunt pale face which seemed to
bleed into his white, scraped back hair, no obvious
delineation between the two. In his youth his black widows
peak had been a distinctive feature but now it was almost
indiscernible - white on white. "Give me a short while and
I'll be along. Just let me gather some things together." Sol
nodded and they left.

Cameron sat for a while looking around his domain. He
still missed his Mary so much. She had served at his side
for most of their married life through thick and thin, each of
them doing what they could for the wounded. He
removing limbs, stitching wounds, she tending the dying,
dressing wounds, comforting and relieving pain where
possible. She had been dead over two years now but the
aching emptiness he felt without her never left him. He
stood up sighing, gathered a few implements and
bandaging and made his way to the boys' cabin.

He found Jake and Sol wiping India's face with a damp
cloth. They stepped aside to let him tend to the patient. The
boy's face was indeed a mess but no bones had been broken
as far as he could see and the splits in the skin were not
deep enough to warrant sutures. The worrying thing was

the boy's colour and clammy skin.

"Where do you hurt lad?" There was no response. He lifted India and removed his shirt - just bruising. He noted the buttons on India's trousers had been torn off and they were stiff with blood. His heart sank, he knew what ailed the poor lad; he was not the first on this God forsaken ship. He looked at Sol. "I need to get his breeches off and examine the boy."

"No" shouted India. "No."

He bent down whispering, "Don't be afraid I won't hurt you."

"Sol, and you lad" pointing to Walden, the tallest boy there. "I want you to stand either side of this hammock and hold up a blanket - give us some privacy."

Sandwiched between the two blankets, he gently eased down India's trousers and lifted him onto his side. He found, as he knew he would, that the boy had been sodomised, and had sustained a good deal of damage during the process. The flesh was badly torn and the boy was still bleeding from internal injuries "Jake, go to my cabin. You'll find a chest of drawers and in the top left you'll find a green glass jar. Fetch it as quick as you can but be careful now, it's very precious."

It was one of the last of Mary's salves. She had used it to sooth many a wound and right now it was the only thing he had that might bring the boy a little comfort. He stroked India's forehead. "I'm just going to swab you down a bit lad then I've some soothing ointment for you." He cleansed the boy as best he could and placed a pad under him to catch any seepage. He applied the salve fetched by Jake, covered him, and then he turned to Sol who was now able to put down the blanket screen. "I'll speak with you outside."

They stood together out of anyone's hearing. "The boy's been buggered and he looks pretty bad to me. Whoever did this deserves to be hanged."

"I think we know who did it, don't we?" said Sol "and if the boy survives they'll want to shut his mouth for good. This is a rum do and no mistake. Look, best you say nothing other than he's taken a beating. I need to talk this over with the others. Something needs sorting but how to do it without landing us all in the brig, that's the thing. Anyway Ian, thank you for helping - keep an eye on the boy will you. Just his condition, that is. Don't want you mixed up in anything else."

Ian patted Sol on his shoulder, nodded and turned to go, "I'll see how he is tomorrow - I'll do my best."

At six bells the next morning the cry went out to rig for action - another drill. All the boys jumped to, folding their hammocks into the side netting, stowing away everything not fixed down. India looked awful, he tried to sit but Jake pushed him down. "Stay there Indy. I'll find Henson and tell him you're sick." Jake scurried out bumping into the very man. He stopped briefly to explain that India was too ill to work today then ran full tilt to the magazine store to collect his powder. When he got to the gun deck all was squared away and his crew had run out their gun, but he was shocked to see India, pale as a ghost, still in stained pants struggling to carry out the scuttle-but to fetch water. "What are you doing? Why are you up?" Without waiting for a reply, and far exceeding his authority, he ran to find Henson again - there must be some mistake - he must have misunderstood.

He found Henson who just shrugged arms out, palms up. "I did report but Lt Bridger said there were to be no exceptions and he must carry out the drill." All the anger and exasperation Jake had stored up over the last few days exploded in his head and, before anyone could stop him, he was on the quarter deck shouting at Lt. Bridger, Captain Coutts looking on stunned.

"How dare you make India work when he's so ill? You set Croucher on him didn't you? I told you all about what he had done to Joe, but you don't care. I thought you were a good person but" turning and pointing to Croucher, "you are just as bad as him. "I'm…"

Before Jake could utter another word Bridger dealt him a stunning blow and knocked him to the floor. He turned to the captain. "With your permission Sir I would have this boy and his accomplice flogged. They are dishonest, thieving, troublemakers and we cannot let such rogues go unpunished." The Captain, who had very little interest in his crew at the best of times, had been shocked at the boys unmitigated display of rudeness and lack of discipline, nodded his consent and retired to his day cabin to obsess once more on the length of time it would take to catch up with the fleet.

Lt Bridger, crimson faced, shouted loud enough for all to hear. "Croucher put this wretch and his half breed accomplice in the brig. Nothing but biscuits and water for them until tomorrow morning, when they will both receive five lashes."

"Aye Sir, it will be a pleasure." Croucher yanked Jake up from the deck and, holding him with one arm bent behind his back, forced him at a pace below decks and thrust him into the brig. "Now I'm going for your little mate. You should have kept your big mouth shut boy; you are both done for now - I'll see to that." Giving Jake the most venomous look imaginable, he slammed the door shut.

News of the incident between Jake and Lt. Bridger had

swept around the ship like wildfire. All eyes were on Lloyd as he dragged India, crying out in pain, away to join Jake in the brig. The drill was completed in relative silence. Nearly every man on the gun deck had heard about Joe's death and India's beating and, given what they knew about Croucher, to a man they believed Jake.

Chapter 12

At eleven the next morning the entire crew assembled on deck under a gunmetal grey sky to witness the punishment. The sea was running high, a brisk wind tugging at the sails, spray from the bows soaking most of those present. The two boys were escorted on deck by Croucher and Lloyd, India stumbling, having difficulty walking. When the crew saw the cat o nine tails, a murmur of unease went through the men. Cats were used on men; boys were caned, but here was that cruel bastard flexing a Cat. The Captain addressed the company, his voice being carried away by the wind so that most of what he said went unheard. When he had finished his rant, he pointed to India, "Him first Mr. Croucher, five lashes." Croucher and Lloyd manhandled India and proceeded to tie him to a cannon, pushing him over the barrel so that his back and rump were exposed.

Ian Cameron stepped out from the ranks "Sir, this boy is too ill to take a lashing. A cane would be too much for him as he is, but the Cat could kill him. Please Sir, may I request that his punishment is postponed until he recovers from his present injuries."

"You can request it Sir by all means but your request will not be granted. Now step back into the ranks before I have you flogged too."

Cameron was astounded; everyone could see the boy was almost dead on his feet. He started to protest but Sol stepped up behind him and held his arm.

"It's no use Ian, we know yon man is not quite sound and it won't do the boy, or none of us, any good if you end up sick and ailing."

Cameron spoke out once again, loudly, so that all could hear. "Then I request that my objection be put in the log.

This boy is not fit for punishment and if it goes ahead I fear he may lose his life."

The Captain stared at his surgeon. "As you wish, Mr. Cameron! Now, if you don't mind we will get on with it." Just as the Captain was about to signal the punishment to begin, Mr. Pointer, the ship's first officer approached.

"Sir, do I have your permission to lower the main sails, it looks as though we are running into foul weather and..."

The Captain, veins standing out on his forehead, spittle at the sides of his mouth rounded on his number one, "No! You do not have permission! My orders are to catch up with the fleet at the very earliest, and that is what we do in this man's navy Mr. Pointer - we follow orders." He waved an arm skywards. "This is only a squall man. We'll make good use of it and run with the wind. Full sail ahead - that is an order."

"Aye Sir, but I must protest and I wish also that my request and your denial of it be logged. I fear for our safety if we do not haul sail now. The strain on the timbers will be too great; she'll open up and we'll be done for."

The Captain, fists clenched, eyes popping, competing with the ever increasing noise of the wind shouted, "How dare you question my judgment man; your insolence will go down in the log along with my request for your Court-Martial. As from this moment you are relieved of all duties." The first officer turned on his heel looking at the menacing banks of cumulus, inwardly cursing the Captain - he was convinced now that the man had lost his senses.

When India had been secured, at a signal from the Captain Croucher raised the cat and brought it down onto the boy's bare back as hard as he could. India gave one long, drawn out cry, then mercifully fainted, his head lolling to one side, his body jerking with each blow that his torturer applied with obvious enthusiasm. A low murmur went around the assembly, every man jack seething at the cruelty and injustice they were witnessing. Jake, afraid of what he was about to endure, could not stop the tears falling for himself and for his dear friend. The ship was pitching and rolling deeper, the wind gathering strength and gusting, making it difficult for the crew to hold ranks. The lanyards were keening as they strained taught, holding firm the sails now trying to break free.

India was untied and Ian Cameron rushed to gather up the boy. Scarcely able to control his anger he addressed the Captain, "Permission to take the lad below - Sir." Without waiting for any acknowledgement he turned sharply on his heel and staggered towards the hatch to below decks; great spots of icy rain beginning to fall.

The sudden deluge caught everyone by surprise and within seconds the sea had become a broiling black mass washing across the deck, men slipping, grasping desperately for a hold as the ship heeled over badly. A huge clap of ear-splitting thunder filled the air; the horizon disappeared; the sky and the sea were now one solid curtain of oppressive blackness cut through now and again by a spear of jagged lightning. Without waiting for a signal the crew disbursed, every man on board going to his station. Sol grabbed Jakes arm and shouted into his ear, "Get below lad, get to your cabin and batten down."

Jake did not need telling twice. He made his way to the boys' cabin, all the time terrified that he would be washed overboard. As he turned to close the hatch a spear of lightning lit up the sky so that he could see those poor topmen climbing the rigging frenziedly trying to take in the sails, and as he watched he saw one man fall onto the deck, another caught in the rigging was swinging by one leg.

Hanging onto the stairs he saw the bow of the ship rising up pointing to the heavens, then saw it smashed back down by the great black fist of a monstrous wave. All the boys were trying to brace themselves against the violent motion of the ship but were being tossed around like skittles in an alley.

The Huron groaned and screamed as the treacherous water worked to pry her open with its long black tentacles, trying to search out and devour all life on board. Jake had never been so scared. All that stood between him and the fearful, black depths were the ships timbers which were being tortured and battered with hammer blows and must surely split asunder. There was an occasional plea to the Lord from someone to save them but most of the boys were petrified and silent, just waiting for the sea to rush in and take them. Many were vomiting uncontrollably but no-one cared - they were doomed.

The storm raged seemingly for hours before gradually the ships movements became less violent. The howling wind quietened and The Huron was once more on an even keel; the seas were still running high but the storm was abating. Jake waded through the foul smelling sea water that was now inches deep in their cabin and warily opened the cabin door looking out onto the detritus strewn deck.

One by one the boys emerged wide eyed and gasping at the scene of devastation that greeted them. The Main and Mizzen masts were broken, sails hanging uselessly on broken spars, rigging draped across the deck like giant lacework. One of the topmen lay on the deck, his limbs twisted into grotesque shapes, his head a pulpy bloody mess. The poor devil Jake had seen when the storm hit was still swinging from his one snared leg. The wind had died away leaving an eerie silence broken only by the low murmuring of the crew as they too took in the destruction that the storm had wrought.

Mr. Pointer was the first officer on the scene, he was obviously shaken and took a few moments to assess the situation and galvanise the crew into action. He ordered that the rigger be cut down and taken below to the medic along with his dead companion and anyone else who had been injured. All hands were set to clearing the decks, taking down the shredded sails and broken spars and manhandling the broken masts onto the deck as best they could. He ordered Midshipmen Henson and Stiles to take stock of all damage below decks and report back to him. It was obvious to all that The Huron was badly damaged and virtually powerless.

As the deck came alive with the movement of so many men, the Captain appeared. Pointer turned to him to report action taken to secure the ship so far but the Captain raised his hand to silence him. "Mr. Pointer, I seem to remember you were relieved of all duties. Now, get out of my sight; from now on you are under arrest." Turning to Lt Bridger. "Escort this man back to his cabin." The lieutenant looked uncertain. "You heard what I said. He is under arrest pending his Court- Martial."

Bridger nodded "Yes Sir." He signalled to Croucher and Lloyd who each took an arm and frog marched the protesting first officer away.

The Captain continued, "I want all tradesmen in my cabin within the hour with full reports of any damage, along with estimates for the time it will take to carry out repairs." He turned and bent to address the four men kneeling over their fallen shipmates and hissed "Get this mess cleared up and out of my sight and make sure the deck is swabbed. I want to be able to eat my dinner from it." Four pairs of hate-filled eyes stared after the Captain as he strode back to his cabin.

Chapter 13

The sky brightened, the sea calmed and the ship was a hive of industry so that everyone was taken by surprise when they heard the watch cry, "Sail Ho to the east."

Lt Bridger looking eastward felt his heart sink, "Call the Captain, we have a French frigate bearing down on us."

To his fellow officer, "Of all the fucking bad luck. The bastard will be on us within the hour and we are just sitting ducks, we'd better run up the white flag."

Hector Coutts strode onto the quarter deck raising his eye glass. Nodding to himself and smiling he ordered Bridger to give the order to rig for action. "But Sir, it would be suicide to take on an armed frigate in the state we are in. We have no power, no manoeuvrability, we're just sitting ducks. The only chance we have of fighting is if they try to board us."

An irate Captain Coutts spat his words at Bridger. "Give the order to rig for action or by heaven I will have you flogged."

The lieutenant was taken aback by the ferocity of Coutt's threat and was afraid. He knew then that his Captain truly was insane.

The order was given and every man went to his station but apart from the grinding of the guns the ship was silent. Every man aboard knew they were helpless, wallowing, waiting to be blown out of the water. Sol put a hand on Jake's shoulder. "Never thought I'd say it young 'un but we have to surrender. What's that mad man playing at? We ain't got a cat in hell's chance." The whole of the gun deck muttered agreement, all they could do was pray that he would come to his senses. The minutes ticked by in complete silence, every man hoping that they would not be their last.

After some time they heard the familiar whoosh of an approaching missile and the far end of the gun deck exploded in a maelstrom of broken timber; immediately men began to scream and for the second time in a few short hours Jake feared for his life. He looked round for India, for some crumb of comfort, but then remembered that his friend was already close to death, but at least he was not here in this hell hole. Second officer Barton gave the order for all guns on the starboard side to fire, but there was no target, try as he might, Sol could see nothing but open water. The cannons were fired re-coiled and pushed back into position just as another salvo burst onto the gun deck taking Wilf Harris's gun with it and turning his crew into mush.

Jake ran off to gather more powder and, wanting to help, he ran onto the deck trying to get a sight of the enemy. He found himself shouting with frustration. The frigate was firing at will from an angle of forty five degrees, thereby avoiding a broadside attack from The Huron which was unable to manoeuvre and was helpless. What on earth was the Captain doing? Sol had been right; they had no chance, why did the Captain not surrender? Once he had collected his powder, he made his way back to his gun crew but it was impossible to tell Sol what he had seen, the noise was deafening and everyone was totally focused on the job in hand.

On his next errand, unable to contain himself Jake once again went on deck, the frigate was maintaining her position - they were done for, but as he watched he saw her main mast break in two, toppling down onto the deck, taking the main sail with it. How could that be, they were not in a position to reach such a target. As he watched part of the frigate's gunwale was blown away. He saw a cannon and men fall into the water below, and became aware of cheering - everyone on deck was cheering! The Huron's guns became silent as the frigate began to heave to, turning to take on their new attacker.

When she turned stern on, Jake was able to see their ally in full sail moving to attack the now disabled frigate. As she passed the French ship, she opened fire hitting the powder magazine. Jake watched, mouth open, as the aft of the ship disintegrated scattering debris for hundreds of yards, some of it glancing off The Huron. He crouched below the gunwale until the bombardment stopped, peering warily over the side just in time to see the remains of the once magnificent French ship disappear beneath the waves. He could hear the cries of men in the water and, although they were his enemies, he felt sick at heart that he did not have the power to help them.

The cheering continued and Jake ran down to tell Sol what he had seen. The gun deck was full of the smell of cordite and choking smoke. There was another smell too, the blood and guts of Wilf Harris and all the other poor souls who had paid the price for their Captains' folly. Jake had been fond of old Wilf. He was so sad and right then he longed for Ma, Pa and home; he so wanted to go back to them, to get away from this hellish world that he had been forced into. Sol spoke "Well done lad. You did real well for your first time in battle, although it were no battle, we were pissing in the wind and all we've got to show for it are dead shipmates; good men all of 'em."

All those that were able made their way topside to get a better view of their saviour, lining the deck to cheer her in. The senior offices were on the Poop deck scanning the approaching vessel. The Captain spoke to Officer Barton,

"What is she Barton? What flag is she flying?"

"She looks like a Brigantine Sir, but I can't see any flag. She's put down a couple of dinghies, looks as though they are hauling in some of the poor devils in the water." Impatiently the Captain snatched the glass from Barton's hand and watched as those men still alive in the water were hauled into the dinghies, small cheers from brother mariners going up as each man was rescued.

Suddenly the Captain stiffened. "She's making way now and by God! She's run up the Jolly Roger! She's a bloody privateer!" All could now see the black flag bearing a skull and crossbones; the cheering died down, everyone wondering what on earth was going to happen now. Blustering and wild eyed, Captain Coutts gave the order once again to rig for action, but this time the whole crew stood their ground, no one moving. He turned on Officer Barton "Damn it man, I gave an order! Now – get these low lives to man their guns and rig for action!"

A loud cry of protest went up as Sol Benson stepped forward. Since word had got round of old Joe being murdered for his money, and India being raped and flogged, a mutinous mood smouldered around the ship. Men had huddled in small groups readying themselves for more trouble and all had agreed that Sol, a natural leader of men, be elected to act as their spokesman if and when, as now, the need arose. Sol raised his voice to address the assembled crowd. "Well lads, do we carry on obeying this madman or do we do what's right and sensible?" At Sol's words, all the officers present gathered round their Captain, unsheathing their swords, pistols at the ready.

Sol spoke directly to them "Put down your arms gentlemen, you are greatly outnumbered and we mean you no harm, we want no more senseless killing, but the whole crew is agreed and," raising his voice and pointing to the Captain, "we will not serve under that madman any longer. We don't want to mutiny or to take over the ship; we just want someone else in charge. You all know men have died needlessly because of him and what we want is for Mr. Pointer to be released to take command and that is what is going to happen whether you agree to it or not - we want no more bloodshed."

He paused gauging their reaction. Swords were returned to their scabbards and third officer Pritchard spoke. "I, er, we cannot condone your actions but, under the circumstances, we have to agree that we consider Captain Coutts has made errors of judgment which might indicate that he is, well, not able to act in the best interest of The Huron and her crew, and that certainly Mr. Pointer, being second in command, should be released forthwith."

On hearing this, the Captain turned to Pritchard and struck him across the face. "I'll have you all hanged for this. On this ship my word is law, I am God – I'll have you all hanged – do you hear – my ship, I am God."

Pritchard nodded to two of the burliest crew. "Take Mr. Coutts to his cabin and remain on guard. He is not to be released."

With the Captain gone Sol continued "With your permission, Sir, the lads think we should surrender to yon vessel before we suffer the same fate as the French. I don't think they will attack us as they came to our aid didn't they, and as young Jake here has pointed out, they rescued all the Frenchies in the water, but we'd best let them know that we don't intend to fight quick as we can."

"Aye," said Pritchard, "it's a sad day indeed that a ship of the line surrenders to anyone, especially thieving privateers, but in view of our situation it may be wise to live to fight another day." Turning to the two nearest midshipmen he told them to release Mr. Pointer from his cabin, inform him of all that had occurred, and fetch him to join them on deck. Then speaking out so that all could hear he continued, "Mr. Pointer is a fine sailor and we," casting his hand around the assembled officers, "would be happy to serve under him, and to follow any orders that he sees fit to give." He shook his head ruefully "No doubt there is going to be a great deal of explaining to do when we reach the fleet, but that is to worry about on another day. Now, the sooner we run up that white flag the better it seems to me - see to it Mr. Henshaw."

....

Charlie Croucher slowly melted away from the assembled men, signalling Lloyd to follow. When they were hidden from view and out of earshot Lloyd whispered "What do you want? Where're you off too?"

"Can't you see the way it's going you idiot? They've locked the Captain up and it won't be long afore they start lookin for us and asking questions. We've got to shut those kids up or we're done for. Cameron is on deck out the way so we can get one little bastard in his cabin and get rid of 'im for starters." Frowning, although uncertain of his lover's reasoning, Lloyd as ever, followed his lead as they went below and crept into the surgeon's cabin.

India lay on a pallet on the floor, bathed in sweat, deathly pale under his olive skin. Croucher gathered the boy up and whispered to Lloyd, "you go ahead and make sure the coast is clear - if you hear anyone coming, for Christ's sake let me know."

"Where are we taking him?"

"He's goin over the side so just make sure you lead us to

a spot where there ain't no-one, should be ok while they are all forward arguing the toss." The two men made their way stealthily to the starboard gunwale. They crouched down hidden from view behind one of the silent deck guns.

Looking around to check that the coast was clear Croucher leapt up, and in one fluid movement tossed India over the side and joined Lloyd back in their hiding place. Not hearing the splash that he had anticipated he stood and casually leant over the side to see that the boy had landed on a large piece of planking which must have come from the stricken French frigate. "Bollocks!" At Croucher's exclamation Lloyd joined him.

"Oh Christ he ain't gone under."

"I can see that you bloody idiot, I'll just have to hope he drifts off while everyone is taken up with yon new ship. See, it's near enough close to boarding us."

Lloyd turned to watch the approaching vessel and as he did so he felt a hard blow at the base of his spine, then another. He stumbled forward propelled by the momentum of the blows, arms scrabbling to reach the handle of the deeply embedded knife. Using this momentum Croucher heaved his erstwhile lover over the side and watched as he disappeared beneath the dark waters. His cruel mouth twisted into a smile, "Two down, one to go; shame about my stiletto though." He paused for a minute or two then, making sure no-one noticed his approach, he gradually mingled with the crew, feigning interest in the approach of the unknown craft.

Chapter 14

Lord Henry Throgmorton (Harry to his friends,) studied the stricken man-of-war as they nudged closer. Her hull was damaged just above the water line, two masts down, sails ripped to shreds and the wheel enmeshed in rigging. She was indeed crippled, almost beyond repair he suspected. He stood on the main deck and raised his voice to address the main body of his crew. "Okay lads, cutlasses and muskets at the ready. When we," acknowledging the four men standing alongside him, "go aboard, I want you to be ready for trouble. I'm not expecting any but you know what to do if they cut up rough." The Catherine nudged up alongside The Huron and the two ships were lashed together. "Lay the ramp if you please Mr. Stiles." Turning to his small boarding party "Gentlemen, shall we?"

Jake and the rest of the crew stared at The Catherine open mouthed. There were small brightly coloured pennants and ribbons fixed to the masts, plants in coloured tubs scattered around the deck, several dogs running around and barking, and the crew lined up to face them were dressed in all manner of strange clothes presenting a riot of colour. The whole spectacle reminded Jake of the summer fairs that Ma and Pa had taken him to, once in a while. The only reminders that the ship was not some sort of floating carnival were the weapons that every man aboard her brandished for all to see, and the black flag billowing above.

All on board The Huron watched silently as a wooden ramp was erected allowing access from The Catherine to the taller ship and a small group of men, led by Harry Throgmorton, climbed it and leapt aboard. If The Catherine had been a revelation, then her Captain and his party were even more so. He was a tall muscular man, with blonde hair that curled around his shoulders. He was dressed in a shirt and hose that were the same cornflower blue as his eyes. The shirt was made of some soft flowing material and had sleeves that billowed out before being gathered in around his wrists. It was open to his narrow waist and around his neck he had a heavy gold chain upon which hung a small key. He wore a black wide-brimmed hat with a huge white feather the like of which Jake had never seen. He was reminded of a picture he had once seen at the market and the seller had told him it was called, Cavaliers on Horseback. He was fascinated and immediately drawn to this handsome stranger. For the first time since being pressed, his spirits lifted; he had no idea why, they just did.

The rest of the party were equally fascinating but in different ways. Two of the men were as tall as their leader, one with the blackest skin Jake had ever seen, the other with nothing to mark him out especially save for his knee high snake skin boots. The other two made Jake shrink back to peer over Walden's shoulder. One appeared as a normal man to the waist down but his legs were no longer than Jake's arm, consequently his whole frame reached only to the elbow of his leader. The other had the face of the devil. It seemed to have been squashed from both sides so that his forehead, nose and chin were like the prow of a ship, and his eyes were uneven in his face, one being half an inch or so lower than the other, both drooping to expose large amounts of white. His yellow hair on his almost bald head was sparse and straight, very much like the strands of hemp Jake had been taught to weave into ropes.

The leading stranger removed his hat setting his golden hair free to blow in the slight breeze, and bowed to the group of officers now lead by Mr. Pointer. In a surprisingly refined accent he spoke. "Good day to you gentlemen, Henry Throgmorton, captain of The Catherine at your service. My crew and I are pleased to have been of assistance to you." Addressing Pointer, "I trust Sir that we can be assured of your good intentions and that my crew is in no danger."

Pointer totally ill at ease and finding it hard to speak, shook his head. "No, no danger. Er, we are indebted to you Sir for coming to our assistance in our hour of need."

"My pleasure old chap; wasn't a fair fight was it? Now, may my friends here join you and your fellow officers to discuss how events should unfold from here? Perhaps we could adjourn to the wardroom."

Pointer, looking totally bemused nodded, "this way gentlemen."

Throgmorton waved the small group on and before following them, turned to address the crew of The Huron. "Gentlemen, we have the word of your captain that you will not attack us but just as a precaution," he extended an arm towards his ship "as you will see we have snipers in the rigging and all my crew are well armed. They have orders to shoot the first man who looks even remotely unfriendly, so please bear with us until we have conferred with your captain." While he was speaking two of his men began to roll two small barrels up the ramp joining the two ships and lower them onto Huron's deck. He extended an arm toward the kegs. "May I suggest that you help yourselves to a little grog with my compliments?" With that he replaced his hat and joined the small party that had gone on ahead.

Every man on board The Huron joined in the queue for grog. They had all heard tales that pirates were cut throats and villains who ravaged women and killed children but so far what they were experiencing could not be further from the truth. There was no need for lookouts, no need for a helmsman. Their ship was tethered to The Catherine and she had complete control. Despite the curious circumstances and the dire straits they had been in so recently there was now a real sense of relief amongst the crew and low murmurings of conversation gradually gave way to laughter and merriment both previously virtually unknown on The Huron. Jake, Walden and the boys all had their share and they sat around on deck marvelling at the strange ship Catherine and this new turn of events. Buoyed up by the grog they began to call out and wave across the gap, and laughed amongst themselves when their calls were answered.

Jake was enjoying the good humoured camaraderie when he saw Cameron hurry across to Sol and several of the gun crew and watched, his mood changing, as they fell into earnest discussion. India sprang to his mind - was he worse? He hurried across to the huddle "Mr. Cameron what is it? Is India Ok? He's not worse is he?"

Cameron put his hand on Jake's shoulder "I can't find him Jake, he's gone. I moved him into my cabin to make way for the wounded and I've just been down to check on him and he's not there. I've looked everywhere but he's just gone. His pallet is there, his blanket, but not him – he's vanished."

Jake's heart lurched making it difficult for him to breath. He knew something bad had happened to Indy. He looked about him wildly to find Croucher's eyes boring into his, a knowing smirk on his face. He knew then. "He's killed him, that bastard has killed Indy." Jake pulled free of Cameron and ran head down, blinded with rage; he wanted to kill the bastard, to smash him to a pulp.

Croucher sidestepped laughing as the boy rushed at him, kicking his backside as he passed. Jake collided hard with the gunwale but undeterred was about to attack again when a shot rang out from one of Catherine's snipers and the deck splintered a few inches from Croucher's foot. Taken off guard the big man had no time to stop Ginger and Jonjo pinioning his arms behind him. Sol grabbed his shirt and spat into his face. "You cock sucking piece of shit; if we don't find the boy you are a dead man; you and that half baked bastard Lloyd. We won't wait for a judge and jury. You deserve to hang ten times over but we'll be content with just the once, slowly. There's no escape Croucher, if the boy don't show up you die."

Croucher, shaken, shrugged his arms free. Smiling, he swaggered off, on the outside full of bravado, but inside he knew the game was up; his only chance was to shut that bloody kid up and hide behind Bridger.

They were still restraining Jake when the two groups emerged from their parley in the wardroom. Throgmorton spoke "Hello, what's this? Have we trouble in the ranks? Aren't you a little small to be taking on all and sundry?"

Sol spoke up "He's just found out his best friend has died Sir, and he's railing agin it. He'll settle down in a while."

"Oh dear poor lad! I have invited your Mr. Pointer and his officers to supper on The Catherine tonight. Why don't you come and bring the boy – we'll try to cheer him up." Sol was lost for words and looked at Mr. Pointer for a lead, this was most awkward.

Harry, knowing full well that his invitation crossed the boundaries of ship's etiquette, took charge. "I'm sure Mr. Pointer has no objection, have you dear chap?"

Pointer stuttered "but, but these are…"

"'Nobodies,' I know. But tell me Mr. Pointer, if a person is always treated as a 'nobody' how can he ever become a 'somebody'?" Once again unsure of what to say, Pointer just shrugged his shoulders. "Excellent, we will expect you aboard in four hours from now, around sundown." Turning to his own party, Throgmorton continued, "Come gentlemen, we will away and make preparations for our guests." The small group climbed onto the plank, boarding The Catherine without a backward glance.

Shaking off his reverie, Mr. Pointer climbed onto the quarter deck to address the crew who were now deathly quiet. "All hands – where to begin - this is the situation. The captain of The Catherine has agreed to escort us to the nearest port in Bermuda where we can set about repairing The Huron. They will have to tow us as we are virtually powerless so we will be at their mercy for nigh on two weeks. In return for their assistance we have had to agree to their taking all the gold on board, which of course, includes all your prize money and pay." At that a roar went up. Pointer held up his hands for silence.

"As soon as we are able we will continue on to join the fleet as intended and I can promise you that in due course, you will all receive the money that you are due. This whole catastrophe is none of your doing and I will make sure that the Admiralty knows how highly I regard you as a crew. We may even get some reward for sinking the French frigate and saving our ship as Mr. Throgmorton has generously assured me that he is happy for his part in the proceedings to be altered to suit our case. Now gentlemen we need to pray for benign weather; with the damage to our hull, anything but calm water and we will be done for, with or without The Catherine."

With the sun setting all those officers not on duty

boarded The Catherine, Sol and Jake trailing behind. They were escorted below decks and ushered through a door leading from the gun deck into a room that seemed to Jake to be magical. Candles in wall brackets gave the room a golden glow and between the brackets were draped beautiful cloths of all colours that glistened in the warm light. There was a long table which also had a golden cloth running down the centre upon which were bowls containing strange fruits, the only ones that Jake recognized being apples. There were platters and goblets arranged at intervals down either side, each platter adjacent to ornate wooden chairs. There was an aroma coming up from the galley which made Jake's mouth water, he looked up at Sol, both of them wide eyed.

Henry Throgmorton waved them in. "Ah, Gentlemen, welcome. We trust you will enjoy The Catherine's hospitality. We will make the most of this night as our journey commences tomorrow and as The Catherine is somewhat smaller than The Huron, it will not be without its hazards. Please, sit gentlemen." He pointed to Sol. "You and the boy come sit either side of me so that we can get acquainted."

Their host remained standing, hands on the table. "I would like to raise just a couple of issues gentlemen." He had everyone's undivided attention. "I have heard myself and my crew referred to as pirates on several occasions and I feel the need to rectify this misconception. My comrades and I operate outside the law 'tis true, and we fly the black flag 'tis true, but there our resemblance to such loose living, deviant cut-throats ends. We are more - you could say - seafaring opportunists. We are all good men and true but sadly most of us a have, in one way or another, been ill-served by the societies into which we were born;

circumstances forcing us into our present occupation. Given a choice we would not have chosen such a life as this, but there you are. Secondly, we, on board The Catherine have no need of officers as each man on this vessel is equal to the next, therefore we address each other by name and not rank. I am indeed the leader, but by consent only, therefore please feel free to adopt our custom and address us all by our given names." As he spoke steaming bowls of soup were placed on the table. He held out an arm "Enjoy!"

The initial tension eased as the wine began to flow, so that before long everyone at the table was deep in conversation with their counterparts, learning about and being fascinated by each other's life experiences. Jake and Sol found it easy to talk to Harry (call me Hal) and, as the wine loosened their tongues, told the tales of their lives so far. Jake relating everything from the night that Eli turned up on that fateful night, to Croucher having murdered Indy. Sol, who had not enjoyed himself so much since he could not remember, admitted for the first time that he had been jilted by his girl as soon as he had lost his money. Jake, remembering despite the wine, not to let on that he already knew.

Jake and Sol had never known that such food existed. Every course was as delicious as the last and there were oohs and aahs of delight as each new dish was tasted. After several courses Jake could hardly move, he was content and happy and folding his arms on the table, fell asleep. Seeing that Jake was beyond hearing, Harry spoke quietly to Sol. "From what you have both said, this Croucher is a very bad lot, and it seems to me that it would be very much in his interest to dispose of Jake here; without him there is no case to answer. If the fellow were innocent he would have no need to fear the accusations of two boys, but now that one has mysteriously disappeared I am inclined to believe he has something to hide. Unfortunately your Mr. Pointer can take no action against these men, especially the two ships officers, as there is no actual proof of any wrongdoing."

Sol, trying to clear his mind, "You're right Hal, the whole ship's crew knows Croucher is a thieving, murdering bastard but he's clever, so all we can think of is getting rid of him ourselves." Harry sat back in his chair, fingers stroking his chin.

"He's not worth hanging for Sol. You are too good a man to be punished in any way because of the likes of him. Best leave it to fate," he said tapping his nose. "Men like that always meet with a bad end – if you know what I mean." He paused, "Little Jake is in real danger; I think it best that he stays aboard The Catherine at least until we reach port. I'll inform Mr. Pointer before you leave."

The next morning a very different mood hung over The Huron, now very sombre after the revelry of the night before. Eleven men had been killed and several wounded during their futile encounter with the ill-fated French frigate. The whole crew stood to attention silently as Captain Pointer led the service committing their comrades to the deep. All smiled fondly when it came to Wilf Harris when some wag pointed out that at least now he would have no more trouble from his piles. When all was done the men dispersed quietly, reflecting on their dead pals and the good luck that had kept them from meeting the same fate. Sol was glad that Jake had not witnessed the burials; life had been hard enough for the boy as it was.

Chapter 15

A full moon cast a shaft of soft light across smooth glassy water illuminating a raft of driftwood rising and falling on the slowly undulating sea, and the small figure that lay prone upon it. The raft rocked gently upon the quiet waters; a small ripple occasionally washing over it, caressing the unconscious boy with cool unguent fingers, soothing sun scorched skin.

India had lain, for the most part unconscious, on the mercifully calm ocean for almost twenty four hours, surfacing now and again, realising the hopelessness of his situation in his more lucid moments but too close to death to care. He had never before considered his own demise, but now that it was inevitable, he found he was able to accept it, indeed almost welcome it; at least there would be no more pain.

As the raft tipped slightly India's arm dragged in the water, the new sensation awakening him. His hand touched something solid and he instinctively snatched it back onto the raft. He had heard lurid stories of mermaids and monsters of the deep which, up until a few days ago, would have terrified him, but now he didn't have the energy for fear; he just let himself sink into the comforting darkness once again - let it be.

Had India been awake he could have made out several dorsal fins surrounding his little craft. He would have also realised that he was now being nudged gently along toward a group of islands inhabited by people who had befriended the attendant dolphins who would prove to be his saviours.

The rhythmic banging of the raft on the sands aroused the boy as he became aware of being lifted and floating through air. This must be what it's like to be dead, he thought. He tried to open his swollen eyes but the light was too strong. The only thing he registered through his slitted eyes were the arms and hands that were carrying him; they had patterns on them and, oh yes, they were brown like him.

He came too again choking. He was being held in a sitting position and he was choking on a bitter liquid, part of which went down his throat, the rest down his chin. He floated off again and from time to time became aware of being turned on his bed and having something cool and soothing smoothed onto his body. Somewhere in the depths of his mind he should have cared but he had no strength and just wanted to go back to the dreamless darkness. When he was disturbed and the bitter liquid was poured down his throat he just let it happen, he had no strength to resist, happy to slide back into oblivion.

India lay in this semi-conscious state, attended to by his nursemaids for sixteen days. On the seventeenth, as dawn was breaking, he awoke with a clear head and clear eyes. He was under a roof of large green leaves which were supported with rough cross beams. The walls were merely screens erected with the same materials. He lay on a mattress which rustled when he moved, the covering some sort of roughly woven material. The morning breeze wafted in a beautiful sweet perfume - was this heaven? He was curious but too weak to worry either way - all he knew was that he felt good. He moved testing his body, no pain. He stood, his legs were very wobbly, but still no pain.

Just as he got to his feet a woman appeared through the doorway. India was immediately struck by the colour of her skin, a vague memory of being carried on patterned arms and brown hands came back to him - she was brown too! He stared open mouthed, she was bare breasted! She had on a bead necklace and her long wavy hair fell half way down her chest but it could not disguise the fact that she was naked from the waist up. When she saw that India was up she clapped her hands, smiling broadly, showing a set of even white teeth which contrasted starkly against her dusky features. She ran from the shelter clapping her hands and calling out. India had no idea what she was saying but she was obviously pleased about something.

He sat back on his bed, head swimming; forehead sprouting beads of sweat. The woman returned in a trice accompanied by another older female and a man. From his bearing and presence, India deduced that this man must be the guvner. He was not much taller than India but he was powerfully built with well-defined musculature. He had a mop of almost black hair and patterns drawn on his face and arms. If it were not for the kindly brown eyes and the smile on his face India would have been very scared, but he relaxed as it was obvious that he was among friends. The older lady was as wrinkled as a prune and, when she smiled he saw that she had one large brown peg in the lower jaw of an otherwise toothless mouth. Her white hair was scraped back from her face and fixed somehow at the nape of her neck with a wooden stick. Although she had no teeth, so that her face seemed to be caving in upon itself, nothing could diminish the brilliance of her black twinkling eyes and the warmth therein.

All three began to talk at once. To India it was just mumbo jumbo, and when he tried speaking to them he could see from their expressions that the feeling was mutual.

Eventually it became clear that they wanted him to eat and, although they were pleased to see him up, he must continue to convalesce. He was happy to acquiesce but eating his first solid food in almost three weeks tired him so that he was asleep within ten minutes of consuming it.

He slept fitfully now. Sometimes the horrors of the rape and the cat morphing into monsters chasing him so that he awoke calling out for Jake, sometimes dreaming of good things like tables groaning under platter upon platter of the best of foods or of being tucked into bed by Miss Bella.

Over the next few days his little shelter was visited by a never ending stream of curious visitors. India noted that all of the women, like the men, wore very little but grass skirts or loin cloths. He had been shocked by his first encounter but now it just seemed natural; he himself, his own clothes having been ruined, now wore one of these and what better!

As the days and weeks went by he learnt that the first woman he had seen was called Narntac Seesah and she had nursed him, sleeping in his shelter every night so that she could administer medicines and potions every few hours. The man was her husband, Narntac, and the old woman Numee, his mother. He was indeed the chief but India noticed that, unlike in England, chief or no chief, Narntac did not have special privileges; nor did he seem to expect them. Gradually he began to recognise the various individuals and to remember their names, although pronouncing them was another matter. For his part, he accepted that from now on his name in this community would be Indee - near enough he supposed.

Under Seesah's care he became stronger by the day; still having to stomach the bitter medicine, but only once a week now. There were several youngsters in the village around his age but there seemed to be no hierarchy, all ages being equal. Everyone, young or old, was expected to gather food, erect shelters, nurse babies - to share in all aspects which benefited the community. India hit it off with one of the youngsters in particular; her name was Narntac Narnsee, the chief's fourth child and only daughter.

India found that she had a quick mind and an amazing memory so that they quickly learnt so much from each other, both being very inquisitive about the other's culture. Under Narnsee's instruction, India was soon able to converse, somewhat haltingly, in his adopted language. By the same token she learnt from Indee, the King's English, albeit with a common accent.

Narnsee was eventually able to explain to Indee that he had fetched up on the shores of the island (the natives name for it, Llenada, meaning home) and everyone had expected that he would die, but her mother had insisted that she could save him. His skin was badly burnt from the sun and his wounds from the whipping and the rape had become badly infected. Her mother had pinched the wounds in his rectum and his back together with tiny sand crab claws and treated them every day with the unction made from the healing plant they called Kwashi. She had made medicine from it too (the foul tasting drink) so that his body would heal from the inside also.

Indy was mortified to hear that Seesah had treated him so intimately but Narnsee was surprised that he should feel so. Her mother, she said, knew he had been tortured and, even though they lived on this island, they knew there were bad things and bad people in the world and there was no reason for him to feel any shame for the dreadful way that he had been treated.

Having mastered the language India set about indoctrinating himself into the new culture. He learnt how to spear fish, build a canoe, climb trees, erect shelters, skin, clean and gut animals, make a fire, read the weather patterns and the ocean waters, make 'Muctar' from coconut milk, and how to drink it (he soon learnt that moderation was a very good thing). In short, he went native very easily. Some 'civilised' folk would call his new kinsmen 'natives and savages' but he had never experienced such a benign, democratic way of life. His thoughts sometimes went to the barbaric practices deemed acceptable at home - prison or even hangings for theft, whippings for insubordination, the huge inequalities between the rich and poor. No, these people were not savages; what they were *not* was tainted by the so called civilisation that he had left behind, and God forbid that they ever should be.

India's irrepressible nature and good humour quickly made Narntac warm to him. He saw that the boy was kindly and eager to share and was not afraid of hard work. He wondered how such a boy could have been so badly treated, and shivered as a premonition that the cruel world from which he had come was moving ever nearer to his shores. He took a moment to wipe the idea from his mind, and then gave serious thought to something he had been pondering for a while. At length, he nodded his head to the affirmative. He would take Indee into his house - make him one of the family. He did not carry his seed but nevertheless he felt some connection to the boy. Narntac admired him and would be proud to take him in as his own. He strode through the small village to find his wife - he would tell her so that she could make room for their adopted son; and so it was that from that day India was known as Narntac Indee.

India felt at home immediately and revelled in having a family at last. He grew to like his adopted brothers who, all three being a little older than he, took great delight in teaching him all they could about their way of life and honing up the skills he had learnt so far. All three took it upon themselves to introduce Indee to the art of swimming underwater. He would sit on the shore while they dove for shells and fished and they were mystified by his fear of the water. Gradually, over many months they helped him to overcome it so that he became an adroit swimmer, diving and exploring a world that he had never dreamed could have existed.

The very best things were the huge fish that swam around them and let them hang on to their fins so that they were pulled along at great speeds. At first India had been terrified when these fearsome creatures appeared but his brothers explained that they were friendly, playful creatures (just look at their smiley faces) and they often brought gifts from the sea - why, they had brought Indee himself.

He would often go down to the shore with Nancy (as he called her) to hunt for shellfish, swim and talk. She told him much about their way of life and their customs, and happily answered his never ending questions. He asked about her mother's skills and the medicines that she made. Narnsee told him that the healing skills had been handed down to her by her mother Bwoona but most of the real healing came from the healing plant, their treasure. She took him to the grove where the plants grew and explained that the beautiful scarlet flowers were gathered and dried and used when needed. Either brewed to make medicine or soaked in water, then ground and mixed with fat to make ointments and salves.

They would talk in English when they were alone as Indee missed speaking in his own tongue, and at times it was useful to be able to converse without anyone else understanding what they were saying. Often their chats would be cut short when the dolphins, Nancy called them sea children, would appear to play and neither Narnsee or India could resist their cheeky entreaties to join them.

Chapter 16

Jake jolted awake. It took several seconds to hone in on the smiling face of Harry Throgmorton hovering above him, the smile exposing even, white teeth. Then his gaze shifted to the much shorter figure of (to Jake) an elderly woman. She was almost as wide as she was high, dressed in baggy blue breeches and a naval officer's coat which was straining at every seam to contain the large amount of flesh that was considerably more than it was originally intended to fit in it. "Good morning Jake. I hope you slept well. You fell asleep old boy; not used to the fruits of Bacchus's larder eh."

Jake did not have a clue what that meant but shook his head anyway. "Why am I here? Where is Sol?" Harry explained that he and Sol thought he was best off on The Catherine for the time being. He pre-empted Jake's next question. "This is our ship's surgeon Mrs. Hardcastle. I thought maybe you would be feeling a little unwell this morning, the wine and all that but..." Mrs Hardcastle interrupted and Jake was surprised that such a stern looking woman would have such a high reedy voice – he watched her double chin wobble as she spoke.

"He looks fine to me Hal. A good looking lad and no mistake, when he fills out a bit he'll be a fine specimen." With that, she turned and left the room moving deceptively quickly for a woman of her bulk.

"If you are wondering about the jacket Jake, it belonged to her husband. She served with him on The Nautilus but sadly he was attacked and killed some ten years ago when they were on leave in Portsmouth by one of the crew who had a grudge against him. She, of course was terribly upset so she did no more than finish the fellow herself. Opened him up like a kipper apparently. She's worn her dear departed's jacket ever since, although I suspect it used to be a better fit then than now. She loved him you see, such a sad loss for her. She left the navy under a cloud and eventually joined us, a fact for which we will be eternally grateful; she is the very best you know, the very best."

Harry made to leave calling over his shoulder, "I'll be in my cabin if you'd like to pop along once you're dressed." Jake snuggled down, luxuriating in the feel of his soft sheets for five minutes longer. His head swam when he stood but he dressed quickly and set off to look for the Captain's cabin. Once on deck he saw that they were making way steadily with The Huron in tow. He wandered along gawping at the crew as they swabbed the deck, checked the rigging, carried out all the duties he had become used to on The Huron. But these people were different, several were fully grown men but shorter than he. There was one man with a yellow skin, one with dark circles painted around his eyes and one with absolutely no hair on his face, limbs, anywhere. Virtually everywhere Jake looked, he saw strange people but they all waved and smiled and put him at his ease.

He reached the cabin and knocked tentatively on the door. "Come" – it took him back to his first day on The Huron. "Ah. Come in my boy. Let me introduce you to some of my section heads, I was a little remiss in not doing so last night I'm afraid, but no matter." The four men that had accompanied him onto The Huron the day before sat in a semi-circle around a large desk placed under a window to catch the light. He pointed to the first man, the one with the distorted face.

"This is George Perez. He is our navigator, mathematician and font of all knowledge. He has the sharpest brain of any man I have ever met and it is he who is overseeing the shepherding of your fellow sailors to safety." Jake shook the proffered hand, noticing that the poor man's teeth were crammed one on top of the other, protruding from his gums at varying angles. "Moving along, this is Thomas Grey; our armourer. He is in charge of ammunition stocks, gun maintenance, gunnery practice, the whole to do and there is no-one who knows more about arms than he." Again Jake shook the proffered hand, lowering his gaze slightly to look Tom Grey in the eye. "Then we come to Abraham, he is in charge of the ship's stores and provisions. He is the purser and general fixer and liaises with the cooks and baker to ensure all supplies are maintained. In short, if we need anything at all we can always rely on Abe to find it."

Jake looked up at the big man who took his hand in his, dwarfing it. In a booming voice he said, "Welcome aboard young man."

"Lastly, this is Beauregard Tasker. He is you may say, our welfare officer. On the whole we have a happy ship and every man here is free to stay or go as he pleases, but Beau keeps an eye out for, and helps out with, any problems that our lads may have. Keeps everything on an even keel you might say." Bo stepped forward, no boots today.

"Pleased to make your acquaintance I'm sure." He had a handsome open face, a firm handshake and a ready smile.

"You met Mrs. Hardcastle earlier. As I explained she is the ships surgeon and a darn fine one too, the best. As for me Jake; for my sins I am responsible for sailing The Catherine, ensuring she is kept in the best shape and for deciding when and where we operate our trade. It is my job to earn us all a living and keep us safe. Jake thought it surreal for pirates to refer to earning a living but kept his

thoughts to himself. Oh, I had better mention old Edward
Wickenden whom I would like you to meet, he is back at
the base as his sight is failing but he taught me all I know
about seamanship and, however hard I may try, I will
never be able to handle a craft the way he can. Even half
blind he can make any ship dance to his tune, he has a
masters touch."

The group had concluded their business so left soon
after the introductions were carried out. When everyone
had gone Harry spoke. "Well Jake, what do you think of
my friends?"

Jake was lost for words and stumbled.

"Well, I thought - I thought."

"You thought that just because they look a little strange
they would all be imbeciles, did you not?" Jake nodded.
"Let me tell you something Jake. Some years ago I thought
exactly like you - and most other folks come to that. I lived
in the lap of luxury with never a thought of anything other
than how I should dress and how I would occupy my days;
but circumstances changed and I had to leave England in
great haste, and virtually penniless. My man servant Pryor,
whom I had also taken for granted and underestimated so
badly, stuck by my side in my time of need and it was he
who got me through those times; he and not my so called
equals.

"To cut a long story short, a dear lady friend of mine
helped me to escape to France – I speak the lingo you see -
and there I skulked not knowing which way to turn or
really what to do. One night, in a dockside Inn – Pryor had
joined me by then - we were befriended by a man with a
disfigured face. I'm ashamed to say that we both thought
him quite repulsive, and he must have read so in our faces,
but nonetheless, hearing of our plight he took us back to his

very humble lodgings. Imagine; a man like that, shunned and laughed at by everyone, took pity on us! He earned a pittance at a freak show – people would throw rotten fruit and vegetables at him for fun, just because of the way he looked! Anyway, he negotiated a cheap passage for Pryor and me on a ship bound for Cuba which used up the last of our money, and I really do not know what would have happened to us without him.

"When we reached Havana we found work on the docks. It was hard, especially for me as I had been an idle layabout up until then, but we soon started up a nice little business of our own selling the 'spare' that we had acquired. We had to keep a low profile you see as there was a price on my head.

"Well I couldn't get that poor man out of my mind, suffering from the day he was born yet still having compassion for others, so once we had established ourselves Pryor carried on running our 'supply' business and I went back to Bordeaux working my passage on a brig. I found George still at the freak show and eventually persuaded him to join us for a better life. He drove a hard bargain though; he refused to leave without his two friends Edward and Jules, so in the end they all three came. Edward and Jules were twin midgets. The tiniest men I have ever seen, but sadly Jules took a fever just six months after joining us and Edward died a few weeks later; I'm sure losing his brother broke his heart."

Harry leant forward and patted Jake on the knee. "My point is Jake that the man I have been talking about is George Perez." Jake's eyes widened "Yes, our George, and far from being a simpleton I discovered that he is verging on being a genius. He'd had no education when we met, but he learnt to speak English in months, then when I taught him to read, we could not provide books quickly enough to keep up with him. His love though, is mathematics. I was considered a good scholar at Eton, but he surpassed me some years ago. So Jake, I can assure you that every man on this ship, despite appearances, is the same as you or I on the inside - in most cases better." He stood, "end of lecture for today. Away now and see what mischief you can get up to."

Jake hesitated. "I can't read or write, just my name letters. Do you, do you think I could learn like George did?" Harry Throgmorton's face lit up "My boy, my boy. I see an obvious intelligence in your eyes and it would give me the greatest pleasure to reveal the secrets of our language to such an eager mind as yours. We start tomorrow noon – sharp. Now, off you go - I have work to do."

Jake could hardly contain himself the next morning, he was so eager for knowledge. At twelve sharp he tapped on the cabin door and walked in when he heard Harry bid him enter. He was greeted by a jaunty little wired haired terrier sporting a crimson kerchief looking every inch the pirate's dog. Jake bent to stroke him, memories of Jess flooding his thoughts so that his throat tightened and he had to bite down on his tears. "Meet Boxer, he likes you Jake, that's good. Boxer here is the best judge of a man I know. He has given the all clear to every one of my crew; anyone he takes a dislike to, does not step aboard my ship."

Harry Throgmorton was sitting as his large leather topped desk dressed in a plain brown shirt and breeches, blond locks tied neatly at the base of his neck. He smiled at Jake's expression. "Gone the peacock eh Jake? Today I am more like the common grouse. This is my working attire, we put on a show for The Huron's benefit but today it is back to business as usual." He tapped the chair next to him in front of which was a large pad of paper, an ink pot and several quill pens. "We'll start by you showing me how to write your initials er, your name letters and see how we get on."

For the next two weeks Jake was so absorbed in his studies that he only thought of home and India if he stirred in the lonely hours of the night. He was shown all the letters of the alphabet and would be tested on their sounds, gradually putting some together so that, to his utter delight, he could make up words. George was enlisted to introduce figures to Jake, using dried beans as a practical means of denoting the quantities in each number. Jake had been used to practical calculating at home but the knowledge that numbers written on a piece of paper could be used as a visual means of expressing quantities was a revelation and he pestered George to set him arithmetical tests daily.

Chapter 17

Sixteen anxious days after setting a course for Bermuda a call of 'Land Ho' was heard from the crow's nest. Three hours later the two ships, once again tethered together, dropped anchor half a mile from shore, officers Pointer, Barton and Pritchard in deep conversation with Harry. "Do you think you can make enough sail to gain the harbour Mr. Pointer?"

"If we get a favourable wind I'm certain of it, but it is too late now. We need daylight to ensure safety. I propose that we take our leave of you at first light tomorrow."

"My thoughts exactly, so it seems we will have the pleasure of your company a little longer. What say you to a last supper on board The Catherine?" Given the lavish food and fine wines to be had aboard The Catherine, Mr. Pointer needed no time to consider the offer.

"Speaking on behalf of my staff, we would be most honoured Captain Throgmorton, most honoured."

"Splendid! Sundown suit? We can discuss the practicalities over dinner so until then, au revoir gentlemen." Pointer turned to clamber back along the boarding plank. "Oh, please ask your man Sol to give us the pleasure of his company also, such an interesting man."

With a rather sour faced smile Pointer replied "To be sure sir, to be sure."

Jake, having heard all this, felt his spirits crashing down. He had been so happy on The Catherine and now he would have to go back to face Croucher, and worse, his studies would end. It would be good to see Sol, Walden and the boys again he supposed, but he was very downcast. He sensed someone behind him.

"Why the long face young man, you look as though

Boxer has bitten you." It was Harry.

"Oh, I just wish I could stay here. I know I would miss my friends on The Huron, but it's so nice here. Everyone is kind and fair and I was really enjoying being 'teached' by you."

"The word is 'taught' Jake, but why do you think it should end? I wanted to speak to you before tonight to see how you felt. Ahem, yes, we are what one might term privateers, but I can assure you that your life expectancy would be far greater if you stayed with us than it would be on that man-o-war." Jake thought he knew what that meant. "I had intended, if you are willing of course, to inform Mr. Pointer that you will be staying aboard The Catherine as the newest member of her crew. I will instruct him to report to the authorities that you were taken prisoner against your will so that there will be no blemish upon your character or naval record. He can surely raise no objection as you were, after all, pressed into the navy against your will in the first place. What say you Jake, are you with us, or with them?"

Jake was overjoyed. Before he knew what he was doing he jumped up and hugged Harry, just as he used to do with Pa. "Oh, please let me stay, I promise I'll be the very best man you've got. I'll do whatever you say, anything - anything."

"No need for all that old chap, we are just as happy to have you aboard as you seem to be. Now, time to become peacocks once again. I've put out some fresh clothes which should fit you, so onward and upwards me boy, onwards and upward."

Jake, grinning like a Cheshire cat, saluted. "Yes Sir. What's a peacock?"

Those officers not on duty, trailed by Sol Benson,

boarded The Catherine all eagerly anticipating the forthcoming banquet. Jake noticed that each man was greeted by Boxer, short tail wagging furiously as he went from one to the other. They all passed muster it seemed. Harry Throgmorton was dressed this evening in a flowing suit of emerald green. His hair tied at the nape of his neck with a green ribbon, a large gold earring in his left ear. All The Catherine's crew were clothed if anything, more flamboyantly than before; but it was Jake who took their eye. His filthy slops had been replaced with fine white breeches fastened over white leggings topped by an intricately embroidered white shirt and navy waistcoat; the whole outfit thrown slightly off kilter by the soft golden oriental slippers that covered his feet.

"Good evening gentlemen, please make your way below. Dinner will not be too long and we can chat over an aperitif while we wait. Ah, Mrs. Hardcastle, so glad you could make it; how is the patient?"

"He's not so bad, just a knock to the head." Smiling. "I should imagine, he must have seen stars."

"Gentlemen, let me introduce you to our surgeon, Mrs. Hardcastle." All eyes took in the short portly woman standing before them. She had on a loose full length soft pink silk dress which would have helped to disguise her girth were it not topped by the same military jacket Jake had seen before and which was still struggling to contain her ample proportions. Laying a hand gently on her back Harry guided her to the stairway. "Ladies first my dear, lead on and we, beguiled by your beauty, shall follow." Mrs. Hardcastle visibly blushed as she disappeared into the candlelit shadows.

The meal went as before with everyone chatting easily, becoming more loquacious with each glass of wine consumed. Most of the conversations going over his head, Jake asked to be excused so that he could play on deck with Boxer. When he had gone Harry excused himself on the pretext of having a little business to attend to and signalled Sol to follow. He gave it a moment or two then did as he was bid joining Harry up on deck.

"Sol, I have told Mr. Pointer that Jake is staying aboard The Catherine and I am inviting you to do the same. I hear that this Croucher's accomplice has disappeared now, as well as the India boy, which leads me to believe that he is clearing up loose ends – getting rid of anyone who could do him harm, and that includes you."

Sol thought for a moment. "'Tis right good of you, and I can't say I'm not tempted but I've good mates on The Huron. We've been through a lot together and I would hate to leave them when we are on the way to fight. Besides, if I jump ship, I'm not sure I want to be looking over my shoulder for the rest of my life, so thank 'ee kindly but my place is on The Huron."

"Somehow Sol I thought you would say that. You are a good man; loyal and true and there aren't many around like you. Rare as hen's teeth old boy, hen's teeth. So now I will tell you what I am going to do. We will escort you into port tomorrow as near as we can beyond firing range – that's just in case any of your crew betray us, you understand. From there a dozen of my men will escort you in a longboat. They will come ashore on the pretext of assisting you to find suppliers, craftsmen and the like, but their main task will be to find and eliminate your Mr. Croucher. What I want from you Sol is for you to identify him to my men; they will take care of the rest. Now, what is really important is that you stay well away from him at all times. You are not to be involved or endangered in any way. What

I would ask of you however, is that you warn them immediately if you have the slightest idea that they are in danger."

In the dark Sol took in a deep breath. "Sounds so cold blooded to talk about a man's death like this but there's no doubt the bastard deserves it; better him than me or any of my mates. Okay, I give you my word I'll look out for your boys – here, shake on it." They shook hands, both men as good as their word.

"One more thing Sol; here take this." Harry took Sol's hand and put a small sacking bag into it. "There is enough gold and a few jewels there to make you a fairly wealthy man."

"But, but..."

"No buts, when you retire from His Majesty's navy you need never worry again. Now, obviously you will have to keep this safe so listen carefully. There is a Franciscan Monastery on the hill overlooking yon port. You will be there for some time so will be able to get away for a bit I am sure. When you get chance, go to the monastery, ask for Father Schulz. Tell him that Henry Throgmorton has sent you and that you want to leave something in his safe keeping."

"You will have to pay a little something in alms but you can be assured that your goods will be kept safe for as long as need be. You will be asked two or three secret things that only you could know the answers to so that when you return to collect your treasure it will be given to you, and only you. If you have a mind to, you can set a time limit; any that you like, for collection day so that if you die and are unable to collect, the monastery can put your riches to good use. How does that sound?"

Sol was overwhelmed. "I just don't know what to say

except why? Why would you do this?"

"Let's just say that it is to atone for my sins Sol. I killed a man over a woman once. He was rich, but you are ten times his worth and much more deserving. Here, tuck this well into your breeches and tell no-one, no-one," patting him on the back. "Come on now Sol; let's enjoy the rest of our time together." The two men made their way below to the sound of ribald sea shanties with Emily Hardcastle's strident contralto leading the chorus.

Chapter 18

At first light the two ships weighed anchor, and as planned, The Huron limped into harbour accompanied by a dozen or so men in one of The Catherine's longboats. Jake had pleaded with Harry to go with them, and only on the understanding that he would be expected to row as hard as the others, Harry had agreed. Once the ship had docked successfully Jake clambered aboard, eager to meet up with Walden and the other boys to say a proper goodbye. Mr. Pointer joined Beau and his crew on terra firma and set· about the business of procuring men and materials for repairs. Hamilton was a cosmopolitan port with all manner of craft moored so the acting Captain was more than glad of The Catherine's multilingual crew who helped enormously and ferreted out a local craftsman who spoke relatively intelligible English.

Only Beau and two other men in the escort knew the real motive for their coming ashore. They found Sol, greeting him like a long lost friend so that he was able to point out Croucher without arousing any suspicion. He then left them to join the general melee that The Huron's arrival had stirred up, wondering what exactly was going to happen. In the meantime Jake had scampered aboard bursting to tell his old friends his news and catch up on any gossip they had come by. Eventually he concluded his reluctant farewells and was looking for Sol when he saw him wandering along the dock. He hurried down to meet him, anxious to share one last word of goodbye.

By the time Jake had made his way onto the dock Sol was quite some way ahead strolling, deep in thought, at a deserted end of the quay. Jake quickened his step and was just about to call out when he saw the familiar figure of

Charlie Croucher step out from behind a stack of bales to follow Sol; the glint of sun on metal revealing that he had a knife in his hand. Jake began to run calling out to Sol who turned just as Croucher lunged for him. Jake screamed out when his friend went down; he began to sprint as Sol raised an arm in an effort to protect himself. Croucher, standing over the prone man, kicked him in the head, and then pulled back his arm in readiness to plunge the knife deep into his helpless victim. He heard Jake's heavy breathing just as the lad ran pell-mell into him, knocking him off balance so that he stumbled onto his knees. Jake, blind with rage, began to kick out disregarding the slashing dagger. His boot thudded into Croucher's chest but before he knew it he was on the ground, one leg held in an iron grip.

Croucher was breathing heavily but still managed his cruel twisted grin. "Now I've got the both of you; you first you little bastard." Kneeling over Jake, he raised the dagger but dropped it as Beau's hunting knife whistled past Jake's ear and embedded itself up to the hilt in his attacker's chest. Croucher, shocked and in pain, staggered to his feet, and roaring, smashed his fist into Jake's face knocking him almost senseless. He screamed out at Beau and his two ship mates Lin Chow and Jeng Yen. "You'll pay for this. I'm taking this bastard kid with me. No-one gets the better of me – no-one."

He staggered to the side of the quay and toppled in, dragging Jake with him. It took a few seconds for anyone to react then all three ran to the edge of the dock to stare into the murky water, seeing no sign of either Croucher or Jake.

"Fuck!" Beau signalled to his two companions who took off their boots and dove into the water. "Find 'em for Christ's sake, find 'em." He knelt over Sol trying to staunch the wound, which was fast staining the grey shirt red. He waved to the small group of men approaching and as soon as they were within hearing he shouted. "Get help. Sol's bad hurt and the boy's in the water. For Christ's sake someone get a rope or a ladder and get Cameron here – now." To himself *"This was not how it was supposed work out. Christ, the bastard got to them both. Shit, shit, shit."*

Before Jake realized what was happening the dark waters were closing over his head and he could see nothing. Croucher still had hold of his leg and he knew that he was being dragged down and down. Terrified he kicked out thrashing furiously trying to free his leg, lungs almost bursting. His foot connected with something solid and suddenly he was free but he did not know which way was up and he could not find his way out of this nightmare. His lungs were burning; he did not want to die like this! Unable to hold off any longer he inhaled, his mind raging against his misfortune - then there was nothing but oblivion.

Croucher had been surprised at the boy's resistance but held on determined to drown him. Suddenly his body was wracked with pain as Jake's foot connected with the blade in his chest. His body convulsed involuntarily forcing him to let go of his victim. Unable to see his own hand in front of him he struck out feeling for Jake but instead found one of the jetty's wooden stanchions which he clung to letting it guide him to the surface. Gasping for breath, he came up several metres away from the commotion that he had caused just a few minutes ago. He clung on, chest on fire, his strength and life's blood slowly draining from him. He knew his only chance of survival, although slim, would be to remain hidden until dark when he may be able to leave the water unnoticed. For the first time that he could remember he prayed to God to let him live and to give him strength to last out until sunset.

The Throgmorton Legacy

Within minutes Cameron was at Sol's side tending to his wound and organizing a stretcher to get him back to The Huron. He heard splashing then Lin Chow calling out "we have boy, we have boy." Kneeling on the edge of the jetty Beau saw Lin Chow and Jeng Yen treading water, holding an unconscious Jake between them.

"Hold on boys, hold on - help's coming; just hold on." He ran back along the quay shouting for a rope, a dinghy, anything and was so glad to see Mel Cartwright and Ginger running toward him carrying a rope ladder. "Thank Christ lads, this way, they're down here." He ran back calling out "hold on boys, we're coming, hold on."

It took only a few minutes to get the boy out of the water. They lay him face down and Jeng began to push him hard on the back. "He not breathe, must try him not dead." Everyone stood around watching, desperate for Jake to revive. Beau found that he had crossed his fingers on both hands, something he had not done since he was a boy. Suddenly water gushed from Jake's mouth and he was choking and gasping.

Beau reached down and hugged Jeng. "You little wonder you; you bloody little wonder." Jeng grinned from ear to ear.

"Him not dead." He thought for a moment then, "him just wet."

Jeng's attempt at a joke broke the tension and, flooded with relief, the small group started to laugh uncontrollably. Jake, slowly turned over and sat up wishing he was in on the joke. When they had all calmed down Beau and Lin made a human chair seat and carried Jake back to The Huron. Beau spoke to Lin as they walked, "Any sign of that piece of garbage Croucher?"

"No," said Lin. "Him gone to Davey Jone locket."

Jake, Jeng and Lin were taken to the ship's galley where they could warm up and given hot soup which was very welcome. It didn't compare with the far superior fare they had become used to on The Catherine, but was very welcome nonetheless. Jake, though ashen faced and unspeaking, nevertheless amazed everyone with his fortitude; shaking off all offers of help and refusing to visit the surgeon, insisting that all he needed was the soup and a warm through. They were all starting to see that this lad had something special and were glad that Cap'n Harry had decided to take him under his wing.

Beau, Mel and Ginger made their way down to the sick bay and were much relieved to find Sol sitting up and conscious, his wound neatly dressed. Cameron greeted them "Ah, come in lads. Sol here was very lucky that he was falling away from the blade when it struck so he has a nasty slash but that is all. He gave his head a nasty crack when he fell though – knocked him senseless. If it hadn't been for you I very much fear he would be a goner."

Beau spoke out "It wasn't us who saved him, it was Jake. True enough I managed to spear the bastard but if Jake hadn't dropped him with that tackle Sol here would be dead meat, no doubt of it," speaking to Sol. "That boy is full of heart Sol, we heard him bellowing like a raging bull, no thought for himself, just you." Sol put his head back, tears filling his eyes. He was overwhelmed with emotion. He realised how much the boy had come to mean to him and now he was going away.

Mel and Ginger said their goodbyes but Beau hung back a little. "Harry says to make sure you visit the monastery - it's well worth the trip."

"Tell him I will as soon as I am able, and tell him privateer or no, he is a good man and I will always think on him kindly, and Beau."

"Yes Sol, what is it?"

Sol reached inside his breeches. That morning he had taken a small golden crucifix from his little sack of treasure before hiding it away. He had tucked it into his waist band and he was convinced that it had protected him. "Just in case I don't see him again, I want you to give this to young Jake once you are safe on The Catherine. I want you to tell him..."

Beau interrupted. "No, you tell him Sol. He's a mule headed young 'un and no matter what; I know he won't leave without coming to see you. You give him that talisman and you tell him whatever it is you want to say; it will mean so much more coming from you. Goodbye now friend, maybe our paths will cross again one day – I surely hope so." He strode across the room and disappeared.

The events of the day, and hearing that Jake had very nearly died in saving him opened the floodgates to all the emotions Sol had suppressed for so many years. He sobbed and sobbed not knowing if they were happy tears or sad, he had opened the dam and was unable to stop the torrent.

By the time Jake appeared he was feeling calm, almost serene. "Sol, I'm so glad you are alright. Mr. Cameron says you will be back to your duties in a day or so." Jake paused "What I really want to say is that I wish you would come with me on The Catherine. I know they are privateers but they only steal from rich merchants and I know that's bad, but they are kind, much kinder than Captain Coutts ever was and..."

Sol held up a hand "I know what you are trying to say Jake but it's best if I serve my time out then settle down in the old country." He beckoned Jake nearer so that he could whisper in his ear. "Between you and me, and no-one else now, your Harry has given me a little something to make sure that I'll be comfortable in my old age – know what I mean."

Jake wasn't sure at all but nodded anyway, but when Sol pressed the golden crucifix into his hand understanding dawned. "Now Jake, I want you to keep this with you always. I'm sure it saved me today and God willing it will protect you wherever you go. I want you to keep it too so that you remember me. I know we can't see into the future but I know yours will be good. You will grow into a fine man – just the kind of man I would be proud to call my son." He put his good arm around Jake pulling him close, kissing the top of his head. "Go on now son. You don't want to be left behind do you? God speed lad and look after yourself!"

Jake left, tears blinding him so that he stumbled up the stairs; he managed only a weak "Bye, Sol."

It was not until they were back on board The Catherine, everyone listening to Beau's account of events, that the enormity of what had happened hit Jake. He had been drowned and but for Lin and Jeng he would be dead! They could all be sitting here now listening to Beau and he could be dead! He thought of India, what it must have been like for him, alone, heart bursting to live, struggling to escape from a hellish watery death with no-one to save him. He imagined his friend's little body floating somewhere under that huge black ocean, gone forever. He thought his heart would break; it was all too much for him to bear and he suddenly began to shiver and shake, the soup he had consumed so appreciatively just a short while before exploded from his mouth, splattering several pairs of feet.

He was carried, teeth chattering, to his bunk and Mrs. Hardcastle was summoned. She forced him to swallow a bitter tasting concoction which quickly calmed him and made him sleepy. Unresisting, he let her undress him and tuck him into his bunk where she remained stroking his forehead until he drifted off. Every now and then he would thrash around and call out but she would calm him again, "there now Jake, there now, you're safe, nothing can harm you."

Jake reached out grasping her hand muttering random sentences "Ma, oh Ma, don't leave me Ma. I'll see to Jess in the morning. Oh Indy I'm so sorry." When she was sure that Jake had really succumbed to her sleeping draft, she kissed his head lightly, tucked his covers under his chin and a piece of wadding under his head to catch the tears streaming from his eyes.

Jake slept until mid morning, missing the bells chiming the time. He dreamt that he was back in the water, struggling to reach the surface before Croucher could catch him. He woke, bathed in sweat, to find that he was fighting to get free from his tangled covers. He had never been so pleased to see the sun! He threw on his clothes and ran onto the deck taking great gulps of precious life-giving air. He was just about to turn fourteen but felt physically weak and world weary. Just a few months ago he had been a carefree boy but what had occurred since then had changed his view of the world irrevocably; he was becoming a man. He now realized what India had been forced to learn at far too young an age; that the world was a hard unforgiving place filled with so many pitfalls, and that justice and fairness were ethereal ideals that fell far short of reality. He resolved that from now on, like Harry's, he would put his trust only in those people approved of by Boxer and George.

Chapter 19

Sol used his neckerchief to wipe the sweat from his face. He had started the climb to the monastery early in the morning and now stood in front of the great wooden doors grateful of the shade they afforded, as the sun was at its zenith directly overhead. He felt nervous, almost childlike. He had lived a relatively good life but now, at the prospect of entering such a hallowed place, he suddenly felt consumed with guilt over all the little misdemeanours he had committed, and was sure Friar Schultz would find him out. He coughed nervously and pulled the bell chain beside the postern gate. He waited a few minutes, and was just about to ring again when a small Judas hole slid open, eyes peering out at his own level. "Yes my son. What do you want of us?"

"I've come to speak with Father Schultz – Harry Throgmorton sent me." The shutter closed and the postern gate opened revealing a short stout man dressed in the rough woven habit of the order.

The friar welcomed him in and pointed to a shaded courtyard. "Come in my son. Rest your legs and I will fetch Father Schultz and a pitcher of water, you look in need of refreshment. I'm Father O'Toole by the way. Oh, who shall I say is calling on him?"

"Solomon Benson. I'm serving in His Majesty's Navy and our ship is anchored below; in for repairs."

"Ah yes, I have been watching the progress – nearly finished I would say."

"Aye, I reckon we'll be sailing in a few days."

Before Sol had finished his sentence Father O'Toole had turned on his heel and strode through an arch at one end of the courtyard. Sol walked over to a rustic bench above which was an open window festooned with sweet smelling jasmine. He felt immediately at ease. These seemed good men, not at all like the fire and brimstone preaching clergy he remembered from his childhood. He sat, leaning his back against the wall – it was so lovely here, serene and peaceful, maybe the Friars had got it right. Life here must be trouble free, leaving them wanting for nothing. He felt his eyelids growing heavy as he heard the soft padding of sandaled feet approaching. He looked up to see a statuesque man whose habit swung half way up his calves. He was perhaps the tallest man Sol had ever seen but it was his vivid blue twinkling eyes that held Sol's gaze. He instinctively jumped to attention. "No. No my man. There is no need to stand. I'm sure you must be pretty tired after climbing all the way up here from the harbour." He took Sol's hands in his. "Now, Solomon Benson, why did that old reprobate Harry Throgmorton send you to me?"

Sol explained everything that had happened over the last few weeks, pulling out his little sack of treasures from beneath his shirt. "So you want to leave this in our safe keeping; very prudent. Come, let us go inside where we can draw up some sort of contract and take the necessary details."

In a bed beneath the jasmine covered window, Charlie Croucher sat straining to hear the conversation taking place outside. He had been in the infirmary for several weeks now, having been found near to death by some Good Samaritan and taken to the monastery. He had been floating on the crest of a drug-induced torpor when his ears had pricked up at the sound of a voice he knew. He hauled himself up, sitting as tall as he could so that he could catch what was being said, and as he listened, his lips twisted into his old cruel smile. So, these monks had riches - what luck! As soon as he was fit enough he'd help himself and go on his way – he'd leave these bastards with their God and as little else as possible! He slid down beneath his sheets and gave in to the desire to sleep, a smile still on his face.

Sol shook Father Schultz's hand, marvelling once again at the strength of the man. He stepped through the small gate back into the outside world happy that his business had been successfully concluded and began to make his way back to the harbour. He paused on a bend in the track, gazing down at the ant like figures scurrying around swarming over The Huron. He sat, pulling his knees up to his chest; funny how life turns out. Who would credit it - thanks to a privateer he was a very happy man and his future was secured. If he survived the next two years or so he could leave the navy knowing that he would spend the rest of his days in great comfort, if not luxury. He smiled broadly. Who'd have thought it, he was a wealthy man, and all was well with the world.

The patient that the Friars had tended so caringly was much stronger now and safe in the knowledge that The Huron had sailed, rifled through the treasure trove that had been left in trust at the monastery. Father Schulz lay slumped alongside him, blood oozing from his slashed throat. He scooped up coins and jewels and let them cascade through his fingers just as a young child discovering for the first time the joys of playing with water. He selected the largest jewels then stashed as much gold as he thought he could carry into a sizeable leather pouch before stepping over the dead monk on his way out. As an afterthought, he turned to rake through one more box pulling out a long gold chain as thick as a man's finger, upon which hung a large solid gold crucifix. He put the chain around his neck smiling as he did so, "the Lord moves in mysterious ways his wonders to perform - yes indeed." He found the irony of him wearing such a thing amusing and the sound of his laughter echoed throughout the monastery as he strode away, leaving behind the usual trail of misery and destruction that had become his trade mark.

Chapter 20

Jake returned to his studies with gusto. Breaking off now and then to play with Boxer and to talk with crew members, all of whom had amazing stories to tell and all of whom had nothing but praise for their captain.

Several days after leaving The Huron, Jake heard the cry of Land-Ho. Peering over the side and squinting to see the dark mass ahead more clearly, he felt a tap on his shoulder, it was Harry. "Jake come into my cabin and I'll show you where home is." They found George leaning over Harry's desk studying a large map. Harry pointed to an asterisk pencilled on the southernmost tip of Cuba. This is our home Jake, take some time to study the longitude and latitude, then commit it to memory, but on no account must you ever tell another soul. It is a safe and secret place and must always stay that way. Meet me on the poop deck in a while. I will be taking the helm and I want you to watch. We'll make a seaman out of you yet."

Jake spent a few minutes studying the map then climbed up to stand alongside Harry at the helm. He saw they were heading toward a rocky outcrop dead ahead. Having every faith in Harry's seamanship he said nothing for a while, but seeing the foaming white water breaking on jagged rocks that were now all around them he could hold his tongue no longer. "Christ Harry, we'll be ripped apart. Turn back! What are you doing?"

Harry laughed, "Welcome to the dragon's teeth Jake; help me to hold the old girl steady. See that cleft in the cliffs yonder? We need to keep that dead ahead. There is quite a wide channel between the rocks but one slip and the dragon will slay and devour all of us. Steady now, steady. Just concentrate on our landmark." Harry laughed again,

"This is the life eh Jake! Pitching your wits against the elements and beating them. This is the life boy, this is the life! If we turn now, young Jake, our old Catherine surely will be ripped asunder, and we wouldn't want to do that to her now, would we?" Jake was really frightened thinking that Harry had taken leave of his senses, felt the colour drain from his face as the seething waters buffeted the ship as they crashed over the menacing black shards of rock. Lost for words and waiting for the dreadful sound heralding The Catherine's demise, Jake braced his legs against the heaving deck and hung on to the wheel not taking his eyes from the cleft in the cliffs ahead, praying that Harry had not actually gone crazy.

After what seemed to Jake an interminable age Harry laughed again. "Watch now Jake. Look to your left – I told you this was a secret place. Welcome to Dragons Lair, our home and our refuge." Just as Jake thought they must run headlong into the cliffs ahead, he saw that they were passing what was a thin finger of land on their port side and turning into a wide channel. Looking directly ahead it had seemed that the cliffs were unbroken, thus concealing the inlet. Suddenly the waters calmed and as they moved slowly through the channel, Jake looked on in wonder at the lush dense vegetation that reached down to the water's edge. It was all very strange to him. Soon the channel opened out into a large lagoon where several boats were moored to a wooden jetty. They were in a valley surrounded on two sides by densely wooded hills. Beyond the jetty there were a number of log cabins behind which, in an enclosed allotment, grew orderly rows of plants some of which he recognized. Goats, chickens and several dogs roamed free, reminiscent of the home and life he had left behind.

"Now then young Jake," said Harry. "I have a few things to attend to so George here will give you a quick tour of our domain and I will see you in a while." He turned on his heel and strode off leaving Jake, George and Boxer looking on. George took Jake's arm and Boxer ran off to briefly greet his canine companions before hurrying back to join the tour. There were three rows of six cabins arranged as three sides of a square; each door facing into the central open space within which stood several large tables and dozens of chairs. The cabins or dormitories had bunks spaced out on either side and each bunk had a straw mattress with a wooden chest and stool alongside, and there was a large table in the centre of the room, presumably for communal eating in bad weather.

Making up the quadrangle of buildings was the cook house. Jake could feel the heat coming from the open fire and the tantalizing smells wafting on the air made his mouth water. "Smells good doesn't it?" said George. "We'll eat soon. Just let me show you the rest of our little kingdom." Set apart from the dormitories, further back into the valley, there were several other buildings. George explained that one was for Mrs. Hardcastle and was divided internally; one side being her private quarters, the other the dispensary. Another building had racks and racks of shelving upon which were sacks of flour, grain, and all manner of non perishable goods. There were also row upon row of bolts of silk in all colours of the rainbow. There were vases and ornaments of china and glass, trays of silver cutlery and box upon box of baubles and beads - a veritable Aladdin's cave. "As you saw, we grow a lot of our food and we have livestock for most of our meat but we use these trinkets to barter for supplies when needed. Truth is the finest silver bracelet is no use to a starving man."

"But all this treasure, and there is no lock on the door."

George smiled "No lad, and that's the way it has to be. We may be outside the law but there truly is honour among thieves, at least with our crew."

The last and most grand cabin had two storeys, with a veranda which ran the length of the ground floor. The front door opened into a smallish entrance hall with a door off to the left and to the right and a staircase in the centre which lead up to the top floor. George showed Jake into the first room on the left, which housed just a map strewn table in the centre, several chairs; a chest of drawers and on two walls, shelves stacked with books from floor to ceiling. These pieces were not roughly hewn like most of the furniture but beautifully carved and finished. He felt his heart tug as he thought of home.

"Anyone can come here that has a mind to. I'll be giving you a lesson or two on map reading soon I don't doubt." The second room, on the right hand side of the hall, was a considerable size with a central table around which were a number of chairs again, all of the finest quality. "This is where we have meetings – all sorts. Sometimes it's to plan our next sortie, sometimes it's to settle arguments or take a vote on things, or sometimes it's just nice to come here to enjoy a little peace and quiet if you want to be on your own."

Jake looked up the stairs. "Now those rooms are out of bounds. One is Harry's; the second one is, if you like, the treasury and the final one is for John Pryor. You haven't met him yet, but he has a room right next to where we keep the gold and such valuables that we come by. Harry will tell you all about it, but putting it simply everything that we accumulate (another word for Jake to look up), barring what you have seen in the stores, is shared out equally.

Every man gets the same and every man is expected to do his fair share of work around here - whatever is needed. John Pryor keeps meticulous accounts and records exactly how much each of us is due. If it proves difficult to share things equally - with jewellery and such, then Harry has the last word. All done here?" Jake nodded "Good, one last thing to show you."

Jake followed George into a secluded clearing where a small waterfall splashed into a natural rock pool. "This is fresh water and needs fetching for the kitchen every day. We also wash in it. It's freezing cold but Mrs. Hardcastle insists we have a good wash at least once a week, and I tell you son, there is no crossing her, even Harry does as he's told." Jake looked at the clear cold water and shuddered. The thought of being immersed in water ever again chilled him to the marrow.

Boxer had abandoned them some time ago lured by the smell from the cookhouse and they found him slavering over a bone. There were several tables scattered around and Harry was sitting at one working his way through a plate of dark aromatic stew. He told Jake, "Go fill your platter and come sit beside me." Jake didn't need encouragement. He scooped as much stew onto his plate as it could take and tore off a chunk of warm fresh bread and hurried back to the table, eager to get stuck in.

"I expect George mentioned John to you and explained that he is our treasurer." Jake nodded mouth too full to talk. "Maybe if you pull your weight around here he will look on you kindly and show you our treasure house; would you like that?" Jake nodded again, mopping gravy from his chin with his bread. "Good. I expect George told you too that we all have to chip in and help to keep things running smoothly, so for the next few days you are in charge of the livestock. Feeding, watering, that sort of thing, oh, and slaughtering for the kitchen. Jake's heart sank, thankful that he had just finished his stew; Harry's last words would have definitely killed his appetite.

Two days later and so far he had only been asked to supply chickens for the kitchen. Pa had shown him how to break their necks but he had never had to do more up until now. It was a grizzly business but he steeled himself to the task and managed to keep cook happy, thus far. He was clearing up the feathers when Beau tapped him on the shoulder. "Harry wants you go see him. I'd clean up a bit before you go though else he might think you're some old rooster come to call." Jake smiled, finished as quickly as he could then reluctantly he went to take the dreaded ice plunge.

"Ah, come in Jake. I thought it was time you learnt a bit more about our merry band – how it all ticks don't you know?" Harry nodded toward his companion. "I've spoken of John here before so let me introduce you to him now. He is my good friend and a man I know I can trust with my life. Jacob - meet John Pryor. John - meet Jacob Faraday, our newest recruit." John Pryor took Jake's hand and gave it a firm shake.

He looked a little older than Harry. He had dark hair which was greying at the sides and temple. Somehow, as he seemed such an important man, Jake had expected him to be serious, even severe but he was immediately set at ease when John ruffled his hair and said, "Glad to have you aboard lad."

Harry continued, "Now, I know George has explained that we get equal shares of any prize money but I thought you might like to see what John here does, so if you follow him up, all will be revealed." Jake, saying nothing, climbed the stairs and followed John Pryor into his quarters. The room was very tidy, furnished with just a bed, small chest of drawers and one chair. John took a key from atop the chest of drawers and opened the door through to the treasury, the two rooms being about the same size. A large, leather bound book and a pen and ink-stand sat upon a desk which nestled against the far wall underneath a window. Against a side wall were two large, dome topped chests. John opened the ledger. "George explained that you are eager and have started to learn your letters and numbers so I don't know if this will mean much to you yet but," pointing to the left hand column, "these are the names of the crew and here at the bottom I am going to add your name. The numbers alongside each name show how much each man has due to him, and each time we gain a prize I put the date at the top here and add the appropriate amount onto his total. He stepped to the chest and lifted the lid. "There are one hundred and twenty six boxes in these two chests, each named and each one containing gold and jewels, and I will be putting another one in there with your name on it in readiness." Jake didn't know what to say. He had never possessed anything of value before, and Pa would never let him keep anything stolen.

Harry popped his head around the door. "What do you think Jake? Quite impressive what?" Seeing the confusion in Jake's face he beckoned him to follow. He crossed the head of the stairs into his own quarters. There was a curtain pulled across one end of the room which Jake supposed concealed a bed. There were two comfortably padded chairs, a small desk, a chest of drawers and a small bookcase with leaded glass doors.

Harry sat and waved a hand inviting Jake to follow suit. "Jake my boy how old are you now? Thirteen?" Jake nodded "Just thirteen and look what's happened to you in these last months. I'm afraid I'm guilty of overlooking just what you've had to deal with and how difficult things have been for you. So, let me say how things are as I see them. You are missing your home and family and want to get back to them as soon as you can – yes?"

"Yes. I mean, you have all been real good to me and I'm very thankful, but I do miss Ma and Pa so."

"Just so Jake, just so. Now, it seems to me there are two options open to you. Firstly, we can arrange a passage for you to England and you should not be charged with desertion as Mr. Pointer assured me he would report you being captured by pirates, but there is a possibility, things being how they are with the French and Spanish at the moment, that you could be pressed back into the service." Jake started at that, the thought of being back on a warship was almost more than he could bear. Secondly, you could stay with us for a year or two and continue with your education; with letters, numbers, navigation, and the like, and of course you would eventually go home not just a scholar but with gold in your pocket, and by which time things should have calmed down and the navy will not be in need of men."

Jake's head was swimming with all this. He wanted with all his heart to go home but the thought of being pressed again frightened him more than he could say. On the other hand he loved learning and he would be so proud to take home money to ease things for Pa. Another thought clouded his mind. "Trouble is, if I stayed, how could I keep things that were stolen? Pa always said that God would punish sinners and thieves are sinners ain't they."

Harry leant one elbow on his desk, chin on his fist. "Things are never that black and white Jake. Your Pa is a good man and from what you have said he works hard and helps strangers, but does he get what he deserves? Is he rich? No! Yet there are many rich people who never do a days' work, or a kindness to anyone, and they are very rich even though they are undeserving." He paused, choosing his words. "What we do is, you could say, wrong, but we take only from rich merchant ships. These merchants trade in slaves, and goods that have been gathered by slaves. Poor souls who have no freedom, who have been torn from their homes, as you were, and who are beaten and worked until they drop. They make fortunes from the misery of those slaves with never a thought for their suffering. They buy and sell men as if they are no more than beasts in the fields."

Harry paused again marshalling his thoughts. "Many of our men have found their way to me, suffering from the real horrors of bondage, or that of ignorance and poverty - of the greed of the rich and uncaring. They have all suffered one injustice or another and that is why, who and whatever they are, everyone in my crew is treated equally and fairly, and I will have it no other way."

Harry stood, sighing deeply. "I was one of those rich undeserving. Lord Henry Throgmorton, a dandy who cared for nothing but rich clothing, good wine and pretty women. I never gave a thought to where my wealth came from, not a thought! Anyway, as I told you once before, I was a philanderer and was challenged to a duel by the husband of one of the many beauties with whom I had a liaison, and to cut a long story short, I killed him. Unfortunately he was a very eminent politician so there was a hue and cry for my blood. That's when I found out that all my so called friends and acquaintances were nothing of the sort. I had only three true friends, one my man servant, John Pryor, my old friend Giles Mason, and the other a lady with whom I should have spent my life but who I let slip through my fingers, my dear Catherine; but for her we would never have escaped."

"Every cloud, they say, has a silver lining, and I suppose that is true as it was not until I was in real trouble that I really began to live, to take notice of and understand people; to get to know them and see for myself how unfairly life treated so many but the privileged few." He sat down again, looking troubled. "Stay away from women by the way Jake, they are nothing but trouble." Jake thought of Ma and, while he understood, sort of, what Harry had said, there was no way his Ma was trouble. Jake sat awkwardly until Harry dismissed him with a wave of his arm and a weary smile. "Off you go now Jake; think about what I've said. If you decide to stay all well and good, but if you want to go we'll arrange for your passage home as soon as we can."

Jake walked to the door then stopped, turning. "Why, er why are you being so good to me?"

"Because my dear Jake, I see something of me in you and you have many qualities that I would like to have seen in a son of mine had I been fortunate enough to have had one, but of course I didn't. I just frittered my youth away, squandering the opportunities I had been given, with nothing to show for it but a life in exile. I want better for you. I want to give you the opportunity to live a life that is worthwhile, which may go some way towards making me feel better about wasting mine. Go now my boy, I expect cook will be looking for you."

Sleep eluded Jake all that night. He was so homesick and yet, his experiences since being pressed had given him a taste for more knowledge of the world. It had shown him that the earth was a wondrous and mysterious place, full of different people living different lives and he was curious, no hungry, to learn more of it. He had been enthralled by the tales of some of the more exotic members of Harry's crew. Their dress, their languages; the different ways in which they prepared food - he wanted to see so much more, and had already learnt so much from George. He could read a little but he wanted to be able to read a whole book, to calculate with numbers. He wanted to do so many things, all of which would be impossible in the small backwater of Poundsmill and Spinnaker cottage. More than anything though, he imagined himself returning home with money and gifts for Ma and Pa; they would be so proud of him. As the camp began to stir, he had made up his mind; he would stay here for a while and work hard. He would do his damnedest to make Harry proud of him too.

Chapter 21

The next four years were the happiest India had ever known. He missed nothing of the life he had left behind, with perhaps the exception of Jake. He sometimes dragged his memory back to those unhappy days on The Huron and silently prayed that somehow his dear friend had survived all the hardship and beatings that he must have had to endure, on that God forsaken ship.

Although life was good for him, as he matured, he worried more and more about his feelings for Narnsee. At first he delighted in her company because she was so interesting and they were such good friends, but lately he had begun to regard her differently and was becoming more and more attracted to her as a woman. He could not help but notice her swelling breasts and rounded hips, and the way she moved when she walked, which aroused him. He did not quite understand his feelings and it weighed heavily on his mind that somehow he was being disloyal to Narntac.

One night, troubled by his thoughts, he walked down to the waters' edge under the moonlight and sat listening to the soothing sound of the water lapping onto the shore. From nowhere Seesah appeared and sat down alongside him. "What is it that troubles you Indee?" He was glad of the night cover as he felt himself blush to the tips of his toes.

"I cannot say Seesah; I think I am not such a nice person."

"Why should you think bad things of yourself when all you feel is good for Narnsee?" India's mouth dropped open.

"But, how do you know what I feel? I want things to be

like they were, but they have changed - I have changed."

Seesah chuckled in the darkness. "We have all changed Indee; you have become a man and Narnsee has become a woman."

"But she is - was my sister."

"Not by blood Indee. We took you into our house because you were a fine boy - but a stranger. If Narnsee feels as you do, and I am sure she does, we will be happy because we will not lose you."

India was both embarrassed and ecstatic at the full import of Seesah's words. "You mean? But Narnsee may not feel as I do and..." he felt Seesah's hand touch his arm.

"I have watched you for many moons now, and I see that you are both of the same mind. Talk with her Indee. You have the blessing of both Narntac and me if you wish to take her for your own." India was lost for words. He wanted to shout his thanks to the heavens but contented himself with thanking Seesah. He reached for her hand and squeezed it until she thought he might break her fingers.

The next morning Seesah, winking at Indee, suggested that he and Narnsee try their luck at fishing. The two of them ambled toward the shore, Indee unusually quiet searching for the right words. He cleared his throat, "Nancy. Nancy I..."

Before he could say any more Narnsee put down her spear, grabbed hold of him and planted a soft kiss on his lips. "Indee, I know you want me for your woman and that's what I want too, but you've taken a bloody long time to get round to it ain't ya! Come 'ere," and with that she put her arms around his neck and kissed him again.

They sank to their knees, right there on the shoreline, shedding their rudimentary clothing, hungry for each other. It all came so easily, so naturally, melting into each other's bodies, each totally lost in the sheer ecstasy of the feelings that they had unleashed. They made love hungrily; passion building to a climax which, when it came, carried them to a place that neither had ever dreamed could exist. They were the only two people on earth, enraptured in the moment. Finally, satiated, they lay on the sand chests heaving, euphoric.

Neither spoke for some time then Narnsee rolled over to snuggle into India, caressing his body. "Oh Indee, you are wonderful, I want us to be together forever." India had never imagined that anything could be so beautiful; he felt his heart would burst with happiness. In all his life he had never felt the warmth and gentleness of a woman's touch and now here he was laying alongside the beautiful Narnsee, his love.

"When we get back," he said, "I will tell old Narntac that I want you to be my missus." Narnsee leant over and kissed him once more

"'Bout time too. I fort you was never gonna get round to it. Come on mate, we'd better get some grub in."

They waded into the crystal waters, spears ready, but all India could think of was how beautiful Narnsee was and how wonderful their love making had been. They were standing up to their waists naked and there was no hiding the fact that he wanted her again. Narnsee looked down, grinned and splashed water in his face. "Now, now! We've got to catch some fish before I'm gonna let you catch me again." She turned and swam a little further out, laughing. "Mind you, I might change me mind if you're quick enough."

India was about to launch after her when he spotted the familiar triangular fin of the sea children. He called out to Narnsee laughing. "Ay Nancy, they're back."

Smiling, she turned to look past her shoulder but cried out and struck out for the shore, her face contorted with fear. As India watched Narnsee suddenly disappeared then, just as suddenly, she erupted from the water screaming, clamped in the jaws of a huge creature, its silver grey body glistening wet. He watched, transfixed as she disappeared once more. He heard someone screaming out her name, screaming, screaming as he stared at the water, now tinged pink, part of the bead necklace he had so lovingly made for her floating lazily, the only sign that she was ever there.

India felt pressure on both arms as he was dragged onto the shore. He lashed out still screaming for Narnsee. Her two brothers, Sammac and Shomoon held him tight as he tried frantically to pull away and rush back into the water. He thrashed and struggled against them but it was no use, eventually he fell to his knees trembling. He tried to form the words, to tell them where she was but they wouldn't come, he could manage just an incoherent jumble. He felt strong arms lift him and carry him back to his hut. He was aware of Seesah forcing something down his throat, then blackness.

He awoke to sobbing. Seesah sat alongside his mat, rocking to and fro arms folded tight across her chest as though she felt it might break open. It was true then, the horror was not a bad dream, Narnsee was really gone. India could not cry, he could not feel, he was trapped inside some sort of bubble; he could see and hear but he was apart. He watched himself moving and talking to Seesah but he, India, was floating above them, a spectator, and so it was for several weeks. Narntac and his family not only mourned the loss of their dearest daughter, they mourned for India too. He was still with them physically but he had lost his mind, maybe they feared, forever.

Very gradually India began to return to something of his old self and marshal his thoughts. He let himself acknowledge that Narnsee had been killed, gone forever. He told Narntac that he wanted to hunt for the creature that had taken her and kill it, and was upset and surprised at her father's reaction. "India, my son. It would be wrong to do such a thing. The creature did not want to hurt you, or Narnsee; it was just looking for food." Narntac's reasoning and the thought of Narnsee's end was abhorrent to India.

"How can you say that? It was your own daughter the beast took! It slaughtered her just as though she was no more than another fish in the sea!"

"But that is just what she was - what we are! The sea is bountiful Indee, it gives us life. We take from it every day, and sometimes it takes from us. My heart is breaking for my daughter but we cannot always take, sometimes the gods demand that we have to give too."

India was incensed, he was angry that Narntac could say these things; that he did not want to kill the monster. Without another word he stormed off, running down to the shore. He ran and ran, until he was exhausted. He threw himself to the ground and, for the first time wept. His sobs wracked his whole body until it hurt to breath but he could not stop. On his knees with his head on the sand he could not hold back the tears or the anguished cries that echoed across the water well into the night.

Several nights later, Indee once more alone on the sands, Seesah came and sat alongside him just as she had a lifetime ago when she had reassured him of Narnsee's feelings for him. "You will be leaving us soon." Her words shocked India, for they crystallized his feelings of unhappiness and uncertainty into something he had known he must do. She had, as usual, known his own mind before he had!

"You came to me before and you knew of my thoughts and now again you understand them better than I do."

"Tell me of your feelings my son."

"Oh Seesah, I have been happier here than I ever thought it possible. With Narnsee I knew I would never want for anything, but now that she is gone I am in such pain. Everywhere I look, every time I hear you speak, I am reminded of her and I just can't bear it. I love you, my family. You have all been so good to me and I know I will miss you and be very sad to go, but even though I tell myself this, the thought of staying here and being surrounded by memories of Narnsee is just more than I can bear."

"It is late Indee, and your soul is tortured, but know this. Whatever you feel you must do, your family will understand. We have lost our beautiful Narnsee and now maybe we will lose you too, but whether you go or stay you will always be in our hearts. Go now, let the spirits guide you. I will pray that they lead you to contentment."

India struggled with his thoughts throughout the night but in the end he knew what he must do. He would go back to his old life, try to make a go of it in his old familiar world. Try to forget that for one fleeting instant he had held paradise in his hands before it had slipped through his fingers.

Chapter 22

Four years passed at Dragons Lair and true to the promise that he had made to himself Jake worked hard at his schooling, both in the classroom and aboard ship under the tutelage of George and old Eddie Wickenden. He had changed considerably in every aspect. Physically he had developed into a handsome young man with long strong legs and a well sculpted body. His chestnut shoulder length hair, now sun bleached accentuated the long dark lashes that fringed his blue eyes. Being around Harry he had developed his clipped cultured way of speaking and reading any books he could get his hands on had massively extended his vocabulary. He had also proved to be a natural sailor, *"A ship's just like a woman son, you have to listen to her, let her show you what she wants; treat her gentle like and she'll always come through for you,"* and was one of only a handful of the camp's inhabitants that could bring a ship safely through the rocky channel into their lagoon. Harry preened with every one of Jake's achievements; he had been right about the boy; he was exceptionally astute, and was a born leader - a special person.

In the early days Jake would remain on The Catherine while Harry and the rest of the crew were relieving some hapless ship of their riches, but as time passed he progressed to being in the front line of boarding parties and then to actually leading some raids. There were a few skirmishes but Harry knew his trade and singled out only those ships with weak officers or discontented crews who were not prepared to risk their lives to protect the goods of some rich merchant so, for the most part, they encountered very little opposition.

Every few weeks one of the Dragon's smaller vessels was loaded with silks and goods to exchange for supplies in Pont la Santa Maria, a small but cosmopolitan port a days' sailing away. These shopping expeditions also presented a good opportunity for the small crew to stay in town carousing for a night or two, and to learn which ships were transporting which cargoes before returning to report to Harry. On this occasion Jake was in charge of the supply trip so he called in on John Pryor to collect the list of goods required, money for expenses and any further orders.

He was just leaving John's room when Harry called out. "It's on Jake. Silas has just come back. The Pride of London sails tomorrow morning and we'll be able to intercept her just off the point here before she can haul full sail. She's carrying sugar Jake – white gold!"

"But she's an East Indiaman, Harry, and well armed, and sugar hogs are perishable. Can you take enough of the cargo to make it worthwhile? If she suspects anything she could run out her guns and..." A look of anger flashed across Harry's face.

"I'm disappointed in you Jake. That cargo is worth a fortune and it belongs to Sir Richard Greebe, an odious snake of a man whom I will enjoy besting."

"I'm sorry Harry. I just have misgivings because of the size of the ship." He stepped forward to shake Harry's hand. "I shouldn't question your judgment, there's no-one knows their trade better than you – good luck and God speed."

Three days later Jake strode purposefully along the quay eagerly anticipating his night on the town. All business had been concluded, to Jake's mind very successfully, and he had left half the crew guarding their supplies, they having had their recreation the night before. He was unaware of the many heads he turned as his small group progressed. He was half a head taller than his companions and devastatingly handsome.

They were soon jostling their way through a crowded smoke filled tavern toward the one table that was free whilst trying to attract the bar keep's attention as they went. The place was filled with the noise of men intent on enjoying their time in port. Some singing, some sharing a joke, some becoming argumentative as the ale took hold. Jake was soon enjoying himself immensely; it felt so good to be one of the lads and the ale was slipping down very easily, in fact in no time at all he and his companions had entered into the spirit of things and were roaring out a well known sea shanty at the top of their lungs.

As Jake staggered to the bar intent on ordering refills an arm slid around his waist, and looking down he saw that it belonged to a very pretty girl with long dark hair and full red lips. He noticed when she smiled that she had the most beautiful white and even teeth as, without thinking, he lifted her off the ground so that her face was level with his. He enjoyed being so close to her and marvelled at the softness of her skin, the feel of her, the roundness of her body, all so soft and pliant. Having limited experience of the fairer sex he misread her intent and assumed she was after him buying her a drink. Her husband however became aware of her interest in Jake as soon as he had entered the tavern, and knew exactly what she had in mind. He was incensed at the blatant way she threw herself as this young whippersnapper and, not stopping to think, he pushed his way toward the pair and without any warning landed a roundhouse to Jake's jaw laying him out cold. Before anyone could stop it, there was a free for all and the tavern now rang with the sound of men shouting, women screaming and wood splintering.

Jake came to with teeth chattering, head splitting and the smell of the dank musty cell that was now his prison filling his nostrils and making him gag. He had no idea how he had ended up in such a place, or how long he had been there, but the narrow window set high in the wall was just discernible in the moonlight, so he assumed that it was still some time of night.

He became aware of others in the room, some mumbling in their sleep, some snoring at varying volumes. He moved so that his back was against a wall, hugging his knees in an attempt to keep warm. The relative quiet was shattered by a low, heart rending cry, "Nancy, Nancy, No, No." This was followed by deep shuddering sobs. Something touched a chord within Jake and he felt compelled to make his way toward the sound of the poor wretch who was obviously suffering greatly.

Kneeling, he reached out and gently shook the man beneath the bundle of rags. "Sshhh. You were having a bad dream but there's nothing to be afraid of in here. I'm too cold to sleep, do you want to talk for a while." A searching hand came from beneath the rags and found Jake's knee.

"What d'you want? I ain't done nothin and I'm warning yer, if you mess with me you'll 'av to take the conserquences." Jake was taken aback and unannounced tears sprang to his eyes as he thought of dear India giving him a lecture that first day they had met. The voice continued, "I asked you what yer up to! Just leave me alone or you'll be sorry!"

"I'm sorry but you sounded so upset and just then, when you spoke, you reminded me so much of a dear friend who I lost years ago."

The figure beneath the rags dragged itself to a sitting

position. "Ok mate. Can't be too careful in places like this, they're usually full of right bastards. Blimey though, you sounds like a bit of a toff, so what you doing in 'ere?"

Jake sighed, "I'm not quite sure. One minute I was enjoying a drink with my shipmates and the next I woke up in here. What about you. What have you done?"

"Long story mate, I 'ad this girl see but she got eat by a bastard shark."

"Oh, that's awful, what rotten luck!"

"Yeh, more for her than me though. Anyway, it broke me heart and I 'it the bottle. I just drink till I can't think no more. I keep ending up in shitholes like this but, you know what? I keeps hoping that one day I won't wake up and then maybe I can be with 'er, my Nancy."

All the while the man was talking Jake was reminded more and more of India. "I had a friend who spoke like you." We were shipmates on a Man of War, HMS Huron, it was called. We were both pressed from a village close to my home but again it's a long story." Jake sighed, "He was killed and I was taken by privateers. I'll never forget him though, never." For quite some time Jake's new companion said nothing. To break the silence Jake said "By the way, my name is..." the stranger finished his sentence,

"Jake." Jake was astonished.

"How the heck do you know that?"

"Well, you do sound like a toff, and I dunno 'ow, but it's gotta be you. I'm India - by the way!"

The two men strained their eyes to see through the dawn light that was now creeping into the cell, both wrestling with the impossible notion that the friend they had thought lost forever could not only be alive, but could have fetched up in the same place, in the same cell, on the same day! "You can't be India. He was thrown overboard by a murderous swine called Charlie Croucher and he drowned."

"No I didn't mate. I landed on some driftwood – that's a long story too."

Jake reached out. "Is it really you Indy? How? What happened? I can't believe it, I can't believe it!" Laughing and with tears in his eyes he reached out and took the stranger into his arms. "Come here you little squirt, come here and tell me how the hell you wriggled out of drowning. Are you a ghost? Have you got a fairy Godmother?"

"Not so much of the squirt and no I ain't a ghost, I was just lucky – for a change."

The two friends huddled under India's blanket. Jake didn't notice their smell and wouldn't have cared if he had. They both had so much to tell each other so talked non-stop as shafts of morning sunlight gradually filtered into their dark dank cell, both oblivious of their three other cell mates disclosed by the morning light.

They were deep in conversation when the heavy cell door clanged open, light flooding in, silhouetting the jailer who stepped inside calling for Jacob Throgmorton. From behind the big man's shoulder a face Jake immediately recognized peered out. "George, thank goodness, I need to get out of here." He threw aside the blanket and strode across the room climbing the small flight of stone stairs and grabbing George's hand. India grabbed up his knapsack which was full of precious Kwashi and was fast on his old friend's heels, but stopped short once he got a good look at George.

"Jesus Christ, who's that ugly bastard? How can he get you out of 'ere? He's a bleeding freak. He should be locked up in 'ere, not us."

Jake turned, grabbing India by the throat, "George is one of the best people I have ever known and far more worthy than a drunk like you. If you ever, ever speak about him like that again I'll break your skull without a seconds thought – understand!" India, shocked and chastened, silently held up his hands in submission.

George spoke. "I've managed to persuade our friend here that you have done nothing wrong - just let your hair down a little. I have paid for all damages incurred at the Inn, rewarded the good man here for taking such good care of you, and promised that such a thing will never happen again. On that basis he in turn has agreed that I can take you into my custody forthwith."

"Blimey, he talks like he's swallered a book." Jake stamped on India's toe. "Ow! What's that for? I only meant that he ain't as daft as I thought he was. Can he reward our friend 'ere a bit more, so's I can come with yer?"

George gave Jake a wry smile as he took a handful of coins and offered them to the jailer. "Go on then. Take the no good with you. He'll be back before you know it; his sort always are!"

The two lads stepped into the bright sunshine shielding their eyes and once acclimatised were now able to get a good look at each other. India was pallid under his coffee coloured skin with dark rings under his eyes. He was half a head shorter than Jake with a slim but muscular build. He was far too thin and it was obvious that he had been neglecting himself but despite that he was still beautiful. Jake couldn't think of another appropriate word, the features were too delicate to be handsome, he was just beautiful. His black hair hung lank around his face which was still smooth with just the hint of a moustache above his top lip. But it was his soulful liquid brown eyes that brought a lump to Jake's throat. He could hardly believe it; after all this time it truly was him, his irrepressible little friend Indy.

India saw that Jake by contrast was a picture of health. His shoulder length hair was thick and lustrous. His blue eyes shone out from his tanned face which was bristling with the need of a shave. He had grown much taller and was well muscled and had a presence of natural authority about him that set him apart. He was, India thought a truly handsome man, and he realized just how much he loved his long lost friend. He spat on his hand and held it out. "Put it there Jake. From now on I'm gonna make sure I never lose you again – my brother, that's what you are."

Jake took Indy's hand and they stood, eyes locked for fully ten seconds until Jake, swallowing back his emotion, ruffled India's hair just as he had done so often in the past. "Well, if you're going to pretend to be my brother you'd better have a wash, you stink."

Turning to George he said, "Thanks George, I should have known you'd sort things out. I've been really worried about the crew and all, is everything Ok? How did you find me so quickly and how did you really wangle getting us out?" George smiled but said nothing and the three walked down to the quay in silence. "See Indy, I told you George is the best. You have no idea." India still had grave reservations. True the man seemed to have a brain but he was so ugly, so bloody ugly.

Trying to lighten the mood, Jake confided, "You'll never believe it George. This is India, you know - the boy I told you about? The one I thought was dead. The one Croucher hurt so badly - he wanted him dead you know."

George looked straight ahead, pushed his hands deeper into his pockets. "Can't think why!" When they climbed aboard and were under sail George suddenly became more animated. "The lad's not too bad Jake, just ignorant." Jake thought back to how he had viewed the world before meeting Harry, George and the others. He made a mental note to apologise to Indy and to try to set him straight.

Chapter 23

Once on course for Dragons Lair, George spoke again. "Things are not good Jake. Harry is badly wounded but is hanging on and insisting that he needs to see you."

"What happened, was it The Pride of London?"

"Yes, we played the usual distress card and managed to board her hiding the rest of the crew below decks until we had secured the ship. The Captain and crew surrendered easily - much too easily - we should have smelt a rat. Anyway, when we went below decks we didn't find any cargo just marines, armed and waiting for us. Someone must have tipped them off. Anyway, as you can imagine, we had a real fight on our hands. We managed to escape but most of us were wounded; Harry caught a bullet in the back – lost the use of his legs. We had a real struggle to get him back aboard; we lost twenty men Jake, twenty!" George was silent for a moment. "They gave chase but being smaller and swifter we made it to the Dragons' teeth and escaped. They probably think we perished on the rocks, hope so anyway; we threw a few barrels and bits overboard just in case they hung around waiting for us."

"Is Harry going to be alright? Can he walk?"

George pursed his lips and shook his head. "Non, mon cher; I'm afraid he is mortally wounded. Mrs. Haitch has done all she can but the bullet has shattered his spine and he is bleeding inside. He's full of fever. When you didn't come back with the stores he knew something was wrong; that's why he sent me. I just pray we make it in time - he is so set on seeing you before he goes."

"Blimey, sounds to me like he should have croaked it by now. Still, I'm still 'ere and you never reckoned on that did yer?" Both men scowled at Indy who decided it may be prudent from now on to speak only when spoken to.

The sloop was in full sail but seemed to Jake to be moving at the pace of a snail. Eventually they rounded the point and turned to look straight into the Dragons' teeth. Indy, who had been silent since imparting his last pearl of wisdom, took in the boiling seas ahead and the cruel, jagged rocks that they seemed to be heading straight onto. He was suddenly transported back on that sandy island shore looking at the fearsome teeth that had savaged his darling Nancy. He froze; they were going to smash onto the rocks and drown or worse, be eaten alive by one of those accursed sea monsters. He heard himself screaming, partly for him, partly for Nancy as he saw in his mind's eye not rocks but the dorsal fins of those huge, dead eyed giants as the white foaming water crashed over granite. George, fearing that the screaming would distract Jake or that the boy would try to turn the ship, stepped behind Indy and clubbed him over the head rendering him unconscious. He looked to Jake who nodded his understanding.

When Indy awoke they were moving slowly along in calm brackish waters that mirrored the lush overhanging vegetation. The air was filled with the sweet cloying perfume of exotic flowers and he could hear the screeching of the brightly coloured birds that swept in and out of his vision like fireflies. He sat up suddenly, head hammering. Jake knelt down putting a hand on his shoulder. "Sorry Indy but George had to stop you from wrecking us. You went crazy back there."

"Where the hell are we? How did we get 'ere and what the hell did you risk killing us all for? I thought I, we was gonners, I really did."

"We are just coming into our camp. It's safe here; no-one dare run the rocks but we know a secret way through.

When you are a bit stronger I'll show you."

"No you bleedin' won't. You know I 'ates water. From now on if I can't walk anywhere, I ain't goin'."

Leaving others to unload the provisions on board Jake and George hurried along to Harry's cabin where they found John Pryor and Mrs. Hardcastle ministering to him as best they could. Although George had warned him, Jake was not prepared for the change he saw in his beloved Harry. The once flamboyant handsome peacock lay shrunken, ghostly white, a sheet pulled up to his neck. His golden hair dull and damp with sweat was tied in some sort of knot on the top of his head. His eyes were sunken, lips dried and cracked with sores. There was a cloying smell in the room that made Jake want to gag but he sat on the stool beside the bed and took Harry's hand.

Sensing someone was there Harry turned his head and seemed to brighten a little when he saw Jake. "My boy, you made it. So glad all well - worried about you. You were right, I got it wrong - you have good instincts son always listen to them. Need to sleep but want talk, lot to say – soon. Pryor knows." Jake looked pleadingly at Mrs. Hardcastle.

"It's no use my boy. He wouldn't want to live like this, even if he could. You just step outside for a bit while I clean him up. I'll call you when he wakes again."

Jake sat moribund, the drink George had pressed into his hand turned warm. Eventually the door opened and he was beckoned inside. Harry raised a smile when he saw Jake. "Come near Jake, and hold my hand once more. I can't feel it but it's good to have you close. Now, I have much to tell you and not much breath, so don't interrupt please. I have pondered often on what I would do should I die as I have no family, nor any likelihood of one. Then you came along, the son I would have loved to have. I saw so much of me in you and yet you are so much more. Tell your Pa by the way that he should be the proudest father on earth to have such a son as you.

Now, I have made arrangements with dear John to pass my share of our prize money over to you, which will make you a very rich young man."

"But..."

"Please just listen Jake, I can't move and I have little strength. I told you that I had to leave England and I was stripped of my wealth but that was not quite true. Thanks to dear John and one or two true friends I was able to sign over title deeds to various properties and land to John, whom I have told you I trust with my life, and so can you Jake. When you get to England you will need to go to my good friend Giles Mason of Mason and Maws in London who has taken instruction from me as to what should happen if I die. He holds a small amount of gold and some jewels which he will hand over to you but the real wealth is of course locked in those deeds." Harry's eyes closed and he lay silent for a few minutes. He rallied and spoke again.

"For security Mr. Mason will ask you several questions the answers to which only I, and my dear John know at present; you must remember them well Jake. Keep them in your head; don't write them down. When he is satisfied with your answers he will hand you a key to a safety deposit box which is in my London bank. He will accompany you and help you, should you need it.

"My dear old Pryor knows all of this and has agreed to travel to meet you in London at a time and date agreeable to both yourselves and Giles Mason, when he will sign over all these documents to you. If you take my advice, once you have inspected the box, you will return the key to Mr.

Mason for safe keeping until you can all get together for the signing. One more thing, you will need to take my signet ring; he will need that as further proof of my wishes. Take it please Jake. As you can see I am unable to remove it myself." Jake hesitated "Please Jake, take it with my blessing".

Jake reluctantly removed the ring and placed it on his own finger.

"Lastly, I would ask a favour. I told you that a dear lady friend of mine helped me to flee to France. Her name is now Lady Catherine Villiers; she is married to Sir Edward Villiers and now lives on their estate, down in the West Country. I would be so grateful if you would visit her and present her with a diamond and emerald brooch that you will find in the box at Coutts, and tell her that I died never forgetting what a great friend and lady she is." Jake was stunned.

"But I know the lady. My Pa has worked for Sir Edward on the great house and there never was a finer gentleman - excepting yourself of course."

"There you are then Jake it is kismet - meant to be. So glad, all sorted. Pryor knows what to do. Leave me now I feel weary. Just kiss me before you go, my boy - my son." Jake kissed Harry's forehead and sat watching him sleep for a while before letting himself out into the fading light.

He heard quite a commotion coming from the shower area - Indy's high pitched shouts of protest as cook forced him to bathe. "Just shut up young un. George told me to sluice you down and that's what I'm a doin. I ain't having you anywhere near my kitchen smelling like a tanning yard; now hold still or I'll box your ears." At any other time Jake would have found it all very amusing but not today, today there was only room for sorrow.

John Pryor approached him. "You holding up lad? We'll go through Harry's instructions later – I expect it's all a bit of a shock."

Before he could reply Mrs. Hardcastle appeared behind them calling softly. "He's gone, God bless him; he's gone."

Jake and Pryor strode back to the house. "There's no need for speed any more lads. He's at peace now. The Lord knows how he kept going as long as he did. Come inside and say your last farewell then I'll get him ready for all the others to pay their respects."

The two men tiptoed up to Harry's bed and Jake was surprised to see that he did indeed look at peace. The dark circles and lines previously etched around his eyes seemed to have lessened and it looked, for all the world, as though he was peacefully asleep. Both men bent to kiss him one last time then left Mrs. Hardcastle to her ministrations. She shaved, washed and plugged his poor broken body, dressed him in his finest clothes then, silent tears forming dark spots on his turquoise tunic, she laid him out before rigor set in.

Boxer, who had not been allowed into the sick room, nudged open the door and ran to Harry's bedside. Standing on his back legs he licked his master's face. "He's gone Boxer, he's at peace now." Boxer turned his head towards her then jumped onto the bed, curling up at Harry's feet. Mrs. Hardcastle had an unexpected rush of love for the loyal little dog. "You loved him too didn't you - I know. Well you do your duty one last time little one. It's better that he is not alone tonight." She bent to stroke the wiry grey head, a pink tongue gently licked away the tears that had fallen onto her hand; they were united in grief.

Somehow the whole camp knew. The general hustle and bustle ceased and men began drifting towards the Capn's house, murmuring amongst themselves; consoling each other as best they could. Beau, who had been injured himself helping to rescue Harry, struggled up the slightly sloping ground leaning heavily on a makeshift crutch. "Come on now lads. That's Harry in there. Do you think he would want us to be standing round like a lot of old women? No, he'd say break out the wine lads and drink his health. He was the best man I ever knew and I for one am gonna drink to him until I can't stand up – on one leg or two! Cookie, break out the rations now – we are all in need of a bracer."

Cook, still wet from his tussle with Indy, nodded his approval. "Yes indeed, there never was such a good 'un as Harry. Come on lads, line up for beef stew and grog, lots of grog. We'll drink to his happy landing in the next world – they are in for treat when he gets there!" The mood lifted slightly as everyone shuffled down to the cookhouse. Indy, cold and still seething at the affront to his person had the sense for once to say nothing and joined the queue, tankard ready. Judging from the men's mood he thought to himself that this Harry must have been quite a bloke, so he embraced the spirit of the wake and slipped into the oh so familiar alcoholic haze that was his comfort blanket. The whole community caroused through the night, laughing and weeping alternately, everyone with a story to tell about their dear Harry. He had been the glue that held them together. They had been lost souls when he'd found them, now they were once more adrift without a rudder.

The next morning the weather was dull and grey, befitting the mood of the solemn procession following the makeshift coffin to the lookout point above camp. The point was a small plateau with just about enough room for the whole crew to stand. At the head of the procession

Abraham and five others carried the open wooden box. Jake and Indy brought up the rear, helping Beau and the other wounded to make the climb up the narrow path. There was little soil on the granite cliff so they laid the coffin in a shallow grave piling on stones to make a cairn. Someone had carved a wooden plaque which was wedged atop it. It read simply, *Lord Henry Throgmorton 1744 - 1786.* George, being the most eloquent of the group said a few words. Each man was lost in his own thoughts as they listened. Most of them had been adrift before they had met **Harry, many heading for the hangman's** noose. He had galvanised them into one brotherhood - what now? Jake thought of the first time he had seen Harry, so exotic and full of life, and his heart twisted in his chest robbing him momentarily of breath - how could he be gone!

Chapter 24

Men gathered around the cookhouse, those that had an appetite eating bread and cold mutton, cook having no stomach for work today. George, who had been deep in conversation with Beau and Pryor went to the dinner bell and rang it summoning those who had wandered off. When the whole complement of Dragons' Lair was present, he spoke. "It is a very sad day lads and none of us thought that it would come so soon, but Harry had an idea that he was hoping to put to you all, not quite yet maybe, but now my friend's, events have overtaken us." He signalled to John Pryor who stood, "John will explain it to you."

Taking a deep breath John began "Harry was thinking – hoping - that before too long, we – all of us, could start up a legitimate business. We've had a good, and up to now, charmed life, but he felt that our luck would run out before too long, as indeed it now has." Most of the men looked stunned. Pryor held up his hands appealing for quiet. "I know it's a strange notion but hear me out. The ship that was our undoing was *supposed* to be carrying sugar - some call it white gold for obvious reasons. For some time now, Harry had been thinking that maybe we could buy a parcel of land and grow our own sugar. Grow it, ship it and sell it ourselves; starting something he called a co-operative. He has always been fair and honest with us and he reckoned that if we found good men to work alongside us, paid them and treated them well, we could all share in a good life. You all know that he hated the way men are kept as slaves and worked till they die; how some men grow rich through the misery of others. I know Harry could have put this so much better than I, but what do you think?"

There was a stunned silence, then a flurry of questions

"Where would we buy the land and how would we pay for it?

"Who knows anything about growing sugar canes?"

"How would we ship it?"

Pryor again held up his hands. "The land would not be a problem and there are plenty of experts in growing sugar canes. The main concern for Harry was how we could pay for it. That is why he was waiting and probably why he took the risk of tackling The Pride of London, but what George, Beau and I would like to put to you is this." He paused, took another deep breath and carried on. "How would you feel about pooling all our bounty money? If we did, by my reckoning we would have almost enough to buy the land and make a start. We have a ship and crew so transport is secured and," with a wry smile, "we know how to keep an eye out for buccaneers!"

A frisson of excitement went around the men. George took over. "The idea is all very new and very sudden I know, so I think it best that we all think on this until tomorrow. Of course you should all do as you feel. We are free men after all and anyone wanting to take their due share and make their own way in the world will have our blessing. We could all stay here and carry on as we have been but somehow without Harry to lead us I'm not sure I have the heart for it. For myself and all of us, I would like to make Harry's dream come true. No more secrecy, no more fearing a musket ball in the head or hangman's noose. As I said just now, let's give ourselves time to think things over and meet tomorrow at noon to discuss it further - is everyone agreed?"

Beau, as he had the night before called for drinks all round. Their lives, for better or worse, had changed forever and he for one was going to get drunk.

As they dispersed George caught hold of Jake's arm. "This does not concern you Jake. You have your life ahead of you and it was Harry's wish that you go back to your home and become the great man he knew you could be."

"I want to go home, I miss Ma and Pa so much but before I do. You said that someone had betrayed you on the last raid and I want to find out who it was and take revenge for Harry's death."

"No Jake. Ling Chow and Jeng Yen have already left. They are the best men for the job. Folk ignore them and speak freely around them thinking they can't understand. Rest assured, they will find the culprit and they know what to do with him when they do. Enough now Jake, you and you friend have things to do in readiness for your leaving, and may God keep you."

The next morning most of the men were gathered around the cookhouse well before the appointed time, and lively discussions went on until George rang the bell to bring the meeting to order. "Well now, it seems our proposal has given you all much to think on. We'll have a show of hands now, for and against, but as I said yesterday, every man is free to choose his own destiny – Harry would have it no other way. All those wanting to leave this life behind and join our co-operative raise their hands." For a few seconds it was only George, Beau and Pryor who did so, then one or two more, then gradually more until all but three of the gathering joined them.

"Well, it looks as though most of us are ready for a new start." Turning to Pryor he asked how that left them financially. The treasurer stood and explained that they were just a little short but he was sure a couple more raids would provide the extra money needed. At that point Jake spoke out.

"If you had my share, and Harry's, would you have enough then?"

"Well, as Harry's share was the greatest, and with yours, yes, but you are not to be part of this."

Jake now stood "I am part of this and I think this is a once in a lifetime chance and could be a new beginning for you all and I wish I could come with you, but as I can't I can at least make it possible by putting in my share; with it you can start making plans now." India, annoyed with his friend and thinking him crazy, elbowed him hard in his thigh. Suddenly everyone was on their feet, patting each on the back, shaking hands, many making for Jake to thank him for his generosity. India sloped off talking to himself.

"He's bloody crazy. Never had a pot to piss in and now he never will 'av, Gawd almighty, what a bloody turnip!"

Jake found India sitting on the edge of the jetty – his body language giving away his mood. "Come on Indy, this place and those lads have given me so much, why should they have to risk any more danger when I had the money to give?"

"You don't get it do yer. We - er you, 'ad the chance to live the kind of the life we could only 'ave dreamed about. Live like posh folks with good food and drink every day, posh clothes and all; and what about your Ma and Pa? We could 'av all been in clover, and now you've buggered it up; you're a real turnip head and no mistake!"

Jake smiled. "I'm not completely stupid you know. Shall I tell you something?"

"Oh for Christ's sake don't say it makes yer feel good or nothin like that – I'd be sick!"

"Well it does make me feel good to help my friends so there, but what I was going to tell you is that I will be rich when I get to London, very rich; so what do you think of that?"

Indy was now all ears "'Ow come? You've just given everythin' away! 'Av you fallen off your carriage? It's only a story about the streets of London being paved with gold yer know; believe me they ain't! Just full of rich folks, who'd spit on yer as soon as look at yer, beggars and footpads. It's a shithole for the likes of us, so 'ow you gonna get rich in that lot – tell me that?"

Jake swore Indy to secrecy and explained that Harry had left a fortune in land, money and jewellery to him. "When we get to London I have to go to his legal friend in Arbuthnot Street who will arrange everything for me."

India visibly brightened "Gawd Almighty Jake, what are we waiting for? Come on let's get some grog and celebrate. I'm suddenly bleeding 'ungry." They joined the carnival atmosphere back at camp, enjoying the cold mutton and slightly stale bread that was on offer; Indy now being full of joie de vivre and goodwill to all men. Cook was re-lighting the fire for tonight's meal and Boxer was having great fun helping to round up the unfortunate chickens that were on the menu.

Over the next two days Jake said his goodbyes to all his shipmates and spent several hours talking over the past four years with his special friends George, Abraham and Beau. He was excited to be going home at last but very sad knowing that it may be years before he saw these men who had done so much for him again, if ever. John Pryor tested him once again on the answers he must give to Mr. Mason in London and presented him with a small box containing Harry's most prized possessions. "He wanted you to have these Jake." Jake opened the box. Inside it was Harry's dagger with its ornately decorated sheath, several silver buckles, a brass compass and an exquisite gold pocket watch and chain.

"But, what about you? He was your best friend! You must have something as a keepsake."

"Bless you Jake, he left me a few mementos but he knows I have no use for such things as those. Believe me, he took my interests into account and I am well provided for."

The following morning the two friends were packed and ready to leave for Pont la Mar where they hoped to board a ship leaving for Calais in France. They were travelling lightly with one valise each and of course India still had his satchel slung over his shoulder, the precious contents rustling inside. Pryor had given them more than enough money to pay for their passage and lodgings and reminded them to make sure not to get duped in France. He said all being well he would set out for London in six to nine months time and would mail Jake as soon as he arrived, and of course he would by then have news of their new co-operative venture.

As they walked to the jetty where Beau, George, Abraham, Tom, Mrs. Hardcastle and Boxer were waiting for one last goodbye, John spoke. "I have to tell you one more thing Jake! Sometime last year we got news that The Huron had gone down at the Battle of Saintes off Dominica; the battle that you and Indy here would have been in, and as far as we know all hands were lost. We kept the news from you but now you are going home you would be bound to find out. All I can say is that we were all so thankful that you escaped such a fate." He held out his hand. "Goodbye lad and God keep you safe until we meet again." Jake fought back tears at the news that all his old shipmates were lost; time to grieve when they were underway. He hugged every one of the small party including Boxer who licked his face as though it was covered in chicken gravy. India shook hands wishing that he'd had the time to get to know these people, especially George – how could he have got it so wrong.

They boarded the sloop waving to their dear friends until they became mere specs in the distance. Jake was pleased to see that Mrs. Hardcastle was holding Boxer in her arms. She appeared to have felt Harry's death more than anyone and he was glad that she and dear Boxer seemed to have become inseparable now that he was gone.

"Oh Gawd Jake." It was Indy looking out at the seething waters and jagged rocks. "If we get out of this lot I ain't never coming back 'ere, never." As the ship began to buck Jake laughed out loud.

"Oh shut up you girl. This is the life eh Indy. Pitching your wits against the elements and winning! This is the life!"

Tom Grey who was at the helm grinned to himself, Jake was right this is the life, and a good one. Indy, sitting on the deck hanging on for dear life felt like screaming but not wanting another smack on the head, thought better of it, closed his eyes and tried to swallow his fear.

....

On the voyage to Calais the friends had time to take stock. Everything had happened so fast! Meeting each other, losing Harry, inheriting a fortune and, hardest of all to absorb, learning that The Huron had gone down with all hands. They talked long into the nights about their days on the ship. The friends they had lost, Sol, Mel, Ginger, Walden and so many others; both of them shuddering at the thought of those poor souls meeting their end in those dark fearful waters. Gradually the shock and grief subsided and they spent more time learning about how each other had spent the last four years.

Once he had heard the full story of Indy's native life and Narnsee's dreadful end, Jake felt less disapproving of his friend's drinking, which anyway was lessening at approximately the same rate that his old sunny disposition was reappearing. Jake was fascinated by Indy's tale and made a mental note to maybe one day try to find the islands and these people.

Jake felt that maybe this was the time to tell of Eli's friend Junti and the flower tattoo that they shared. Indy was fascinated and said it helped in some way to explain why he had felt so at home on the islands with Narntac and his family. Seesah had said that the gods had brought him to them, so maybe it could be true, maybe Junti was his father, and maybe all that had happened and would happen in the future was meant to be. Who knew?

Indy wanted to hear more about George and the other unfortunates who had the misfortune to have been born different. He, like most people, had a closed mind when it came to physical abnormality, assuming that it went hand in hand with idiocy. He was astounded to hear that Jake had learnt so much from George and that he could now read and do figuring, and was chastened by his own previously bigoted outlook. Much to Jake's enjoyment Indy was keen to learn too and they spent most days of the voyage, in the roles of master and pupil.

Chapter 25

Before they reached the harbour they could smell the port of Calais. A cocktail of turgid water, fish and tar filled their nostrils and their ears were filled with men shouting in an unintelligible language, the screeching of winches and shrilling of herring gulls. The two friends disembarked and made their way into town to find lodgings grateful to leave behind the smell and hubbub of the busy port. They took the first room available, changed into the only other set of clothes they had with them and went out to find some food and a little relaxation on terra firma.

A couple of hours later, after a meal of some sort of fish soup and potatoes accompanied by a tankard of heavy red wine, Jake was having difficulty staying awake and suggested they go back to their room for an early night; they would try for passage to London in the morning. Indy, who was enjoying the ambiance of the town, and took a liking to the wine, opted for a walk around, maybe popping into a tavern before turning in. They parted company with Jake warning Indy not to get drunk and thrown in jail.

Jake made his way back, undressed and sank thankfully into his bed, eyes closing almost as soon as his head hit the pillow. His peace was shattered when the door to their room flew open and a wild eyed, ashen faced Indy rushed in slamming it firmly behind him. He bent, hands on his knees, struggling to get his breath back.

Jake - "What the hell have you done now?"

Still puffing Indy struggled to speak "It's 'im, I seen 'im, that bastard from hell! You told me he was dead but he bloody ain't. I just seen 'im large as life. Bastard. Bastard!"

Jake sat on the edge of his bed, "What the hell are you talking about? You've seen who? Who's not dead?"

"Croucher, that's who! You told me he was dead but he ain't, he ain't!"

"Sit down Indy! Get your breath back and tell me exactly what you mean – who you saw."

Indy sat on his bed and started talking to Jake slowly, as though he were an imbecile. "I was 'avin a look around and I 'eard music coming from this tavern so I fancied takin a look."

"Go on."

"Well, I walked in. It was busy like, full up. Then I 'eard this laugh that made my blood run cold; it sounded just like Croucher. I looked over and could just see across the room an there he was large as life, sitting at a table with some other geezer dressed in real posh clothes, looked like a gent but I'm telling you it was him! It was that murdering bastard Croucher laughing an' drinking without a care in the world. He looked right at me Jake. I know it was him."

Jake, knowing how traumatized Indy had been by Croucher, humoured him. "Well it must have been someone that looks like him. He nearly killed me but he drowned, so it can't actually be him." Trying to reassure his friend he suggested, "I'll tell you what. I'll look for a ship first thing in the morning so we can get out of here as soon as we can. You can stay safe in here until the ship sails; what do you say to that?" India climbed onto his bed pulling his blanket over his head.

"You can go. I'm not leaving here. I ain't moving till our ship sails."

Indy was plainly very scared which rattled Jake a little so trying to sound more confident than he really was he said, "As you like, I'll bolt the door now and let's get some sleep."

Both men lay awake until well into the early hours,

memories that they had tried to suppress re-surfacing. Every time Jake drifted off he woke with a start, gasping for air, arms thrashing, trying to break away from Croucher's iron grip, thankful to wake and climb out of his nightmare. He heard Indy tossing and turning and wondered what demons were haunting his dreams - poor devil. It was well past mid-day when they awoke to a grey cold April day; a steady drizzle falling from the oppressive leaden sky. Jake dressed, wishing that he had such a thing as a cloak or overcoat. He shook India. "Indy, I'm off to the harbour, maybe we'll get lucky and be able to leave today."

India looked up drowsily and nodded, "I bleedin 'ope so".

Jake wound his way through the narrow cobbled streets down toward the harbour, head down and chin tucked into his chest warding against the drizzle and cold wind that seeped into his very bones. After a few enquiries, he tracked down a merchant vessel carrying hemp that was due to leave for England on the first tide the next day. He paid a small deposit to secure a passage for two and turned for home, anxious to get out of his now wet clothes and back into a warm bed.

He started back for their room, the wind this time at his back blowing droplets of cold rain onto his neck. He hurried eager to tell Indy the news; he would be so glad to hear they were leaving soon. Tomorrow they would be on their way to London and home.

Jake suddenly became impatient to see Pa and his Lizzie, to sit around the table in the warm welcoming parlour with the smell of baking flooding his nostrils. Despite being cold to his marrow he smiled; just wait until they heard all he had to tell them. He couldn't resist a hop and a skip - just wait.

He turned into their street passing the café in which they had eaten the day before. As he approached their lodging house his mood darkened, the hairs on the back of his neck stood on end. Harry's words came back to him. "You've got good instincts lad, always listen to them." What was it? What was wrong? Then he remembered the man sitting at the window of the café just now. He was out of place in this quarter; well dressed, a toff as Indy would say. He remembered too Indys words, "He was sitting with some other bloke, real posh clothes."

With a niggling unease he entered the house silently climbing the stairs then stood listening outside the door of their room. He heard something that sounded like a loud slap then Indy's cry of pain. Opening the door slowly his heart did a summersault in his chest as he saw Charlie Croucher standing over Indy who lay prone on the bed, terror etched into his every feature.

Jake could barely believe his eyes, gone were the rough clothes and filthy hair, but the man who stood before him was undeniably the hated Bosun's mate of yesteryear. He was handsomely dressed now and wore fine jewellery, most noticeably a thick golden chain upon which hung a large ornate crucifix, but his hard black eyes and cruel face were unchanged.

Hands trembling, shaking with fear and full of loathing for this man Jake stepped into the room pushing the door to behind him. Sensing the movement Croucher turned to face him pulling out a dagger. "Don't know who you are son, but you made a big mistake coming in here." He lunged for Jake, "I'll have to do for the two of you now."

Croucher was a big man, so as he lunged Jake, remembering his lessons with Lin and Jeng, feinted to one side at the last minute and landed a heavy blow with his foot on his attacker's arm making him drop his weapon. As he bent to retrieve it, Jake, in one smooth action, jumped onto his back drawing Harry's dagger from his belt and, clinging on with his left arm plunged it into his adversary's neck with all his strength, ripping it from side to side.

Indy watched on in horror. It was as though the two men were performing some sort of satanic ballet as Croucher staggered around with Jake clinging on, arms and legs wrapped around his victim, waiting for his strength to give out. Croucher fell to his knees choking and gagging as his head went to the floor, blood gushing from the grievous wound. As darkness began to engulf him the last thing the big man heard was Jake whispering into his ear, "Remember me you bastard? Jake Faraday, the boy you tried to drown. Now go to hell you twisted bastard, go to hell."

For several minutes the two stayed locked in their deadly embrace until Jake was sure that Croucher was dead. He stumbled to his feet, treading in his victim's fast pooling blood, and sat on the edge of Indy's bed, the adrenalin which had fortified him gone. He began to shake uncontrollably in the aftermath of the action, mind numb, unable to take in what he had done. He was hardly aware of Indy's voice. "Gawd Jake, I thought I was a gonner. I woke up and that bastard was standing over me. I shit me pants - couldn't help it. He said he was gonna do the same to me again and then cut my balls off. He started pullin me pants down and he hit me when he saw what I'd done in them. Blimey Jake what we gonna do now?" The two friends sat in silence for some time. Anyone passing the door to their room would have been shocked to the core to witness the grisly tableau that it concealed.

At length Indy repeated, "What do we do now Jake?

Gawd Almighty what a mess." Jake suddenly snapped to; he instinctively knew that the man in the café was Croucher's companion and that he would come looking for him.

"We leave – now! Just grab what you need. We've got to get out of here." Jake, avoiding the macabre sight of Croucher kneeling as though paying homage to some deity, waded through the pool of blood to reach his valise, checking to make sure their money was still safe inside. India snatched together the few clothes that were to hand and stuffed them into his valise, hoping he had a change of trousers, together with his backpack.

"Jake you can't go out like that you're covered in blood."

Throwing a blanket around himself, Jake opened the door. "No time to bother now Indy, I think Croucher's mate will be here any minute – just let's go." They crept out; a trail of bloody footprints leading from their room to the head of the stairs.

They had just reached the front door when they heard shouts from above. "*Assassiner! Arretez ces deux hommes, non les laissez pas s'en tirer!*"

"What the 'ell is all that about?"

"I guess they've found Croucher. No time to talk Indy, save your breath." Stepping out into the street Jake saw in the distance the man from the café striding purposefully towards them. "Oh Christ Indy run, just keep with me and run."

As they set off several people poured out of the lodging house shouting. "*Assassiner! Arretez ces deux. Assassiner!*" The two friends ran hell for leather through twisting streets heading as best they could toward the harbour. Hiding in a small alley they stopped to catch their breath; the hue and cry seemed to have died down for the moment.

"Where we goin Jake? Did you get us a ship?"

"Yes, but we can't get on it, they'll be looking for us now that's for sure."

"Oh Gawd, we come all this way just to end up on the gallows, and all 'cos of a shit like Croucher!" The shouting started up again getting closer every second. They ran on stumbling onto the quay, a dead end. "Christ! Where to now?"

Jake spotted a fishing dinghy moored near the end of the harbour wall next to a wooden ladder, a tarpaulin stretched over the deck. "Over there." He ran to the dinghy, climbed down the rickety ladder and slipped under the tarpaulin. Peering out, he could see Indy hesitating. "Come on Indy, it's our only chance. For Christ's sake get yourself down here – now!" Puffing and panting, complaining at every rung, Indy reached the small craft and slid into the dark space beneath the cover. Within minutes they heard footsteps thudding above their heads and voices, seemingly dozens of them, all calling out for the murdering thieves who deserved to be hanged there and then.

Both men lay holding their breath, India gritting his teeth against the pain of pins and needles in his leg which had folded in under him as he had scooted into the boat. Trapped and with no way of escape should they be discovered Indy, probably for the first time in his life, prayed to God for help. Eventually all went quiet as the posse moved away and Jake risked poking his head from their hiding place to take a look around. "They've gone."

Grimacing in pain as he stretched his leg Indy burst out "Oh, lovely, that's alright then innit! What do we do now then clever Dick?"

"How the heck do I know? And don't start on me you ungrateful sod. Would you prefer to have been raped and had your throat cut?" Silence, "No, I didn't think so!" The outburst from both released the tension between them and they lay in the darkness of their shelter, thoughts whirring around, trying to make sense of how their lives had changed so drastically in the last hour.

In a much more conciliatory voice Indy spoke "Well, what are we gonna do Jake? Lay here till the morning?"

"I don't think we dare try boarding as passengers; they'll be looking for us. All we can do is hope no-one comes for this dinghy before we can make sail for London at first light."

"What! Stay like this in ere all night. It's freezing, your shirt is still wet and bloody and..."

"And you stink, but we'll have to put up with it so shut up."

"But this ain't a proper boat; we can't go out in all that water in this."

"We'll be alright. I've got a compass and she looks sturdy enough. Anyway at least we've got a chance this way. How the hell can we walk around like we are? Me covered in blood and you stinking of shit?" India remained silent. "No, we can't, can we? So that's that, we hang or we drown so I'll take my chances on the water thanks; you can do as you please."

"Don't be like that Jakey. I didn't mean to get at yer but you knows I hate water and I'm freezing and..."

"I know Indy, I know. But I can sail pretty good – we'll be fine." They settled down to endure a miserable few hours waiting for dawn, cramped and shivering under the tarpaulin.

At first light, with India keeping a look out Jake undid the tarpaulin, hauled the single sail and gave Indy the nod to push off from the harbour wall with one of the oars that had made his enforced sojourn overnight so uncomfortable. He clambered back into the boat and began rowing while Jake held the tiller. Both men were silent, waiting and listening for the alarm that would mean they had been discovered. The little boat handled well and as she edged out of the harbour their spirits began to lift as a weak watery sun fought its way into a new day; all they had to do now was head for England, London and safety.

Once in open water Indy reached for his valise and pulled out a pair of clean breeches and shirt. "Ere Jake, put this on and chuck that bloomin thing away." He pulled off his soiled breeches and, wetting them used them to clean himself up before throwing them overboard. "Cor that water's bleedin cold, especially round me nuts." Pulling on his spare breeches he looked up at Jake who had taken off his shirt and shrugged into Indy's offering which, he being taller and broader than his friend was much too small. Indy burst out laughing. "Gawd you looks like a fat sausage wot's burst it's skin." Jake, holding out his arms so that the cuffs rode almost up to his elbows saw the funny side and joined in, their laughter ringing out across the water.

Eventually, chests aching, they gradually conquered their hysteria and eased back to reality. India sitting with elbows on his knees, face cupped in his hands said, "How did we get here Jake? I mean, look what's 'appened to us! I reckon we must be the unluckiest bastards alive. Gawd Almighty! If only I'd nicked a smaller pie." The ludicrous statement and the seriousness with which he said it started Jake off once again, his laughter infecting India until they were both curled up, tears streaming down their faces, gasping for breath, India asking, "What? What we laughing for?"

Eventually they lapsed into thoughtful silence. The only

noise the sail flapping and billowing in the gentle winds. Jake emerged from his world of memories to the sound of silence. "Oh shit."

"What? What's up now?"

"Listen."

"I can't hear nothing."

"Exactly, the wind has dropped, we're going nowhere, and I can smell rain." Almost as soon as Jake had spoken grey skies appeared in the distance and within the hour the same freezing saturating drizzle that had blanketed Calais was upon them.

"What can we do now Jake? You're the sailor here."

"We've got oars, we'd better start rowing; no telling how long it will be before the wind picks up. You first, then we'll swap and you can take the tiller." With some tuition India eventually managed to get the boat moving in a relatively straight line and the friends alternated at the scuppers. They made tortuously slow progress but, even though the freezing rain persisted, when the wind picked up they gave each other the thumbs up.

They sailed on in a world completely grey, the soft drizzle blanketing the sky, cutting visibility down to just a few yards. Jake began to worry. He had no idea how long they had been afloat but it seemed like an eternity. They were completely reliant on Harry's compass which thankfully still showed them to be heading north. He silently thanked his mentor for his gift and prayed too that it was accurate. India, sensing Jake's unease narrowed his eyes trying to peer through the gloom. All he could see was water. He became very uneasy, water surrounding them for miles and water beneath them. He had to fight down sudden panic at the thought of what was lurking there. He had a mental picture of the huge beast that had taken

Narnsee exploding through the surface to overturn the dinghy and drag them down into the dark freezing depths. "It's alright Indy, there are no sharks in this water; it's too cold for them. There's nothing below that can harm us, the cold is our worst foe. Slide under that tarp and try to get some sleep. If I see anything I'll holler."

Indy curled up with the two valises and his knapsack on his chest in a vain attempt to stave off the cold then pulled the cover right over his head. He woke with a jolt when the dinghy struck land. They had beached in a small shingle inlet surrounded by a rock face about ten feet high. He looked over to Jake who was slumped over the tiller and was suddenly afraid for him. "Oh Gawd, please let him be alright." He threw aside the tarpaulin and clambered over to his friend shaking him awake. "Jake, Jakey boy we landed, we landed." Jake's speech was slurred

"Where are we? Are we home?"

"No mate but we're off that bleedin water."

In the gloom he thought he could make out a trail leading from the inlet through the rocks. He wrapped Jake in the tarpaulin and using strength he didn't know he possessed, manhandled him out of the boat and propped him up against the rocks alongside the trail. "Stay here Jakey, I'm gonna see where this path goes. I won't be long, just don't go nowhere." There was no reply from the dark bundle prone on the shingle.

India scurried up the trail and stood screwing up his eyes trying to see through the fading light. With a rush of relief he could just make out what looked like a single farmhouse not more than two hundred yards from the cliff edge. He slithered back down to the beach knowing he needed to get help fast before Jake froze to death. He climbed back into the dinghy, which was rocking from side

The Throgmorton Legacy

to side with the ebb and flow of the sea, took out their meagre but precious luggage and slumped down next to Jake. He thought for a few seconds before taking out Jake's money and letters of introduction and stuffing them into his knapsack. Then taking Jake's knife he sliced off a piece of the tarp and wrapped up their valises before wedging them in a rock fissure. All being well they could collect them later, but if not, he was happy that at least he had the important things safe. He dragged an almost unconscious Jake to his feet, "Come on now turnip. Just a bit further and we'll be in clover."

Staggering, now and again tripping on the uneven ground, they reached the garden path of the house. As they started down it a light appeared in one of the windows and India could see the dancing shadows of a fire playing on the walls inside. They reached the front door and, holding Jake upright; he leant forward and lifted the brass horseshoe door knocker letting it fall back to the door with a bang. A shrill voice called out "Whose there on such a miserable dark evening? Who is it?"

"We was lost at sea missis and my friend here is near freezing to death. Have you got somewhere we can shelter till morning? We got money!" The door opened letting out a thin shaft of light

"Who is it Bosun? You go see."

The door opened a little wider and the huge grey whiskery head of an Irish Wolf Hound appeared eye to eye with India who had never seen such an enormous dog. "Well Bosun, what they like?" The door opened wider still and Bosun stepped out exposing his front quarters.

India went to take a step back but Jake put out his hand, "Nice dog." Bosun sniffed then began to lick the proffered hand with his huge pink tongue.

The disembodied voice spoke. "I see a tail wagging. Thank 'ee Bosun, shall us let them in?" The door opened to its full extent revealing the silhouette of a plump woman wearing a mob cap. She held out a candle, took a good look at the boys and, seemingly satisfied she stepped back into the room and waved them inside. "Come in, come in, you looks like a couple of drownded rats and no mistake."

The room was warm and welcoming with a roaring log fire in the blackened brick inglenook. Mrs. Daisy Halfpenny ushered them toward the two wooden chairs on either side of the fire. She was fairly portly, almost as round as she was high, with thick dimpled arms that she folded under her ample bosoms as she surveyed the strangers in the firelight. She had a shiny round face with pink cheeks, a button nose and sparkling jolly blue eyes under a head full of grey corkscrew curls that were winning the battle over the Mob Cap, trying in vain to restrain them. She stood in front of Jake, putting her hands on his shoulders. "Gor lummey lad, look at you; you'm almost blue with cold." She turned to India. "And you, look at you," hesitating while she took in the colour of his skin, "you looks cold too." She nodded her head as she came to a decision. "You get them wet clothes off while I go to fetch blankets for thee. Take care of 'em Bosun, make sure they stay by the fire and get warmed through."

She was back in a minute with two multi-coloured woollen blankets. "These will keep you warm till your clothes dry. They smell a bit but that's Mugwort – keeps the moths away; tis good for the guts too. My Ruben, he suffers so with his guts. I keep telling him 'tis all the ale he drinks, but he won't 'av none of it." Jake's heart lurched - the brightly coloured blankets reminded him so of Ma's rugs; he suddenly had an overwhelming longing to see them again which brought tears to his eyes. "There, there now lad, you're safe now. I'll put on some milk to warm and put in a drop of honey and a tot of Ruben's best brandy; you'll feel much better with that inside you. Now, Bosun and me'll look away while you undress."

The boys sat in the glow of the fire supping the warmed milk, limbs gradually coming back to life. Mrs. Halfpenny let down the clothes rack which was suspended from the ceiling just in front of the fireplace. She hung on their wet clothes then hauled it back up to catch the rising heat. "Now lads, how on earth did you come to be getting lost on a day like this? Where did 'ee come from and where does 'ee want to go?" Not having discussed what they were going to say, both friends were silent for a few moments before quick thinking India took up the tale.

He explained that they lived in London and his father and two uncles had a very humble business importing silks which they sold to dress makers and haberdashers for their rich clients. He and Jake had been sent across the river in his uncle's dinghy to a Chinese medicine man to collect some plants to make into a potion for his father who was nearly crippled with painful legs and feet. He picked up his knapsack and rustled the dried contents as proof.

On the way back, as Jake could sail, they thought they would take just a little trip down the river before going back to work, but Jake couldn't handle the boat as well as they had thought and they got swept out to sea. They weren't sure how long they had been adrift but had been scared that they would drown, and worse than that, no-one would know what had happened to them and now thankfully they were safe, but they still had to get back to London and were very afraid to face India's parents. India launched into his tale with relish, embellishing it here and there so well that Jake began to half believe it himself.

Mrs. Halfpenny became more and more agitated as India detailed how cruel his parents were to him and how hard they made him work, and as he described the cold and the hardships they had endured in the dinghy. Jake raised his eyebrows; at least some of that bit was true. She fetched out a large loaf to the table and, venting some of the anger she now felt towards India's fictitious parents, proceeded to cut thick slices which she spread liberally with butter and slapped onto two plates.

"I've a good mind to get my Ruben to go up to London and box your father's ears. He'll be 'ome on the morning tide. He's a big man you know, strong as an ox. Treating you like that, a disgrace I call it!" Jake scowled at India, trust him to overdo it! "I'll do you some coddled eggs to go with that bread and I've got a bit of cold bacon left, and plenty of honey. You two lads need feeding up it seems to me! Feeding you potato peelings indeed! Just you wait till I tell my Ruben."

Dipping the bread into his eggs, watched over by their hostess, India tried to ameliorate the situation, owning up to maybe having been a little deserving of his harsh treatment and assuring her that all in all his parents weren't too bad. Jake kept his head down; least said the better.

Warmed through, well fed and with another of their hostess's special concoctions inside them, both friends were stifling yawns, longing for sleep. Mrs. Halfpenny smiled indulgently at them, she was really rather enjoying having someone to fuss over, but seeing that both boys were exhausted suggested they bed down in the barn before they fell asleep at the table. She gave Jake a lantern and India a wicker basket. "If you put your shoes in there and give 'em to Bosun to fetch back I'll put them by the fire to dry –

they'll be good as new by the mornin."

Eyes drooping Jake said, "Thank you Mrs. Halfpenny, we don't know what would have become of us without your help. Could you tell us where we are; how far we are from London?"

"Oh, it's not worth a mention. Two nice lads like you lost and in trouble, anyone would 'ave done exactly the same. We're just outside of Folkestone my dear. My Ruben could tell you how far you've to go to London; he'll be here by morning, he'll know."

The two friends shuffled along to the barn wrapped in their blankets, accompanied by Bosun. The pair had seen the dark underbelly of mankind; they had seen and done so much more than Daisy Halfpenny could imagine or was ever likely to, and yet they had so enjoyed being mothered by her, acceding to her kindly ministrations, letting her take charge. Bosun waited patiently while they put their shoes in the basket, then picked it up and returned to the house - a gentle giant. They made nests in the dry straw, Jake blew out the candle in the lantern and within a few seconds both were dead to the world.

It was so, so cold, they were lost in the mist on the dark, threatening sea. Suddenly the dinghy began to rock violently from side to side. India hung on for dear life, so afraid of being tossed overboard and swallowed up into the cold fearful darkness. Suddenly the biggest shark he had ever seen erupted from the water nearly overturning the boat and wetting him through; but suddenly the shark was Charlie Croucher lunging for him, his eyes ablaze with hatred. He was deathly white save for the livid red blood pouring from the slash in his neck. He rose higher from the water, looming over India, strong hands grabbing him by the shoulders, striving to pull him down into the dark never ending depths. He screamed knowing that this time there was no escape.

"Indy, Indy, wake up. It's alright, you're safe, you're safe." Jake was shaking him by the shoulders as he opened his eyes and stared unseeing for a few seconds, still trying to break free from his nightmare. To his enormous relief he took in the sunlight filtering through gaps in the barn walls, remembering how and why they were there. "There's someone at the door, cover yourself up." Indy realized that he had kicked off his blanket and was naked; no wonder he was cold.

Jake opened the door to find Bosun waiting patiently, a basket containing their dry clothes and shoes at his feet. Jake knelt and hugged the big dog. "Why thank you Bosun, come on in while we get dressed." Seeming to understand, Bosun picked up the basket and trotted into the barn, tail swinging from side to side. He sat watching the two shrug into their clothes, then stood ready to escort them back to his mistress when they were finished.

"Ah, come in my dears. Did you manage to get some sleep? This is my dear husband Ruben. I've told him all about you – all about you getting lost an' that." Ruben Halfpenny was a big man. He stood smiling, shiny red cheeks set in a round pleasant face, sparse salt and pepper hair tied back. He was half a head taller than Jake, his rolled up sleeves exposing arms like small oaks and hands as big a shovels. He proffered one to Jake who shook it, trying not to wince at Ruben's vice-like grip. Inevitably, when it was India's turn he could not of course resist commenting – "Watch it mate, you nearly broke me fingers. I wouldn't want to pick no trouble with you and that's the truth." Ruben, being a jovial sort of man, roared with laughter and smacked his fist down onto the table.

"You're a lively one that's for sure. Are you the one that's got the strange name?"

"It's as good as any, ain't it?"

"To be sure lad; it's not the name a man has, it's the name he earns amongst his mates that counts, wouldn't you say?"

"I would as it 'appens, that's right that is, ain't it Jake?" Jake nodded, his attention having turned to the aromatic fresh bread and butter and the great pan of eggs slowly frying over the fire.

"Come on now, let's all sit round before these eggs go hard and you lads can tell your story to my Ruben just like you told me." So India launched once again into his tale, remembering it almost word for word but trying not to make his family sound like the ogres of the previous night, being fearful that Ruben would indeed take it upon himself to find them and box their ears. Ruben sat in silence for a while, wiping the yolk from his plate with chunks of the delicious bread. With the last vestiges of his breakfast still churning around in his mouth he said, "I got some bad news for you boys. I walked over to yon cove to check on your dinghy and it ain't there. It must've drifted off on the tide." The two looked at each other – what now? How were they going to get to London? India, remembering that the loss of the dinghy, which was supposed to belong to his family, would be a disaster, covered his face with his hands and pretended to be even more mortified than he already was.

"Now, I can't do anything about your dinghy lads but I can help get you to London. There's a Dutchy in the Pent stream harbour and she's leaving for Hay's Wharf on the next tide. I knows the master and I'm sure he'll take 'ee on; what do 'ee say to that? But I'll tell 'ee what. Afore 'ee goes young Jake you'd better take one of my old shirts as that one ain't no more use to 'ee than a nose rag." He roared with laughter at his own joke and both lads joined in. Jake did look ridiculous in his tiny ill-fitting shirt but more than that, they were laughing out of shear relief at their good fortune.

And so it was that the two Halfpennies, Jake, India and Bosun walked the half mile along the coastal track to the estuary of the Pent stream where the Dutch cargo ship lay at anchor preparing to set sail in the next hour. On their way India slipped off the track and ran down to the small inlet where he had stashed their valises the night before; to his great relief they were still there, and undamaged. Tearing off the now shredded tarp he tucked their only worldly goods under his arm, scooted back onto the track and caught up with the others.

Ruben introduced the two friends to the captain of The Magdalena, and a small passenger fee was agreed. The four said their goodbyes and the two lads watched as their new found friends retraced their steps back home, waving as they disappeared over the horizon. Jake smiled to himself as he imagined Ruben's reaction when he found the silver shilling he had slipped into his pocket earlier. He would like to visit them again one day; that bread was second to none, even as good as Ma's. Ruben saying nothing to his dear wife, smiled to himself as he pondered on what those two little rascals had really been up to.

Chapter 26

As soon as they stepped onto the wharf, India chirped up. He was on his home turf and for the first time in years felt that he was where he really belonged. They were now virtually destitute with just about enough money for one night's lodgings; India having complained non-stop once finding out that Jake had left a whole shilling with the Halfpennies.

He led the way across London Bridge, Jake marvelling at the bustle and noise of London. Traders shouting above the general hubbub trying to sell their wares, horse drawn carriages clattering along cobbled streets, throngs of people scurrying along, some dressed in grand clothes, others in rags; Jake had never seen such a place. Leaving behind the maritime smells of the river and the market stalls selling their wares, he followed India into progressively dirtier and narrower rubbish strewn streets filled with the smell of stale ale leaking from seedy run down taverns, foul sewage filled puddles and the acrid smell of unwashed humanity. Jake had never encountered such squalor and he picked his way carefully through the filth, trying to breathe as shallowly as he could. Eventually India stopped at the weather beaten door of a terraced house with the word 'lodgins' painted above the door.

In the absence of any kind of knocker he beat the door with his fists turning to Jake as he did so. "I know it ain't much but we ain't got much money thanks to you, and Ma Woodley don't ask no question, and it's best not to draw attention, not since you done that bastard Croucher." Before Jake could think of an answer the door creaked open to reveal Ma Woodley. She was a scrawny woman with rheumy blue eyes and a thin wrinkled face framed with faded ginger hair most of which was poked beneath a mob cap that had probably at some point been white. Her rust coloured dress, which was almost the same shade as her hair, was made from coarse heavy cotton and the petticoat beneath it bore stains that were probably as old as the dress. Everything about her was worn and faded; Jake imagined that if caught by one blast of wind she would disintegrate leaving just a pile of rust coloured ash where she had once stood.

She stared at them taking in their dishevelled state and Jake's well oversized shirt. "You wantin a room?"

"Yes Ma, I speck for just one night, but maybe two. Do you 'av one?" Ma Woodley turned and started up the stairs beckoning them to follow. Jake hated the place. It smelled of old cabbage and stale urine, and the sounds of children shouting and babies crying echoing throughout the house did not bode well for good night's sleep. She stopped on the first landing opening a door to reveal a room overlooking the street outside. The wooden floor was bare, and the only furniture some kind of mattress on the floor covered with a stained blanket, and a chamber pot in the corner. She put out her hand. "Four pence now for the two of yer, another two if yer stay tommorer. Don't bring no-one back 'ere."

"Four pence for this shit hole! Come on Ma, that's bleedin' robbery!"

"I ain't short of takers so if you don't want it, get out and don't waste my time."

"It's bleedin' daylight robbery!" Indy sighed. "Oh, give the old crone the money Jake and I 'opes she falls down the stairs and breaks 'er scrawny neck."

Jake placed four pence into the landlady's dirty, claw like hand and after checking the money carefully she left them, slamming the door shut as she went.

"Gawd Almighty, what a greedy old cow! Still, we'll be safe 'ere Jake, she might be greedy but she don't never 'ear nothing an' she never says nothing. I suppose that's 'ow she keeps going."

Jake sat on the straw mattress. "I wish I hadn't been taken by Daisy's kindness. I suppose it was stupid to give them so much; I got carried away and didn't think and now look where we are! How can we go to see this Mr. Mason dressed like this? We won't even get through the door." India joined Jake on what passed for their bed.

"Don't you worry about that Jakey boy; just leave things to me. I need to go out for a bit but best if you stay 'ere; keep out the way of things." Jake didn't argue; he was too disconsolate and he certainly did not want to walk around in such a dreadful filthy place more than he absolutely had to. They had no money to speak of, no decent clothes without means of getting any and he had no idea where to find Mason's offices; how the hell could India be happy with things the way they were?

He sat daydreaming for a while, thinking of all that had happened since that fateful day he had lied to his parents and left Spinnakers. A lump formed in his throat. He was desperate to go home and the nearer he got the harder the separation was to bear. He strolled over to the window just in time to see India darting into their doorway wearing a frock coat that did not belong to him and looking very fat. He listened to feet thumping up the stairs then India came in all smiles. "Take a look at this Jakey." He pulled several bundles from under the coat dropping them onto the floor. Picking them up and shaking them out one by one Jake saw that there were two pairs of breeches, two shirts, two waistcoats, and two sets of stockings, all of the finest quality. "You just need a coat and I might find a couple of hats, but shoes ain't so easy so the ones we got will have to do." He went through the door again. "Stay here. Back soon."

Jake sorted through the clothes picking out the bigger of each article. He tried them on to find that everything fitted perfectly and for the first time since reaching London his mood began to lift. India soon returned with a second frock coat, a loaf of bread, cheese and a small fruit cake. "Gawd, don't you look the gent. Try this on." Jake slipped into the coat, another perfect fit.

"But where did they come from. How did you pay for them?"

India tapped the side of his nose, "Let's just say as how the Lord provides in time of need." The penny dropped and Jake said nothing, having to accept that ends sometimes justify the means. Laughing while they ate the food the Lord had provided, they changed back into their poor clothes and called into the nearest ale house spending the very last of their money.

After enduring a restless night scratching flea bites and listening to drunken singing intermingled with drunken street brawls the two dressed in their newly acquired finery and set off for the offices of Mason and Maws gladly leaving behind the misery that was Ma Woodley and her lodging house.

As they walked through the city away from the squalor of the night before Jake gazed in wonderment at the size and splendour of some of the buildings. The narrow filthy roads became wide thoroughfares and bewigged gentlemen and ladies dressed in the finest silks and brocades paraded through the streets, some on foot, some in sedan chairs and the lucky few in smart horse drawn carriages. Once through the city centre the streets became a little more modest, the tempo slowing to suit. They rounded a corner into Arbuthnot Street, smart dark brick houses lining either side. "Here we are Jakey, here's number two so it must be just a bit further along."

They saw that number twenty four was a red brick building four stories high with a basement below the pavement. The windows and door were framed with white stone and on the wall to the right of the black glossy door was a plaque confirming that these were indeed the offices of Mason and Maws. It read Mason and Maws, Solicitors, est. 1752. Beneath it was another plaque informing that these were also the offices of Worthy & Sons - Undertakers. Plucking up courage Jake walked up the four steps to the front door and pulled the brass chain causing a bell inside to chime.

The door was opened by an elderly, kindly looking man wearing a short powdered wig and, save for his cravat, dressed from head to toe in black. "Can I help you gentlemen?" Jake felt his voice quaking a little.

"I have come on the recommendation of Lord Henry Throgmorton to see Mr. Mason."

"Oh yes, do come in. Mr. Mason's offices are on the first floor. Do go on up, his clerk, Mr. Frobisher will be able to help you I'm sure." They were invited into a large oak-panelled hallway with a wide staircase, at the bottom of which was a stand supporting a glossy blackboard upon which were painted in gold lettering the names of Mason and Maws; a golden arrow pointing the way upstairs. There were three doors to the right of the stairs, all having similar boards also with gold lettering affixed to them. The first door which stood open, marked Clients, the next marked G. Worthy, the next J. Worthy.

They crossed the hallway, feet sinking into the deep pile of the maroon carpet which covered the entire floor and wound its way up the stairs. The hairs on Jake's neck stood out, he had never felt so out of place and he had to fight the desire to just turn tail and run. They reached the next landing and Jake coughed to alert anyone of their presence. In answer a tall gangly man appeared walking ponderously toward them, he immediately reminded Jake of a grey marsh heron. His short body sat on long thin legs that were completely out of proportion. He had a small head with dark hair parted on the side and seemingly wetted down so that it stuck flat to his head. His large beakish nose and small close eyes completed the picture; to Jake he would always be a Heron.

Mr. Frobisher looked the two friends up and down, and an unfriendly, "Yes," was all he said.

Jake cleared his throat and holding up his letters said, "I have a message for Mr. Mason from Sir Henry Throgmorton and we, I, would like to see him urgently."

"He's busy, give them to me."

"I will not Sir. I was told to hand these to Mr. Mason only and I will see him now if you please."

From Jake's tone it was obvious to Frobisher that this nuisance would not be deterred. "Wait here, I'll see if Mr. Mason can spare you both a minute." He turned on his heel, knocked discreetly on the door facing them and let himself in. The two heard mumbled voices, then the door flew open and a man they presumed to be Mason strode out smiling from ear to ear. He was a well-built man about Jake's height, dressed in brown breeches and waistcoat, with a plain white shirt and neckerchief underneath. He wore a short powdered wig which accentuated his thick black eyebrows and dark brown eyes. "Good morning my dear chaps. You have news of Harry? How is the old scoundrel? Come in, come in and tell me all there is."

He beckoned them into a room containing a huge leather topped desk set in front of the only window in order to catch the light. Behind this stood a single ornately carved wooden chair. On its opposite side sat two large arm chairs covered in gold brocade, presumably to accommodate clients. Between them, a small table upon which sat a silver tray holding several crystal glasses and a decanter of port. Three walls were oak panelled to half way and topped with a very ornate wallpaper displaying a large boldly coloured, floral design; the fourth wall was shelved and filled from floor to ceiling with books. There was a white stone Adam style fireplace with a small fire flickering in the grate. The mantel shelf above it held a large ornate turquoise and ormolu clock and a ship in full sail; Jake thought a Corvette, in a bottle. The whole room was sumptuous and comforting and Jake took a liking to Mr. Giles Mason immediately.

"Sit, do sit. Would you like a glass of port gentlemen before we begin?" India spoke up for the first time since they had entered the building.

"We wouldn't say no would we Jake; very kind of you I'm sure."

"Help yourselves gentlemen, please do, then we can settle down and I can hear all the news."

Jake felt very uncomfortable knowing that the information they bore would not be welcome. "I have two letters for you Sir, one from Harry er Lord Throgmorton and one from Mr. John Pryor. I... I'm afraid we do not bring good tidings." Giles Mason's face clouded over, he took the letters opening them as he sat at his desk.

Jake and India sat in silence, India helping himself to a second glass of port. After a while their host walked over to the fireplace and leant on the mantel, his head buried in his folded arms. His shoulders shook as he cried silently for his dear friend. India pulled a face at Jake not sure what they should do. Jake put his finger to his lips; there was nothing they could do but respect the silence.

After a few minutes Giles Mason gathered himself together, and wiping away tears with his hand sat back down to face the two friends. "Please forgive me gentlemen but Harry and I knew each other as youngsters from our early school days, we went to the same university together too. He was one of the best people I have ever known, poor dear Harry." He sniffed; pulled himself up to sit straight in his chair and having composed himself was the professional once again.

"Now then gentlemen which one of you is Jacob Faraday?" Jake raised his hand. "Well young man, you come highly recommended and if you can answer Harry's conundrums correctly you are about to become very wealthy, so let's get down to business; but first would you be so good as to pass me a glass of that port, I feel I am in need of it."

India jumped to, poured and passed the port as requested at the same time filling his own glass once more. "Jacob, at Harry's insistence I have to verify that you are his chosen heir in private so," looking at India, "I'm afraid, young man that I will have to ask you to leave the room for just a few minutes."

India, now full of bonhomie, stood to leave. "No bother mate. Give us a shout when you've finished." He stepped out onto the landing to find Frobisher hurrying to sit down at his desk. "Wotcha cock - bit tall for key holing ain't yer?" Flustered a little by being caught out, the clerk gave India the most disdainful look he could manage and pretended to be engrossed in his ledger. The awkward silence lasted only a few minutes as Jake soon peered out and beckoned India back into Mason's sanctum. He filled all three glasses with the fast diminishing port before he sat down.

"Now Jacob, it seems that you know most of what has happened with Harry's estate but just let me clarify things. As you know he fled the country rather hurriedly but before doing so he 'sold' his lands and properties to Mr. Pryor for a nominal sum and left most of his valuables with me. I deposited them with Thomas Coutts and company for safe keeping and hid the keys to the box awaiting Harry's return. Now however all that is in the box belongs to you, so I suggest that we visit the bank tomorrow and you can decide what you want to do from there.

"With regard to the Throgmorton Estate, it borders that of the Villiers Estate with which, as I understand from Pryor's letter you are familiar. After expenses it brings in a good annual income with which I, having Power of Attorney, and on Harry's instructions of course, have bought parcels of land on the outskirts of this fair city. He was far-seeing was Harry; that land increases in value virtually year by year as the city grows. Anyhow I digress. The estate is managed by a very capable man, a Mr. Dobson and his two sons, all of whom have always been well paid for their services at Harry's insistence.

"The Manor House is occupied by Henry Fredericks and his family. He is, was, a mutual friend of Harry and myself and he lives there free and gratis on the understanding that he maintains the house and grounds to a good standard. He is an honourable but too trusting man who lost a great deal of money in a financial exercise orchestrated by some mountebank, and was left virtually penniless. I took the liberty of removing the most valuable paintings and articles from the house before he moved in and have put them in safe storage; some of them are in my attic, actually, well secured and safe from harm. So there, basically, you have it. You are, or will be, a man of fortune. How do you feel about that young Jacob?" Jake's head was spinning but he wasn't sure if it was from learning of the extent of his fortune or the port.

"But how about you? You have done all this for Harry over the years, how much must I owe you?"

Giles Mason smiled. "My dear boy, it's touching that you should think so, but I have taken an agreed sum annually for all I have done, and following Harry's lead I have purchased land which will, in the not too distant future net me a handsome profit. So you see we all owe dear Harry a debt which unfortunately we will never be able to repay. I think I have covered most things but do you have any questions gentlemen?"

India, who had been dying to speak up said. "Yes, ain't you scared of being here with all them dead bodies down below?" Giles Mason laughed.

"Well actually from a practical point of view, the arrangement suits us very well. The Worthys own the building and have all but this floor. They live in the rooms above, so as to be available at all times so as to speak, and the basement is eminently suitable for their work, and of course they receive remuneration from us. There are stables and outbuildings out back which house the horses, my carriage and their two rather larger ones, and there is a track from the rear for access. You could say also that we have a well, long established and symbiotic relationship with the Worthys. When the grim reaper calls, usually unexpectedly, we are on hand to help out in the bereaved's hour of need with any necessary legalities. By the same token we are able to recommend the services of our good neighbours should any of our clients be too bereft to deal with such matters as their loved-one's final journey."

India shuddered, "I still don't like it knowing there's dead 'uns down there."

Giles Mason stretched his arms above his head "Do you know? I really don't feel like working now. Can I take you out for luncheon, or back to your lodgings perhaps?"

Jake embarrassed, "Well, we haven't really got any lodgings nor sadly the money pay for any."

"Excellent, then we shall go to my club for luncheon and then my dear wife Martha would I know, be delighted if you would agree to stay with us overnight, or even for a few days if that would suit. What do you say to that? Please say yes; Martha and I would love to hear all that Harry has been up to." The two friends readily agreed, this was a change in their fortunes and no mistake.

Giles summoned Frobisher to inform him that they would all be away for the rest of the day and probably tomorrow too. As far as Frobisher was concerned this was manna from heaven as he could please himself as to how much work he would do, which basically amounted to nothing. "Yes Mr. Mason, no need to worry about coming back, I'll take care of everything."

Excited now and looking forward to an evenings' entertainment with his two guests Giles slipped into his frock coat. "Any more questions gentlemen before we leave."

"Yes", India said, "'ow the 'ell did you get that boat into that bottle?"

Chapter 27

After a 'light' lunch consisting of some of the finest food either had ever eaten and which left both Jake and India fit to burst, Giles insisted that they call on his barber to spruce the lads up with a haircut and shave. Then on to, as he liked to jest, the Maison of Monsieur Mason - the pun being lost on both newcomers. They entered a crescent of houses that looked out onto a small park with seating scattered among trees, seemingly at random. Giles halted the carriage outside a house more or less in the centre of the crescent. All the houses were three stories high with basements on view from the pavement. They were constructed of a light sand coloured stone and all had large bay windows on either side of the front entrance. A stone porch over the front door of the Mason house was supported by two circular pillars, one of which bore the number ten painted in large black numbers. The front door had eight panels carved into it and was painted a glossy holly green. In the centre sat a huge brass knocker in the shape of a lion's head.

Before they had alighted from the carriage the door burst open and a small pretty woman with a heart shaped face and chestnut ringlets stood in the doorway holding a babe in arms, two small children clutching at either side of her cornflower blue gown. "Giles, how lovely, what brings you home so early and who are these fine young gentlemen." Giles ran up the steps, kissed his wife on the cheek and ruffled the hair of all three children.

"Let's get inside and I'll tell you all about it. Come Jacob, India, come and meet my dear family." He called into the house "Sims, would you see to the carriage please, I have company." A grey haired man appeared, nodded at the group, climbed onto the carriage and proceeded to drive it to the other end of the crescent where he disappeared. By way of explanation Giles said "Sims takes care of the horse and carriage for me, amongst other things; the stables are at the rear."

They entered the house in a huddle, everyone talking at once until Giles held up his hands. "One at a time please; one at a time."

Martha spoke up. "So, my dear husband, are you going to tell me who our guests are?"

Giles explained their appearance at his office; the letter from Harry and that he had invited Jacob and India to be their guests at least overnight. "We can talk over dinner but I wonder if now my love you could make ready rooms for our guests as I'm sure they must be in need of freshening up. Also, and I'll explain that later, they have no luggage and no spare clothes so would it be possible to find a few bits from your father's old chest and lay out two of my nightgowns; and one more thing my love, could we have some..." turning to his guests, "would you like, port, ale or tea?"

Being thirsty they spoke in tandem "Ale would be most welcome."

"Some ale in my study then my dear, at your convenience of course."

Martha smiled, and babe still in arms, whirled on her heels calling on their housekeeper Mrs. Moffatt for assistance as she left, the two young Masons running in her wake.

The three men drank their beer making small talk. Giles was itching to hear all they had to say but he had promised his wife that they would wait until all four of them could sit around the table and talk at leisure. Mrs. Moffat took Jake and Indy to their respective rooms and as soon as she had gone they each ran to the other's inspecting them and marvelling at the sheer luxury and softness of the beds.

The house was beautifully furnished with delicate, richly covered furniture, much of it with ormolu embellishments. Tables, display cabinets, sideboards were all of warm yew with the odd piece of oak adding gravitas. Huge gilt framed mirrors hung on the walls, each reflecting the beautiful display of flowers set in front of them, filling the whole house with their perfume.

Eventually, freshly washed and changed Martha, Giles, Jacob and India sat around the dinner table. Giles opened the conversation by introducing Martha properly. He had married quite late in life, hence the difference of fifteen years in their ages. She was the light of his life and, judging by the way she hung on his every word the feeling between them was mutual.

"Now, let's begin with you Jacob; start at the beginning and tell us how, why and where you got to know Harry." Haltingly at first, Jake explained how, at the age of thirteen he had come to be in Poundsmill just at the wrong time and been pressed into the navy. By the time he had got to the end of their tale in Calais they had eaten three courses, no-one paying particular heed to the food, and consumed copious amounts of wine; Jake's story having wetted their appetites in more ways than one. Martha was agog. "Go on. So what happened to this beast of a man, where is he now?" Before Jake could open his mouth Indy spoke up.

"Jake done for 'im, slit his slimy throat." Jake, horrified and having visions of a noose around his neck said.

"Um, yes, we had a fight, I hurt him quite badly. I had to you see he was about to – to hurt India; not sure quite what happened to him though, we had to leave."

Giles Mason had not missed Jake's warning look to his friend; he was a man of the world and had come across the likes of this Croucher from time to time in his line of work. "Well Jake my lad. It's a shame you didn't actually rid the world of such a loathsome creature." Leaning towards him and winking broadly, "you would have done us all a favour! So what happened then, how did you manage to get from Calais to London?" Jake, realizing that Giles had guessed the truth and in some way approved carried on telling the unvarnished truth; he really liked this man.

Martha suggested that they move into the drawing room where they could sit in more comfort. She asked Mrs. Moffat to bring in more wine and brandy as no-one wanted coffee. Then they settled down to hear from India. He explained how he had fetched up in Poundsmill, also at the wrong time. Jake had covered most of what had happened on The Huron so he went on to tell how he had been rescued from the sea by the dolphins and how he had befriended the island people who had nursed him back to health. He talked of Kwashi, the medicine plant; how Narnsee's mother had shown him where it grew, how to harvest and use it. He described his life on the island and his love for Narnsee and how she had tragically been killed. He explained that his life from then on had been meaningless and viewed largely through the bottom of a bottle until the fates had brought him and Jake together again.

"You knows the rest, it's like Jake said."

Giles, Martha and Jake had sat spellbound by India's story, much of which Jake had never heard before. "You mean you learnt to speak their language – can you say something now?" India spoke a few sentences and then explained them.

"I just said, *I love you Narnsee and you will always be in my
'eart. I'll never forget you, never.*"

Martha rose with tears streaming down her face. "Oh,
you poor, poor boys!" She hugged Jake and India in turn. "I
have to go to bed now. Goodnight to you all," and weaving
her way a little unsteadily, she left the room. Giles refilled
their glasses, he had lost count of how many they had
consumed but who cared.

"You must tell me more about your medicine plant
India, sounds incredible."

"I'll show you some tommorer, I got some in me bag."

Giles lifted his glass. "To Harry, God rest his soul. He
didn't deserve to be treated like that y'know. Blasted bloke
he killed asked for it; engineered it in fact but it back fired
because Harry was a damn fine shot."

Jake was curious "What do you mean engineered it?"

Giles took another sip of his wine and leaned forward in
a conspiratorial manner. "Bloke was a bad un. Name of
Shorcross – we called him snotty. He was at Cambridge
when we were undergrads; left before us and went into
politics. He was a bully and a thief and he hated Harry for
giving him a good hiding once; never got over it. See, Harry
was so clever. Granted he was a bit of a rake in our young
days but he was beginning to settle down; even talking of
going into politics himself – hated the way the poor were
treated. He used to say that one's wealth and position in life
was merely an accident of birth and he hated the way
society treated the downtrodden, but for the grace of God
and all that.

"Anyway, snotty Shorcross was consumed with jealousy
and I'm sure he was afraid that if Harry did get political he
would wipe the floor with him and expose him for the
corrupt devil that he was. He pretended to be outraged and

The Throgmorton Legacy

heartbroken that his wife, Marina, was being indiscrete with Harry, but in truth the whole thing had been arranged you see so that snotty could challenge him to a duel. Marina Shorcross is a beautiful whore of a widow woman with a heart of granite and a son who I gather is a chip off the old block; a bad 'un through and through. Anyway, they had some scheme to get their hands on Harry's estate. Rumour has it that they had arranged for one of their seconds to swear to hearing that it was Harry's last wish - as he lay shot and dying - that Shorcross should be forgiven and granted some kind of monetary bounty as a penance, but as soon as their plan went wrong and milady lost her hubbie she was baying for Harry's blood. Called him a murderer and wanted the state to freeze all his assets as he was a murdering fugitive. She probably wanted to give herself time to find out who would inherit so that she could get her claws into them next, of that I have no doubt! Of course Harry was ahead of the game; scuppered that whore's plans and no mistake. He had everything made over to his man Pryor and gathered together his mother's jewels and a few thousand pounds which he left in my safe keeping. He had intended to take them with him but didn't get chance."

Giles took a sip of his drink before continuing, "That was a time I can tell you, it seemed that the whole country was out looking for Harry; there was a huge bounty on his head – Madam Shorcross had friends in high places see – all of 'em as corrupt as her dear dead husband. Of course as I was known to be his friend, people came knocking at my home. Luckily he was in our offices, my father's at the time that is, so I sent Sims to warn him, told him to hide."

"'Ow did you get 'im out of the country then if everyone was watching out for 'im."

"Well, I told you we have a good relationship with our neighbours so through Sims I arranged for a Monsieur Dupont – as we named him - to be transported back to his fictitious loved ones in France under the benevolent auspices of Worthy & Sons. He was escorted by his grieving widow Catherine Villiers as she now is; you know of her Jake, I think, and the rest, as they say is history. He loved her you know, Catherine. Poor Harry was in France virtually penniless and without Pryor who had to stay around for a week or two so as not to give the game away and also of course to sign all the necessary legal papers."

Jake was glad to have heard the missing pieces of the jigsaw. "That's quite a story - poor Harry."

"Yes, I've had the odd letter from him, but to think I will never again see my old friend is really most distressing. Things will never be the same again."

"That Shorcross woman sounds a real bitch. Let's 'ope she gets what she deserves like old Croucher. But I'll tell you what's worrying me, Giles Sir. 'Ow do you know you can trust this Pryor bloke to sign over all that stuff to Jake 'ere. I mean, why would he?"

"Because he is a man of absolute integrity, and anyway Harry has left him well provided for. He said in his letter that he will return to England within six to nine months and I have no doubt whatsoever that he will be true to his word."

"Well you trust 'im, and I trust you, and that's something new for me I can tell yer. Only one I ever put me trust in before was old turnip head 'ere." Jake stood shakily,

"I'm for bed."

"Me too."

"Me too."

All three wove their way across the drawing room, bounced off the architrave in turn and staggered up the stairs.

Late the next morning; everyone refusing breakfast to the obvious annoyance of Mrs. Moffat, the three men set off for Thomas Coutts & Co with Sims driving as Giles said he didn't feel quite up to it. After satisfying all security measures they were taken into a small side room where Harry's chest was placed on a table. Giles produced two identical keys. "Here you are Jake, you do the honours." Jake, still suffering from the excesses of last night, steadied his hand, turned the key in the lock and lifted the domed lid. What he saw made him sit down in one of the wooden chairs provided, head swooning, and mouth agape.

Layers of jewellery lay one upon the other. Jake exclaimed with delight at each piece he picked out; they were the most beautiful things he had ever seen glistening in the candle light as though they had a life of their own. Diamonds, Pearls, Emeralds, Rubies, Sapphires, some of them huge, all woven into the most beautiful golden filigree, they were breathtaking. There were earrings to match most of the necklaces and rings and brooches of all manner. The bottom of the chest was lined with bank notes and scattered on top of them, gold sovereigns. All three sat in silence. Jake knew he should feel happy about his good fortune, but all he could think of was Harry. His hands were the last ones to touch these things, his dead mother's jewels, the money; he should be elated but all he could feel was a deep sorrow. India on the other hand was cock a hoop.

"Gawd, how much money do you reckon is there Giles? And what about them stones eh! They must be worth a bleedin' fortune. Jakey boy you're bleedin' rich."

Giles spoke "Well Jake, what do you want to do? Take this with you or leave it here? It's up to you, it's all yours." Only then did Jake realize what he had been given. In some ways owning nothing had been easy, having all this on the other hand, required responsible thought.

"I think for the moment I will take a little of the money, and leave everything else here."

"A wise decision if I may say so. How much do you think you want?"

Having never had such responsibilities, or any money to speak of, Jake was at a bit of a loss. "I don't know Giles, what do you think?"

"Well, and this is only a suggestion of course, you intend to go home and it will be at least six months before you return to London, so I would suggest you take enough to cover your needs. At the moment they are few but, as you have the money, if I were you I would consider purchasing new clothes, and maybe at some time your own small carriage, and then you will need money for the stage, and board and lodging, and..."

"Yer own carriage, fancy that Jake; you with yer own carriage".

"I'm not suggesting that you do so immediately but I do think you should take maybe three thousand pounds or so; enough at any rate to cover most eventualities. You may for instance, probably will in fact, wish to take home a gift for your parents. I'm sure a great many things will occur to you later, so I'm just saying that it would of course be foolish to take it all, but don't leave yourself short my boy, there is just no point."

India echoed, "No point!"

They left the bank taking some money, the emerald and diamond brooch as Harry had requested and a delicate gold necklace entwined with turquoise and pearls, together with a pair of matching earrings as a present for Jake's Ma Lizzie. Jake also secreted a diamond brooch in the shape of a flower into his pocket; he wanted to surprise Martha with a parting gift as a thank you for all she and Giles had done to help them.

On the way back to Newlands Crescent they called in on a tailor frequented by Giles, where Jake and India purchased several sets of clothes. Jake also ordered a complete outfit in finely woven soft grey wool for his father. They then called on Martha's dressmaker who had in stock a beautiful pale blue damask gown which Jake thought perfect for his mother and which complemented the jewellery he had chosen for her. Not having measurements for either parent he was fortunate enough to find a tailor and a seamstress who were, as far as he could judge, approximately the same size and build as his parents. Unfortunately both outfits would have to be altered a little to suit but could be ready in another day or two. This was a disappointment to Jake but he reasoned that, as he had been away for nigh on five years, another two days would make little or no difference to anyone except himself. He set aside his feelings of homesickness and determined to enjoy his time with Giles, Martha and the children who took great pleasure in giving their guests a tour of London pointing out the sights of interest and giving a potted history lesson with each.

The days passed quickly enough and it was soon time to say goodbye to the Masons. Having purchased a trunk Jake began to carefully pack all his new belongings, gently folding his mothers dress as though it was made of gossamer. India came into his room and sat on the bed. After some time Jake noticed that he had not said a word.

"You're quiet Indy; cat got your tongue?"

"No, I just don't know what to say. I... I'm gonna miss you so much turnip. I mean, I'm glad for you and all that, being rich and everything, but in lots of ways I wish you wasn't. We've 'ad some strange times ain't we? Saved each others' hides a coupla' times and, well I ain't never 'ad a friend like you before, and now you're goin'."

Jake looked up in astonishment. India sat on the bed, looking at the ceiling with tear filled eyes. He rose and sat on the bed next to his friend, putting his arm around him. "What are you saying Indy? I thought you were coming home with me, don't you want to? I thought we would be friends forever; you're the brother I never had. Please don't say you won't come with me, and anyway Giles has booked us both onto the stage this afternoon so you owe me the ticket money if you're not coming."

Indy turned to look at Jake. "D'you really mean that? You really want me to come with yer? You're goin 'ome to yer Ma and Pa - yer 'ome! They won't want me."

"Now who's being a turnip head? I'm not going anywhere without you. You've got no-one but me, and you're stuck with me and that's an end of it. Now, go and fetch your things and let's get them packed." Shaking his head in genuine bewilderment "I can't believe you ever thought I'd leave you behind especially as you are always so fond of telling me I need you to keep me out of trouble."

"I'm coming? I'm coming with yer? Oh Jakey boy, you won't never be sorry. Yeh, we got lots to get packed ain't we, I better get a move on." In less than a minute India was back with the first bundle of his new clothes and threw them onto the bed. He disappeared again and Jake smiled and shook his head as he listened to the laughter and solitary running commentary coming from his friend's room.

Having given over the children to their Nanny for their lunch and afternoon nap, the four who had now become firm friends, sat round a dining table spread with cold meats, fresh bread and various pickles and pastries. Jake presented Martha with the diamond brooch he had chosen for her, which moved her to tears. She would genuinely miss these young men.

"I just don't know how I can repay you Giles, except to say that I will forever be in your debt and you can always call on me if you have the need."

Giles, slightly embarrassed tutted, "Having your friendship, and that of India here, is more than payment enough, and I've told you, thanks to Harry, I stand to make a small fortune from land deals. He chose wisely in you Jake. I know you will prove him right and someday make a difference in this world."

"You too India. You've not had the best start in life and yet you are a fine example of good triumphing over adversity." India didn't really understand every word that his host uttered, but he got the gist of it. "We really ought to sort out a name for you though. If you're going up in the world you should at least have a full name to hang your hat on. You could take your mother's name if you know it, or if not, choose one and I will apply to have you and your new title registered."

"What; 'av another name like you an' Jake?"

"Yes, you could be India Faraday, India Smith, India whatever you like."

India sat for a moment wrinkling his forehead. "I ain't met many toffs, not to speak to like, an' those I 'av, either kicked me out the way or looked at me like I was a piece of dog shit. I seen them step over beggars and old soldiers with no legs, never giving the time of day, treating 'em like rubbish left around the street. But you, you're a toff and you ain't like them. I never known such a good man, doing all you 'av for Jake here, an' letting me stay when I'm just a common no-one like. So, and I won't mind if you say no - there's plenty other names – but well, would it be alright with you and your missis if I called myself Mason, India Mason?"

India's little speech elicited yet more tears from Martha and it was obvious that Giles too was very moved. "My dear boy that is possibly the greatest compliment that anyone has ever paid to me and of course I wouldn't mind; Martha and I would be delighted. I'll see to it when I return to work. Now, we had better eat up and get you two on your way." They ate in silence having to swallow hard to get the food over the lumps in their throats.

With their trunk securely tied down, Jake and India climbed into the waiting carriage that would take them to the staging post in time for the afternoon run.

"Goodbye then. We'll see you again in a few months when Mr. Pryor arrives."

"Yes, I'll send word to you care of The Jugged Hare as soon as I hear from him. Goodbye now. God speed and we hope you have a good journey."

Giles, Martha, young Harry, Letitia and Giles junior stood on their front step waving at the two boys until the cab turned the corner, leaving them and number ten Newlands Crescent behind.

Chapter 28

The travel weary pair arrived at The Jugged Hare on a brewers' dray having begged a lift from last night's coaching inn. They ordered a plate of whatever dish was giving rise to the delicious aroma coming from the kitchens, and sat in anticipation with their trunk alongside them, supping a pint of ale. When the steaming bowls of mutton stew arrived Jake asked the landlord if they could leave the trunk in his keeping until they could return with a pony and trap to collect it.

"Surely me lad, 'tis no bother. Where'll you be stayin' then, I might be able to get old Josh to deliver it for ee."

"Do you know John Faraday? His place is about a mile along the coastal track."

"Surely I do. Him and is missis 'av never been the same since their boy got taken. The blasted press gang took 'im an'..." He stopped mid-sentence. "Hold on now, it's you ain't it? Well I'll be jiggered! You're young Jake aren't you? I can see it now." Before Jake had chance to speak his host called out to his wife "Nelly, Nelly, come 'ere quick. It's young Jake Faraday, he's home, he's back from the navy."

Nelly appeared, mob cap askew, face red and shiny from the heat of the kitchen. She stood hands on hips and took a good look at Jake. "It is 'im too, well I'll be jiggered."

They finished their meal, the landlord refusing to take any money and assuring them that old Josh would be more than pleased to deliver their trunk that evening. Jake was impatient now to get home so, after a little friendly haranguing, he promised to call back in a day or two and tell him and Nelly all about their adventures.

The two friends set off to walk the mile and a half to Spinnakers; Jake carrying his valise containing his money, more money than he could ever have dreamed of, and India with his pack slung on his back. It was a beautiful spring day and they walked along in virtual silence listening to the birdsong and the sound of bees gathering nectar from dog roses entwined in the hedgerows. India, who had only ever seen sparrows in London, was enchanted to see the variety and beauty of the birds and butterflies busily darting to and fro. He breathed deeply savouring the muted perfumes coming from the sweet meadows, so very thankful he had not had to return to the putrid unwelcoming streets of his childhood.

They turned off the main track and walked the twenty five yards or so to a five bar gate. Jake leant on it "Here we are Indy - home." He slid the bolt and pushed open the gate and as he did so a dog appeared in the track ahead which lead to the yard that separated the cottage from the barn and outbuildings. The dog stood on guard silently watching until Jake called out "Jess, Jess, it's me." The dog stiffened, head on one side, tail quivering. "Come on Jess - here girl." Her tail began to wag as she walked tentatively forward then, sure that her old master had come home she rushed headlong, hurling herself at Jake nearly knocking him to the ground. He knelt down and gathered her in his arms, as she made whining noises of joy alternately nuzzling into him and licking his face. Jake had waited so long for this moment and had missed her so much that he could not stop himself from crying. Tears sprang to India's eyes as he watched, the bond between boy and dog had never been broken and it touched his heart to see them together. Another dog stood in the yard barking, "Hello, who's that then Jess, did you keep one of your pups? Come on let's go and you can introduce me."

They walked along the track, Jess pressing against Jake's

leg, glancing up at him every few seconds as if she could not believe he had actually come home. Jake heard his mother's voice, "What's all the noise for Shiner." She came into the yard shielding her eyes as she watched the two strangers approaching. Eventually she was able to make out their features and recognising her boy in this approaching stranger, stood frozen to the spot. She put out her arms to him but was unable to move, hardly daring to believe that her beloved son was home.

Jake was shocked to see how much Lizzie had changed. Her once trim but rounded body was now so thin that her clothes hung on her. She still had traces of her old beauty but the vitality and freshness had gone. She was pale and gaunt, her once lively twinkling eyes now dull and sad. Jake rushed into her arms picking her up and twisting her round. "Ma, it is me Ma. Don't cry now, I'm well and it's so good to be back. You've no idea how I've dreamed of being here with you and Pa." He planted a kiss on her wet cheek and swept her up into his arms to carry her indoors. "I've so much to tell you Ma, you'll never believe what's happened." He waved an arm in India's direction, "This is India by the way, I'll tell you and Pa all about it, where is Pa?"

As he spoke Eli came out to meet them. He had changed too, but for the better. He looked strong and fit and much younger that Jake remembered. "Eli! God, it's so good to see you; I never expected that I would." Turning to India "This is Eli, the man I told you about, the one who has the tattoo." Turning back to Eli "I've got so much to tell, is Pa around? I can't wait to see him anywhere."

"He's inside." As Jake neared the door Eli stepped into his path holding up a hand. Keeping his voice down he warned Jake that John had cut his leg badly several weeks past and he was in a bad way. "Lady Villiers from yon estate sent her physician to tend to him; he said he'll have to lose his leg if he's to survive." Jake, shocked to the core, looked at his mother as he put her down.

She nodded. "He's inside by the fire, it will do his heart so good to see you my love; we've not had a moment's happiness since the day you left."

Jake felt so guilty that his stupidity had brought his parents so much grief. He'd been so foolhardy and now regretted having stayed away so long. He had wanted to come home with money for them yes, but now he realized that no amount of money could compensate for the unhappiness he had caused. He resolved that from now on he would take care of their every need and they would want for nothing.

He walked into the old familiar parlour. This is not how he had envisaged his homecoming. The fire was lit but the room, once a haven of comfort and safety, now had an air of sadness about it and the same sickly smell that he remembered from Harry's sickbed hung in the air. Under his breath he prayed "*Dear God. Please don't let Pa die; not him too.*" His father was asleep in his old armchair covered with a blanket, his leg elevated, resting on a pile of cushions. Jake shook him gently. "Pa, it's me – Jake." John Faraday started and opened his eyes staring unblinking at his son.

"Are you really here or am I dreaming." Jake leant down to hug his father.

"It's me Pa, I'm home and I'm going to look after you – forever."

John sat himself up, wincing at the movement and reaching out for Jake's hand; he looked just like Harry had. His face ashen white, skin cold and clammy, dark rimmed eyes sunken into his head, lips sore and cracked. Jake found it difficult to maintain his composure. "Oh my dear boy, my Jake's home! We prayed every day for you to come back and now you're here. Let me hold you close son." Jake knelt beside his father's chair and they hugged, tears mingling.

India, who so far had gone almost unnoticed, spoke up. "Can I 'av a look at your Pa's leg Jake - when you're ready of course, I might be able to 'elp." Lizzie looked uncomfortable at this intrusion but with encouragement from Jake she lifted the blanket and gently unwound the bandaging on her husband's leg moistening the last winding to help ease it away from the wound. From above the knee down the leg was red and hugely swollen. The wound from knee to ankle was full of puss the edges pouting open and raw. The smell released by the removal of the bandage left no one in doubt that the leg was badly infected.

India stepped across and bent to examine the injury. Taking off his backpack he pulled out a handful of brown dried leaves and handed them to a quizzical Lizzie. "Them's Kwashi, can you brew them up in some 'ot water missis, quick as yer like, the sooner we get some o' this potion inside 'im the better. And, can you lay yer 'ands on some maggots?" Lizzie, having never seen anyone with dark skin before, was taken aback by the way he looked and the way he spoke, and now he was asking for maggots! She put the dried plants into a tankard and poured on hot water. "That's it missis, right to the top. When it's cooled a little, make 'im drink half of it then give 'im the rest in a couple of hours. It tastes like shit but that don't matter, he's got to drink it." He turned to Jake. "D'you reckon you could find some maggots Jakey? We really need 'em."

Jake, knowing of his past experience, had faith in India so without question he went outside to the slops bin. Lifting the lid, shuddering slightly, he put his hand into the white writhing mass and scooped up a handful. "That's good Jake. Now be careful but put 'em right in the centre there, right in all that muck."

Lizzie held her hands to her face. "No, this is madness. Jake, don't let him do this. Please Jake, stop him." Despite his mothers plea Jake dropped the maggots into the wound. He had grave misgivings too but India seemed so sure of himself that, as crazy as it seemed, he must be right.

Loosely winding a clean bandage India said "It's alright really missis. Them maggots will clear up all that mess and then we can start the healing. I 'ad a back as bad as this once, and those little beggars saved my skin and no mistakin' it."

Lizzie collapsed into a chair and began to cry. She was a strong woman but Jake's arrival, the strain of watching her husband's health ebbing away, the sorrow she had bourn from the day she lost her boy all became too much to bear. The floodgates opened releasing all the emotion she had locked away for so many years and she sobbed, deep anguished cries wracking her body. Jake wrapped his arms around her to comfort her, her hard bony body beneath his hands shocking him. Eli poured a tot of brandy which Jake helped her to drink. He then carried his mother up the stairs laying her gently on her bed, stroking her lovely face until she fell asleep.

Somehow John liked this strange boy. "My poor Lizzie, she's exhausted. It's been so hard for her since I've been ill. Eli works so hard, but it's just too much for the two of them. It's strange you know but those maggots don't hurt at all."

"No they won't – er..."

"John, call me John."

"They won't 'urt John, they'll just get nice an' fat eating up all that muck in yer leg and then we can start to get you better. Speaking of which, you need to drink this down now it's cooler. Drink half of it. It tastes like shit but believe me it's bloody good stuff. It makes yer sleepy too but that ain't no bad thing, not in the state you're in." He handed the tankard to John who took a deep breath, then drank. Shuddering, he handed the tankard back to India.

"I've never tasted anything so foul in all my life. Are you sure it's meant to cure me and not kill me?"

They all laughed at John's attempt at humour, Eli especially. The last few weeks had been so bad with seemingly no hope for John and now suddenly there might be. Things had shifted for the better. He poured out four measures of brandy. India held up a hand. "Not for 'im, just his medicine and water for a while. He's noddin' off already see, best thing for 'im." India lifted his beaker and downed the drink in one gulp, "Shall I 'av the spare?"

While John snored softly by the fire, Jake introduced India and Eli to each other. He asked India to tell what little he knew of his father and Eli sat incredulous. How could it possibly be that he was sitting opposite Junti's son? The coincidences were just too incredible but there was no doubting it, everything the boy said fitted, even down to the tattooed flower which matched his own and there was no denying the similarity. The lad was of a much more slender build and his skin was lighter, but his mannerisms and those brown expressive eyes had belonged to his father, miraculous though it seemed, there was no doubt that he was looking at Junti's boy. India in turn was eager to learn all he could about his father and sat riveted as Eli told of their friendship and their escape together from the bloodbath on the island all those years ago.

Chapter 29

Jake wanted to know how they had fared while he'd been away so Eli started from the day he had disappeared, telling him everything that had happened when Cyrus Mallett came back looking for him, not leaving out all the grisly details. India woke John to pour down the rest of his medicine then poured hot water on a fresh handful of Kwashi in readiness for the morning.

"Your Ma sounds a bit like you Jakey boy. I wouldn't fancy getting on the wrong side of either of you, and no mistake."

Eli explained that from then on he had felt indebted to Lizzie and John and had stayed on working for his keep. Life had been sad and pretty uneventful in Jake's absence, all three just getting on with the chores of day to day living. Jake was saddened and very angry to hear what had happened to poor Jess. He rubbed his stockinged feet along her back as she lay under the table, regretting bitterly that he had not been there when she had needed his help. The one pup left, Shiner, had derived his name from the black patch he had over one eye. He sat contentedly alongside Eli and it was obvious to all that this man was the centre of his world.

Eventually, unable to stay awake any longer they all opted for bed. Jake gently placed another pillow behind his father's head and added another blanket. He stoked up the fire to last through the night. "Good night Pa, see you in the morning."

Jake's room had been kept as it was, Lizzie never giving up hope that he would return. He and India climbed the stairs and kicking off their shoes fell onto his old bed fully clothed. "Do you think you will be able to help Pa to get well?"

"I 'ope so mate, otherwise your Ma'll be looking for me with a pitchfork!"

Although it was very cramped in the little bed, they fell into an alcohol induced sleep instantly.

When Jake woke India had gone. He lay for a moment, memories of his childhood flooding back, until he heard his mother stir. He peeked into her room. She looked so small in the big bed, and in repose, beautiful, her hair spread out over her pillow like a chestnut sunburst. She opened her eyes. "Morning Ma, how do you feel? I expect you've got a fuzzy head; that was a big tot of brandy we poured down you."

"Oh Jake, you are here. I was afraid to wake up in case it had all been a dream." She started to sob again.

"Come on now Ma, it's me alright." He stroked her hair. "I'm home, thank the Lord, and I'm not going anywhere."

"I'm sorry Jake, it's just that you went away a boy and now you're a man and I can't help grieving for those lost years, and then there's poor John. He has suffered so and I can't help him. Oh! What time is it? I must get up, he'll need seeing to and..."

Jake put up his hand. "From the smells coming from downstairs I would say that breakfast is under way and everything is being taken care of. You've a house full of helpers now so let things be." Lizzie threw her legs out of bed. "No arguing now, you take your time. Change your dress and make yourself beautiful for Pa."

Lizzie frowned creasing her brow. "That young man, he's very strange and I'm really scared that he'll do more harm than good."

"I've seen men die Ma and I'm afraid Pa is real poorly. You said yourself there's nothing to be done; even if they take his leg it may be of no use, so please give Indy a chance. He nearly died himself once - I'll tell you all about it soon - but he was saved by natives using that Kwashi of his. He is a really good person Ma, apart from Pa and maybe Harry, he's the best and truest person I've ever known. We've been through some hard times together and the only things that kept me going were him and the thought of coming back to you; but Indy, he's got no-one, he's never had a home. His Ma died when he thinks he was about two – he doesn't even know how old he is, or even when his birthday is! He used to ask me to tell him all about you and Pa so that he could pretend that he had a family too. Give him a chance Ma - you'll see." Lizzie stood and hugged her son. He was still the same thoughtful compassionate boy that she loved so much and was so proud of.

"You go on down, my love; I'll just be a minute or two."

She came into the kitchen to find that everything had indeed been taken care of. There was a pot of broth on the trivet, a kettle steaming lazily alongside it, and from the smell wafting through the kitchen someone had a loaf cooking in the Dutch oven hanging above them. John was snoozing, freshly shaven in his chair, India standing over him inspecting his leg. "Morning missis, this is lookin better already, them maggots are doin a good job, I reckon they'll have cleaned it out by tommorrer, then we can pack it and," nodding towards John "really get im on the mend."

"Lizzie, please call me Lizzie."

"As yer like missis Lizzie. See this mash that's left from his medicine?" Lizzie nodded. "Well, when his leg is clean I wanna pack the 'ole out with it, but not loose, it needs to be wrapped in some cloth so we can take it out and put in fresh every day, 'av you got any?"

"I've some muslin that I can make into tiny bags, would that be any good."

India smiled, "The very thing! On the island they wrapped it in fresh Kwashi leaves but we ain't got any, but your muslin will likely be just as good. Now, can I rely on you to make up his medicine like I showed you and make sure he takes it about every three hours? That's important mind; it will stop 'is pain and keep 'im sleepy but most of all it will kill what's poisoning 'im."

Lizzie was warming to this boy. He was fine boned and she thought, slightly effeminate with his large expressive eyes and long thick lashes. He had a quick wit and a ready smile and was so caring of John that her heart went out to him. Watching the way he dressed her husband's leg so tenderly, she found herself saying, "Indy why don't you just call me Ma?"

Jake and Eli came in together. We've done the chores Ma and collected quite a few eggs, so now I'll show you how much I've learnt about cooking them." Hooking the lid off the Dutch oven he speared the bread inside and lifted it onto the table.

"What do you think Jake? I've asked Indy to call me Ma. It's easier than Lizzie and you said you loved him like a brother so from now on John and I will have two sons – just mind the pair of you turn don't turn us grey before our time!"

India was stunned and overcome with emotion which he hoped to disguise with a wide smile, but Jake gave his mother the biggest hug and said jokingly "Now I'll never get rid of him!"

The light-hearted mood in the kitchen was interrupted by Jess and Shiner heralding visitors. All four went into the yard to greet old Josh who had arrived with Jake's trunk.

"Sorry I didn't make it last night but I was busy till it got dark." Jake and India, who had completely forgotten about the trunk until now, unbuckled it and carried it into the house. Josh was invited in for some ale and ended up having breakfast, ears pricked for any gossip as he tucked in.

When he had gone and the dishes cleared Jake unlocked the trunk and lifted out his mother's gown. "This is for you Ma, I hope you like the colour. It should fit, although you are a site thinner than I remembered." Lizzie was overcome; she had never seen anything so beautiful. "Go on Ma, don't stand there with your mouth open, take it upstairs and try it on." He pulled out his mother's arms and laid the gown across them. She, speechless, did as she was told and disappeared. A few moments later she called out for him to help her – she had never had such a beautiful and intricate gown and was having difficulty finding her way in. Jake took the stairs two at a time and in a few minutes, mother and son re-appeared.

Eli and India were taken aback. Even though she had lost weight, so that the gown was a little loose, and the strain of the last years showed on her face, Lizzie was still a handsome woman, but neither of them had been ready for such a change in her. Now rosy cheeked, eyes glowing with excitement, with the low necked gown exposing her creamy white skin she looked absolutely beautiful.

"Oh Miss Lizzie, you look like a real lady; you're a real beauty and no mistake."

"Thank you Eli. I just never want to take it off. Listen to the way it rustles when I walk. Oh Jake, where on earth did you find such a beautiful gown? How did you get it?"

"No questions Ma, you look an absolute picture, but there's just one more thing." He went to his valise which was still in a corner by the door where he had left it the day before. He took out the necklace he had chosen for her. "I thought this would be just right for your gown, what do you think?" The only piece of jewellery Lizzie had ever owned was her wedding ring. She held the necklace out in front of her, then against her gown all the while shaking her head in disbelief. Jake took it from her and fastened it around her neck, the shape perfectly mirroring the neckline beneath it. He took the mirror from the wall and stood it on the table so that she could see her full reflection. Turning round and around she swished and rustled giggling like a young girl.

"Is that me? Is that really me?" She went to her husband and shook him gently. "Look John, look what Jake brought home for me."

John opened his eyes and managed, "Beautiful, angel," before sailing off into oblivion once more.

They unpacked the rest of the trunk and Jake, feeling very uncomfortable, apologized to Eli for not bringing him anything, not thinking that he would be around. "No need for that young Jake. I owe your Ma and Pa a debt that I can never repay and you bringing back so much hope and happiness is more than enough for me." He looked from Jake to India. "God bless the pair of you." He turned on his heel and went outside, he was getting emotional and that would never do.

Over the next few days Jake and India recounted their tales to Lizzie and Eli, starting with their being thrown together on The Huron, giving their separate accounts of how they had both thought the other dead and what they had done when separated, and then how they had then come together once more. Jake explained all about Harry's death and their journey home; how they accidentally came across Charlie Croucher in Calais and how he had eventually killed him and had to escape. He told of how India had saved him from freezing to death, of the kindness of the Halfpennies and Giles Mason and how, in the course of the next few months he was to come into a fortune. All this was almost too much for them to take in; the boys had suffered and seen so much of life in the time they were away, and now Jake was rich; it was unbelievable, just more than they could deal with at present, so they all carried on with life as though nothing had changed while grappling with the realization that it undoubtedly had.

Under India's watchful eye John gradually began to show signs of improvement. The wound in his leg was cleansed and re-packed every day and each few days showed a discernible improvement. The flesh around the wound lost its' angry redness and the swelling began to subside. John was gradually given weaker solutions of Kwashi and consequently was more alert. Almost a month from the day Indy had started his treatment John was able to put some weight on his leg and, with the aid of Eli's crutches, move around a little. During the next three weeks he had improved so much that, although he limped quite heavily, he could walk unaided.

Chapter 30

Satisfied that John was absolutely out of danger Jake decided that the time had come for him to fulfil his promise to Harry, and deliver his gift to Lady Catherine Villiers. He hitched old Prince to their wagon and, he and India dressed in their finest, set off for the Villiers Estate.

They pulled up at the gatehouse. "I'm Jake Faraday and we've come to see Lady Catherine, can we leave old Prince here with you? It's such a lovely day and I would love to show my friend here the beautiful grounds." The gatekeeper nodded his assent and Jake led Prince to a shady spot where he tethered him. They set off on the long driveway toward the house, Jake pointing out things that he remembered from his childhood; Indy wishing they still had the use of old Prince.

Jake's guided tour was rudely interrupted when a huge dog, almost the size of Bosun, charged at them from behind a thicket of rhododendrons. Indy cried out. "Gawd, love us," and began to run back the way they had come.

"Please don't be afraid, it's only Horatio, he's really just a pup and absolutely full of fun. He won't hurt you." The disembodied voice belonged to a young woman who eventually stepped out from the shrubs. "Horatio, come here you naughty boy; be nice to the gentlemen." She was around the same age as Jake and possibly the most beautiful creature he had ever seen. The words he was about to utter died on his lips, his mouth dried up, and the usually self-assured young man, back from travelling the world, was struck dumb.

Seeing that the dog was safely under control India trotted back all smiles. "Gawd, 'ee 'ad me scared I don't mind admitting; thought he was gonna eat me."

The girl giggled. "Oh don't worry, he may look the part but I can assure you he is an absolute baby, no use for protection at all."

"Glad to 'ear it. I'm India, India Mason and this 'ere is Jake Faraday. 'His Pa done a lot of work 'ere for the geezer what owns the place."

"That would be my father; can I help you with anything?" India nudged a tongue-tied Jake who felt himself blushing as he explained falteringly that he had a message for Lady Villiers from an old friend.

"Oh that is fortunate as Papa is in London on business but Mama is here. Let me walk with you to the house. I'm Alice by the way, Alice Villiers – nice to meet you."

They walked on to the house, Indy chatting all the while to Alice, who, not being used to his mode of speech, had to ask him to repeat himself a number of times. Jake trailed behind trying to think of something to say that would not make him look like a complete idiot.

When they reached the house Alice showed them into the drawing room. "Please take a seat and I'll fetch mother – just one moment." She closed the door behind her and they heard her instructing the butler to inform Lady Villiers that she had visitors. "Gawd, she's a looker ain't she? Seems nice enough too." Jake nodded there was nothing he could add.

A few minutes passed and they sat taking in the vastness of the room, marvelling at the sumptuous furniture and huge paintings covering most of the walls. Eventually the door opened and an older version of Alice entered the room. The only slight difference was that her titian hair, which was gathered on top of her head allowing small ringlets to cascade around her face and neck, was flecked with grey at the temples. Her skin was as smooth as alabaster and her kindly green eyes edged with black lashes indicated a lively intelligence.

"Ah gentlemen! Alice tells me you have a message for me." Addressing Jake. "Is it your father? Have you need of our physician? I'll send..." Now that Alice was gone from the room, Jake was able to speak more freely.

"No Lady Catherine, my father is out of danger and very much better, but we are very grateful for your concern. I've come at the request of Harry, Lord Throgmorton." At his name Catherine's eyes lit up.

"Harry, what of him, is he well?"

"I'm afraid I have to tell you that he died a few months ago. He asked me to convey to you that you were often in his thoughts and never forgotten, and he wanted me to give you this." He carefully unwrapped the brooch and laid it on the small ornamental table between them. "He said he chose it for you because when he looked at it he saw your eyes."

Lady Catherine was visibly shaken. She picked up the brooch and after caressing it tenderly she pinned it onto her gown. Harry had been right the emerald was exactly the same colour as her eyes which were now brimming with tears. She got up and walked through one of the huge open windows which lead onto a terrace overlooking formal gardens and manicured lawns. Birds sang gustily splashing and preening in strategically placed ornate Romanesque bird baths totally unabashed by the presence of humans and any lack of privacy whilst they carried out their ablutions. "Please give me a moment gentlemen. It's been rather a shock you know." The two friends waited until she had composed herself enough to come back inside. "Won't you stay for lunch and then perhaps you can tell me how you came to know Harry, dearest Harry." Her eyes filled with tears again.

"Don't mind if we do. Jake 'ere said he used to come 'ere with his Pa and the grub was really good."

Their hostess smiled. "Ah yes, Mr. Faraday was a very skilled workman; my husband was taken with him, I remember that. But I'm really intrigued now Jacob as to where on earth you met up with Harry." She pulled a thick tapestry bell cord summoning a uniformed maid. "Could you arrange lunch for four please Emily, we'll eat on the terrace as it's such a lovely day." She turned to face her guests. "One thing though. Neither my husband nor my daughter know how I assisted Harry in his hour of need, so I beg you, if you know anything of it please keep it to yourselves."

Catherine Villiers sat with her daughter and guests, enthralled as Jake, at first finding it difficult to relax in Alice's presence, slowly began his tale with India, as usual, embellishing his own role on board The Huron; both of them omitting the more unsavoury details in deference to the ladies. Jake went on to describe the circumstances of his meeting with Harry and how he saved the day for all those on board their ill-fated ship. Catherine clapped her hands with delight. "Oh dear, dear Harry. He was such a gentleman you know, a perfect gentleman. Do go on Jacob; tell us what happened then."

Jake gave the women a précis of his four years at Dragons Lair, leaving out the fact that it was a Privateer's enclave, preferring the version that it was a base for the trading co-operative that Harry had set up for the benefit of his crew. He explained that Harry had been injured when Pirates tried to steal their cargo and, knowing that he was dying and looking to the future, he had urged those men who were willing, to invest in land in Jamaica where they could set up a sugar plantation. It was at this point, he explained, that he and India had decided to return to England. Fortunately the luncheon was to India's taste and swallowing the food made it a little easier to swallow Jake's story without comment.

Jake did not lie though when it came to how Harry had treated him. How, during his time at Dragons Lair Harry and George had taken him under their wing; how they had educated him to a reasonable standard in literacy and numeracy and coached him so that he was now a proficient mariner able to command his own ship. He concluded with their short visit to Giles Mason, but felt it inappropriate to mention the extent of Harry's munificence or that he was in fact soon to be the heir to the Throgmorton fortune.

Having finished lunch Lady Catherine stood. "Alice my dear, why don't you show India the stables; I'm sure he would love to see our new foal, he is an absolute darling, and Jacob and I will take a turn around the arboretum. He may recognize some of my dear husband's new acquisitions." The two pairs split up, the sound of India's chattering slowly receding as the distance between them increased. "Now, Jacob, I will not press you any further but I somehow think that there is a good deal more to tell but that you chose not to and I must respect your decision, but please tell me this, did Harry have a good life, and did his end come peacefully?"

She was such a compassionate and beautiful woman that Jake found it hard not to unburden himself completely. "He had a good life and gave one to all those he gathered round him. He saw men for what they were you see; not for the way they looked, but for what was inside. In answer to your question, yes he was well cared for at his end, Mrs. Hardcastle, our sawbones, she was the best. He died thinking of you and he wanted me to tell you so – it would make him happy to know that I had been able to do so."

"I loved him you know. Oh, I love my dear Edward of course, but Harry was my first love and I never stopped hoping that I would someday see him again." She looked so sad that Jake, before stopping to think, reached out to hold her hand. "Thank you Jacob, you have brought me some comfort and I will cherish my gift until the day I die." They stood together hand in hand, one man in both their thoughts.

"Jake, 'ere Jake, look at this little fella." Jake turned to see India leading a chestnut mare across the lawns, her foal trotting by her side. He had a sleek black coat with a small white star shaped blaze on his forehead. "Ain't he lovely! And guess what! Alice is gonna call him Indian Star, what do you think of that, an 'orse named after me? Gawd! who'd 'av thought it?"

A short time later all four walked down to the gatehouse and Catherine and her daughter waved to their two unexpected but highly entertaining visitors until they were out of sight. Catherine haunted by memories of Harry and what might have been, Alice excited, looking forward to her next meeting with Jake Faraday, not quite sure yet how or when that would be, but determined that it would happen, and sooner rather than later.

Jake gave Prince the reins and let him amble along for home at his own pace. India, full of wonderment at the grandeur of the Villiers estate, talked non-stop, not noticing that Jake was totally preoccupied. Had he been able to read his friends thoughts he would have seen that they were full of Alice Villiers, the way she walked, the way she talked, the colour of her hair, the colour of her eyes, her even gleaming white teeth and the full red lips that he so wanted to kiss. She was the most beautiful thing he had ever seen and oh, so far out of his reach.

Chapter 31

A warm breeze wafted in from the yard, carrying with it the sound of birdsong. For the first time in many weeks John Faraday felt the desire to be out amongst his livestock and tap once more into the throb of life in the natural world all around them. He took himself to the parlour door, and with a little assistance, negotiated the one step down into the yard where Eli had placed a blanket covered bench with a stool upon which to rest his bare leg so that he could get some sun on it. Still in his nightgown he sat with his face turned up to the sky, breathing in the cool fresh air. He could smell mayflowers on the old hawthorn tree beside the barn and the primroses that clustered in pale yellow posies beneath fence posts. The sudden rush of fresh air made him feel light headed but he had never been so thankful to be alive.

His heart was near to bursting with gratitude that he was going to be fit and well once more and able to carry on looking after his family. He could not help but smile as he heard Lizzie singing as she pottered in the house. Dear Lizzie, life was so good and he loved her so much, probably more now than ever before. His train of thought was interrupted as Jess barked, alerting her charges to the arrival of visitors.

John called out. "Lizzie, it's the physician from Lady Villiers, and there's someone else with him." Jake, Lizzie and India stepped into the yard eager to meet their callers. Jake's heart skipped a beat as he recognized Alice. He rushed indoors and brought out a blanket which he thrust at his father. "Cover yourself up Pa it isn't right for a lady to see you like that."

The visiting carriage came to a halt at the entrance to the

yard and a booming voice called out. "Good day to you Mr. Faraday. Lady Villiers told me that you were recovering well from your injury and well frankly, I just had to take a look for myself." Being a man of ample proportions, the bluff physician's exit from the carriage was a somewhat awkward affair. Slightly short of breath, he continued, "I found it quite difficult to believe you see, and I'm still not sure I can trust my own eyes, but by heaven you look well man; it's a miracle and no mistake. Can I take a look at the leg?" John pulled up the blanket to expose the subject of interest. The wound had knitted together leaving a livid red scar but his leg, which had been swollen and blotched purple and red, was now perfectly normal.

St John Lyons leant down to take a closer look. "May I?" John nodded in assent so he ran his hand gently down the length of the scar. "Well I'll be damned. As far as I was concerned you were a dead man unless you lost that leg, and even then I didn't hold out much hope for you – you were full of poison you see. I can only say again that it's a miracle – nothing else for it – a miracle."

Alice spoke to Jake. "Mama sent a few things as a token of her well wishes, would you help me with the hamper please." Jake, embarrassed by being caught out with his father improperly dressed was even more tongue-tied than before. He blushed and nodded following her to the carriage. Unbeknown to her mother, Alice had packed the hamper and had engineered the whole visit so that she could meet with Jake again. In truth Mr. Lyons had been incredulous to learn that John was recovering without surgery so Alice had seized the opportunity and suggested that they pay a visit to satisfy his curiosity and to deliver a few luxury items to aid the patient's recovery.

Refusing to let Alice help, Jake carried the hamper into

the parlour, still feeling thoroughly ill at ease. His discomfort was matched by Lizzie's who was completely thrown by having such a fine lady descend on them; she was also painfully aware of the difference in their attire. If only she had known they were coming, she could have put on the fine gown which hung upstairs.

Sensitive to the atmosphere Alice set about putting them at their ease. "Do you have an apron Mrs. Faraday? This is my very best dress and Mama would be furious with me if I marked it." Lizzie scurried around and found one. "Thank you so much. Now, I have no idea what Mama has sent, she can be such a fuss you know. Shall we unpack? Don't worry, I can take back anything that you don't want, she need not know." Whispering in a conspiratorial fashion, "She means well and I'm sure none of us would like to hurt her feelings."

The girl's natural air and practical manner put Lizzie at ease. It was comforting to know that her ladyship's very best dress was not as fine as the one Jake had given her. She had to admit that it was very nice, but hers was better. They unpacked game pies, cheeses, fruits, puddings, bottles of wine and even some sweet meats. By the time they had emptied the hamper Lizzie's table was completely covered with some of the finest food she had ever seen. "Oh my Lord, your mother has been so kind, however can we repay her?"

"Never mind that now, she wants only for your husband to get well. I know there is work for Mr. Faraday when he is better, but he can discuss that with Papa once he is up and about."

This sudden and completely unexpected turn of events lifted Lizzie's spirits. She liked this girl. "It's such a beautiful day, won't you stay and eat with us. We've all this beautiful food and we could put a table outside, so that my dear John could join us and still enjoy the sunshine."

Feeling more like her old self than she had done in weeks she whipped Eli and India into action getting them to fix a make-do table in the yard and carry out chairs. Jake helped his father into the house so that he could dress, and within the hour everyone was seated around the picnic table laughing and chatting like old friends. Emboldened by the wine and ale Jake began to chat with Alice and found that conversation flowed freely between them, her quick wit delighting him and making him laugh. They were completely wrapped up in each other and it was obvious to everyone present that love was in the air.

Mr. Lyon was engrossed in conversation with India, fascinated to hear how this strange young man had apparently achieved John's miraculous recovery. He cringed inside when he heard how maggots were introduced into the wound, and found it hard not to scoff when told that it was then packed with Kwashi to cleanse it and allow the poison to seep out; in truth he had never heard such humbug in all his life. He listened politely and attentively biting his tongue; it was all so far-fetched and so out of tune with current medical thinking, and yet there was John Faraday large as life and undoubtedly on the mend. Try as he may though, he could not begin to accept that a simple dried plant could bring about such a recovery. He felt he was a reasonable, open minded and practical man and so concluded that, although India had made a valiant attempt to save John Faraday's life he alone could not possibly have done so. No, this miracle was surely down to the good Lord who had chosen to save this particular lamb for some greater purpose.

The sun was beginning to set and there was a chill in the

air when the two visitors, Alice reluctantly, climbed into their carriage. She leant from the window. "Don't forget now India, you must visit us again soon. I swear Indian Star has grown quite a bit since you last saw him. He is going to be so handsome – sleek and dark just like you." India smiled and Jake felt a pang of jealousy until Alice clasped his hand. Her voice softened as she gazed into his eyes. "I have had such a wonderful day Jacob." Her face was so close to his that he had to stop himself from clasping it in his hands and pressing his lips against hers; the lump that had appeared in his throat rendered him speechless. "Please thank your parents for making us so welcome, and you will come along to visit us with India won't you? We could teach him how to sit a horse - maybe go for a hack."

Jake felt himself blushing again, his desire for her was so strong that he was sure everyone could see and all he could think to say was, "Of course, that would be very nice." India smiled to himself. His friend had really got it bad, not that he blamed him, Alice Villiers was truly beautiful, but more than that, she was everything that he could want in a friend; he truly hoped that their friendship could last forever.

Six months passed with Jake and India frequent visitors to the Villiers mansion. India spent hours in and around the stables fascinated with all things equine. He proved to be an excellent horseman, even joining in the hunts, although having been the subject of the odd hunt, he was secretly pleased when the quarry escaped. He felt the odds were very unfairly stacked. Apart from enjoying the run of the stables, he had begun to very much enjoy the company of Sarah, a petite young parlour maid who had caught his eye on their very first visit and who had taken to slipping out to the stables with cakes and pies which she assured him were only going to be thrown out anyway. When he was in her company he found that for the first time in as long as he could remember, he could forget about his Nancy.

Over these months it became obvious to Lord Villiers that his daughter was head over heels with young Jacob Faraday and, while he had grown fond of the lad and could not help but like him, he began to worry that things could get out of hand and his strong headed daughter may begin to consider something ridiculous like marrying beneath her station. He decided that the best course of action would be to introduce her to London society and invite weekend parties to the estate in the hope of eclipsing young Faraday so that she may take a fancy to someone more suitable.

The Faraday household was back to normal and with all four men sharing the workload things were ticking along smoothly. The only indication that John had ever been ill was a very slight limp which developed when he tired. Breakfast was finished and everyone was about to start on their own particular chore when Old Josh arrived with a sealed letter addressed to Mr. Jacob Faraday. Lizzie took the letter thanking him and went inside to find Jake. She fetched Josh a flagon of ale and asked him to wait a while just in case they needed him further.

Everyone clustered round as Jake broke the seal. He studied it for a moment then. "It's from Giles Mason. He says John Pryor has arrived and he wants me to meet with him as soon as I can to sort out my inheritance. He says his family and Mr. Pryor are looking forward to seeing me and they have much news of the sugar plantation in Jamaica." Everyone was dumbstruck. They all knew that this was supposed to happen but somehow, despite Jake arriving home with more money than any of them had ever seen, they never thought it would. John's illness had been paramount in everyone's minds and once he was on the mend, no-one wanted to refer to Jake's would-be inheritance for fear of jinxing it.

India said what was on all their minds. "Gawd, so that John geezer is really gonna 'and everything over to you! I never thought I'd see the day. Shocked I am! He must be a bleeding saint! When you going then Jake, d'you want me to come with yer?"

"We'll all go." Lizzie went to protest but Jake held up his hand. "No buts. Eli; will you be able to cope with things for a week or so if I ask young Josh to stay and help?"

Eli nodded. "Take as long as you like, I'll have old Jess and young Shiner for company."

"That's it then, Ma, Pa, India; get some clothes packed, we're off to London! I'll arrange for Old Josh to take us to meet the stage tomorrow and then I'm off to Alice to let her know we will be away for a while." He ran outside to Old Josh grinning from ear to ear.

The excitement was palpable as they packed and unpacked having no real idea of where they were going or what clothing would be suitable. Not having large wardrobes though made things a little easier so in the end all of them packed their very best outfits, leaving their everyday clothes for travelling.

Jake returned in a sombre mood and in reply to Lizzie's inquiring look said, "They aren't there. They all went off to London yesterday and didn't say when they were coming back."

"'Tis just as well then; neither of you young folk will have time to miss each other."

India said nothing. He had overheard some of the

servants' gossip that Alice was being taken to London to get her away from Jake as her father wanted her to mix with more of her own sort. He had been waiting for the right time to tell his friend, but now with the arrival of the summons from Giles Mason events had overtaken him. He decided to let things lie for the moment, at least until Jake's future had been resolved, one way or the other.

Chapter 32

Three days after leaving Poundsmill, four dusty and travel-weary visitors arrived at the offices of Maws and Mason. Giles seemed genuinely pleased to meet Jake's parents at last, and insisted that all four of them stay as his house guests until their business was concluded. Leaving Frobisher in charge as before, he ushered them all into his carriage with instructions to his man to return later to collect their luggage. In no time at all they arrived at number ten Newlands Crescent. Giles ushered them inside where they were greeted warmly by Martha, the three young Masons and John Pryor. Introductions were fairly brief as Giles could see that all four travellers were very tired. He organized refreshments to be sent to their rooms and suggested that they take a few hours rest before freshening up to meet again for dinner that evening.

Initially things were a little stilted as John and Lizzie were overawed by the opulence of the house and by being the guests of such an eminent lawyer. But Giles and Martha put everyone at their ease and before long, lively conversation flowed back and forth, everyone eager to have their say.

Dinner was served in the oak-panelled dining room, the polished wood reflecting the warm glow issuing from the beautiful, strategically placed candelabras. Lizzie marvelled at the flowers and silverware that dressed the huge table so beautifully. She felt like such a lady as Giles pulled out her chair in order that she and Martha may sit before the gentlemen, and was very grateful to Jake that the array of cutlery held no fears for her or John; he had instructed them beforehand on their use.

The first course was a delicious soup which was

accompanied with a light white fruity wine, the crystal glasses turning it to amber in the reflected candle light. The food was exquisite each course being accompanied by a different wine. The evening passed with everyone in the best of humour; a never ending stream of lively anecdotes, mostly from India, keeping everyone amused. Anyone taking a clandestine peak into the dining room of Newlands Crescent would have witnessed what was surely a group of old friends gathered together in a warmly lit, cosy room, shiny faces aglow, totally at ease in each others' company.

The subject eventually turned to the progress being made in the setting up of the sugar co-operative that Harry had dreamed of. Everyone listened intently as Mr. Pryor told them at length of the group's journey from Dragons Lair to find and purchase suitable land. How they had set about preparing the land, recruiting workers, organizing and undertaking the building of their homes and, crucially, the set of rules by which every member of the co-operative agreed to abide. There had been a few problems but on the whole he was very pleased by the progress made so far. As an aside he told Jake that before they parted company he would provide him with a map giving directions to their plantation with Dragons Lair as a point of reference. He said he would use some of his time in London to visit merchants to gauge the demand for sugar, price structure etc. in readiness for their first harvest. It was evident to everyone present that here was an intelligent man with good business acumen and it was no wonder that Harry had adopted him as his right hand man.

It was growing late and the effects of all the wine consumed were beginning to show, nearly everyone yawning in between sentences. Giles Mason picked up his glass and addressed his guests. "Dear friends, it is late and I am sure we would all welcome going to our beds but I would ask you to join me in one last toast to Harry." Turning to John and Lizzie, "John, Elizabeth; I know that you did not have the pleasure of meeting our dear Harry – Lord Henry – but nevertheless I would like to include you as he loved your boy and I know that, had you known him, you would miss him as much as we all do today. So please raise your glasses and drink to Harry, a true gentlemen and friend to all, God rest his soul."

Everyone drank and collectively – "To Harry."

"And now my friends, last one upstairs has to deal with Mrs. Moffatt."

Everyone made their way wearily upstairs, no-one daring to look back at the glaring disapproval of the teetotal housekeeper.

After breakfast the next day Martha whisked Lizzie off to do the rounds of fashion houses and dressmakers. Being the only woman in an otherwise male-orientated world, she was delighted to have a female companion. Lizzie was absolutely enthralled by the bolts of satins and silks in the most beautiful colours, the variety of ribbons and lace, the beautiful gowns in the latest fashions and the most exquisite shoes, some embroidered, some covered in beading; she had never seen such a treasure trove.

Martha had enjoyed the day immensely and when they returned home she hurried Lizzie up to her bedroom where she pulled out several gowns from her wardrobe. "Try these on Elizabeth. I love them but since I have had the children, I just can't get into them." Lizzie was speechless. The clothes were beautiful, and with the exception of Jake's gift, way better than any she could have dreamed of owning. "You are welcome to them if they fit, that is of course if you don't mind. I do hope I haven't offended you."

"No, no – it's just that they are so beautiful, and..."

Martha waved away Lizzie's objections "This is my favourite of the three, let's see if it fits." She helped Lizzie off with her old day clothes which now seemed so shabby and into the offered gown of russet taffeta with an oyster coloured petticoat. The sleeves finished just above the elbow and were edged with lace. "Oh, it is perfect Elizabeth. You must have it – please say you will. You look absolutely adorable – don't say anything to anyone and wear it at dinner tonight." She clapped her hands and laughed. "Oh Elizabeth, I so love having you here, I wish you could stay."

"Call me Lizzie please. I love being here too. I know you're a lady and all but, do you think we could stay friends, even when I go back home?" Fearing she may have overstepped the mark, "Oh, I won't be offended if you would rather not, really, I would understand."

Martha, surprised that Lizzie should so put herself down, crossed the room to give her a hug.

"Dear Eliz... Lizzie. I would absolutely love to count you as a friend, how on earth could you think otherwise – friends always – yes?"

Lizzie nodded, "Friends always. Now, could we go and find your children. I've been itching to get my hands on them ever since we arrived."

While the two women had been away the men had gathered in Giles' study. He stood one hand on the mantel shelf while the other four men sat in the comfortable wing backed chairs. "Now down to business." Speaking to Jake and John Pryor. "The situation at present is this. I have prepared all the necessary paperwork for the transfer of the

Throgmorton assets to Jacob here for a nominal fee, where it sits in my office awaiting both your signatures. I think I have attended to every detail correctly but, in order to avoid any problems, I intend to ask, have already done so in fact, two of my most learned colleagues to examine the details of the transaction and to witness the signings. One specialises in, and understands the vagaries of our taxation system, and the other in land registry and the like. I intend to visit their respective chambers tomorrow to arrange a mutually convenient time for them to witness the signings, any questions?"

Everyone shook their heads to the negative. "The estate earnings from last year are in the bank but there will be taxes and fees to be met from the income, so at present the actual liquid balance is unknown. However the estate is very productive and the earnings from it can, in my opinion, easily cope with the demands and fees that I am envisaging." He paused then took the chair next to Jake, addressing him.

"I hope this isn't too confusing for you but you have had a few months to get used the idea what? Have you thought what you are going to do with your wealth; how you may like to run the estate?"

Jake pursed his lips, "I've tried to think about it but I'm no gentleman born to riches and there is so much I don't know. You said that the estate is managed very well and the tenants are fairly treated, so the way I see it, there seems to be no need for me to interfere. You said the house is well maintained and the Fredericks family that live there were good friends to Harry and I would hate to turn them out of their home. I have no need of a big house like that – wouldn't know what to do with it, so again I don't see any reason to change anything. You are a well educated man

Giles, and true, fair and honest and I would be daft to think that I could manage my affairs as well, let alone better, than you do. So, at least for a while I would like things to remain just as they are, provided of course that you would be willing to carry on, and that you take an adequate fee for your services. What do you think – would you be willing?"

Giles paused for a moment "For what it's worth Jake I think you are being very wise and of course I will carry on. In truth managing Harry's affairs has provided me with an appreciable part of my income, and I've always been grateful for it. I am touched that you trust me as you do, and can only say that I will do my very best on your behalf just as I have always done for Harry. But surely you have some plans, some need of extra funds. You are an extremely rich young man Jake, extremely rich."

"I was coming to that. Harry wanted me to live a good and useful life, so firstly I want to give Mr. Pryor money to take back to the lads in Jamaica."

John protested. "Jake you already gave us your prize money, we don't need more."

Jake held up his hand "I'll not take no for an answer. I'm sure we can agree on a sum, and there never was such a thing as too much money now, was there?"

Jake turned to look at his Pa. "Secondly, I know Ma and Pa would never want to move away from Spinnakers so I would like to either build them a new house or make the one they have bigger and better – whatever they wish. And I'd like to build some new outbuildings, and now that he's well, a right good new workshop for Pa so he can carry on making his beautiful furniture." He leant across and put his hand on his father's knee. "It's a rare talent you have Pa, too precious to let lie."

"Thirdly I want to charter a ship so that Indy and I can

go find his Kwashi. I'm thinking that maybe we could bring some plants home and cultivate them. Maybe take some on down to Jamaica and grow them alongside the sugar canes. Just think how good it would be if everyone had Kwashi; how many people it could help. Surely that would be a good and useful thing to do for Harry wouldn't it?" Jake looked to his companions for reassurance, all three nodding in unison.

"Fourthly, I don't want anyone to know about my change of fortune. I just want to carry on being me until I'm ready for other people to find out. So I'm asking everyone here not to breathe a word of this. Apart from us here in the house and Eli, no-one else knows and as far as I'm concerned I would like to keep things that way for a while."

"Of course dear chap, whatever you say and if I may say so Jake, for a young man in command of so much wealth your wishes, though honourable, are very modest, so I'm sure that even as things stand at present you will have more than sufficient funds to fulfil them."

Indy, who had at first been horrified at the thought of a long sea voyage, not sharing Jake's altruism, nevertheless began to warm to the idea as he began to see the financial advantages that would present if they could cultivate his Kwashi. "'Ere 'ere Jake. Very nice like Giles 'ere says, and I reckon we could make a fortune selling the old Kwashi. Gawd, the sooner we goes after it the better, if you ask me." Realising that he may have come across as a little mercenary; "Just think - Kwashi for everyone."

Later that afternoon Jake lay on his bed mulling over what had been discussed earlier. He heard a soft knocking on his door then Indy's face appeared. "Got a minute Jakey boy? I need to talk to you". Jake waved him in. "I wanted to say something before but I ain't bin able to get yer on your own. Anyway, no time like the present eh. See, just before we came up 'ere I 'erd a couple of servants talking about Alice." Jake sat up, all ears. "They was saying that 'er old man wanted to get 'er away from you, wanted 'er to mix with their own kind, and that's why they 'bin away a lot." Jake's brow furrowed. Indy's words were like a hammer blow. He had thought Lord Villiers had a liking for him, but it seems he had misjudged his Lordship.

"I'm sorry Jake but I had to tell yer. Anyway, it don't matter now does it? You probably got more money than his nibs. He can't stop yer seeing Alice now – no chance."

Jake suddenly felt much better; Indy was right. He was a wealthy man now and could give Alice at least as much as, if not more than her own father. He'd sort things out once and for all when they got back home. He was troubled though, he didn't want to buy Alice and he felt resentful that the man he thought he knew should value him only by his wealth, or lack of it. Indy opened the door grinning from ear to ear. Clapping his hands he called out "Eureka."

"What the hell does that mean" said Jake.

"I dunno but me old Ma Miss Bella, said she knew some old bloke what said it when he got a good idea, so when she had a good idea she used to clap 'er hands and say it too. Well, we had a good idea about Kwashi didn't we so I said it, see."

"Oh yes, WE had a good idea – I'd almost forgotten."

Still grinning Indy waved and closed the door.

Within a minute of India leaving John Pryor knocked once then poked his head around Jake's door. "A quiet word Jake if you don't mind."

"Of course not John, is something troubling you?"

"No, but I wanted to tell you that Harry's betrayal has been avenged - not for everyone's ears you understand."

Jake sat up eager to hear what his friend had to say.

John moved over to sit on the edge of his bed keeping his voice low. "Jeng and Lin returned to Dragons Lair the day after you left - they send their best wishes to you by the way and were sorry to have missed your departure, but I digress. I'm sad to say that it was in fact some of our lads who gave the game away." He held out a hand to calm an agitated Jake, "unintentionally of course, but unnecessarily foolish. Apparently they were in the local whore-house speculating on the likelihood that The London Pride would be carrying a rich cargo and how much it would be worth. They were overheard by one of the more - shall we say - enterprising ladies, who put two and two together and saw how she could make some extra money by warning the merchant, Richard Greebe, to expect some sort of attack. He took the information seriously and well, you know the rest."

"But what happened to the woman?"

"Apparently she showed no remorse for causing such a loss of life and was in fact boasting about the reward she had received, so Jeng and Lin dispatched her in a way - they said - that befitted a woman of her calling."

Jake shuddered - at least it was good to know that they had not harboured a traitor in their midst at the Lair. He shook John's hand and thanked him for putting his mind at ease then lay back to rest a while before dinner, Harry filling his thoughts.

Lizzie had enjoyed the most wonderful day. She had not been so happy for years, apart from the day her darling Jake came home. She had played with the children in the nursery, given them their tea and helped to bathe them ready for bed. They were delightful and she had truly welcomed the chance to mother them. A fleeting shadow of sadness passed over her when she remembered how she had longed for siblings for Jake but she brushed off the thought, washed and climbed into her beautiful new gown ready for dinner.

John sat on the bed watching her as she twisted and twirled in front of the long mirror, laughing with pleasure at the rustling the dress made when she walked. He loved her so much and he felt his heart lurch with the strength of his feelings. She was everything to him. If it were possible he thought he loved her more now than the day they were wed. She brushed her hair as he watched, piling it on top of her head and fixing it with pins so that tiny tendrils fell around her face and neck. "Come on John. Don't sit there gawping. We've got to get down for dinner." She hunched her shoulders and giggled. He smiled and shook his head in wonderment that this adorable, beautiful woman had ever agreed to be his wife.

Chapter 33

Their time in London passed very quickly as the best times are wont to. All business was successfully concluded and Jacob Faraday left for home and Poundsmill, a very wealthy man and the new owner of Throgmorton Estate. He had been correct in his assumption that his parents would not want to leave Spinnakers, so within a few days of being home the family started making plans for alterations. They were now very glad of their foresight when, unable to track down the owner of the property or the surrounding land, they had fenced off ten acres around the cottage. As advised all those years ago, they had claimed the whole parcel and become the legal owners of the cottage and plot just a few months before Jake had been impressed. They decided to completely re-site and improve the barn and outbuildings so that the cottage could be extended considerably leaving plenty of room for John's new workshops. Architects and builders were summoned, plans drawn up, an air of excitement rippling through the very walls of the old place.

Jake travelled to Bristol looking for a suitable vessel for his expedition. He had intended to charter a ship but by a stroke of good fortune fell into a conversation with a genial man called Martin Coleman. It transpired that Mr. Coleman was the owner of a three-mast barque, The Fair Wind, which was in need of repairs that he could not afford to undertake. Having taken a look at the ship Jake saw that she was a beauty so he struck a bargain. He bought the ship for what he thought a very reasonable price, agreeing to pay for all necessary works on condition that Mr. Coleman, who was a very experienced seaman, would oversee the repairs and accompany Jake on his search for Kwashi as

ship's Captain, and that he would agree to her being re-
named The Elizabeth.

This agreement suited both men well as Martin Coleman
reasoned that he would come home from his final voyage
with a nice little nest egg waiting for him, and Jake would
benefit from all his experience as a sailor and ships master.
Having secured the deal, they drank a toast to each other
and to the Elizabeth, being ready to set sail the next Spring.

With work underway on all fronts Jake kept himself
busy, but despite trying not to think of Alice, the days
dragged by with no word of her. He spent a miserable
Christmas and New Year wondering where she was, how
she was celebrating the festivities, and who with. At last,
towards the end of March, news went around the village
that Lord Villiers and his family were home and better still,
in two weeks time they were holding a garden party to
celebrate their 25th wedding anniversary to which all and
sundry were invited.

The news created a flurry of activity with every woman
in Poundsmill rushing for her sewing box hoping to add to
or embellish her best frock wanting to look as smart as
possible for such an occasion. Lizzie, who had been longing
for a chance to wear one of her beautiful gowns, went
through all her clothes like a whirlwind calming down only
when she had selected what she considered the very best
from the items they had brought down from London. An
invitation to the big house indeed! No-one could remember
such a thing happening ever before.

The big day arrived and Jake standing with old Prince
could hardly contain his impatience as they waited for Ma
and Pa to make an appearance. Indy, waiting alongside
Jake drew in his breath at the sight of Lizzie. She had on the
blue gown and necklace that Jake had bought on his return

home and her hair was piled high to show off the matching earrings which sparkled like blue fire in the morning sun. She was wrapped in a blue silk shawl and her tiny feet were clad in pale blue, beaded silk shoes. Dear Martha had shown her how to apply a little rouge to her cheeks and lips, and she had smeared the merest shading of soot on her eyelids to give her eyes depth. "Gawd Jake, look at your Ma! She looks bloomin' beautiful, and yer Pa, Gawd they look like real toffs don't they?" Jake had to admit that they did make a handsome couple, although the old pony and trap they climbed into detracted a little from the grandeur. He made a mental note to exchange it for something a little better.

Eli, who had decided that hobnobbing with all and sundry was not for him, waved the group off smiling. Jake and Indy, well dressed and straight backed on their horses made a striking pair, dark and light, both so handsome. John, completely well now, had regained his strong physique and good looks and Lizzie, the way she looked today, was probably one of the most beautiful women he had ever seen. His heart fluttered as he watched them leave. They were his family now and he loved them dearly. He looked down at Shiner and ruffled his head, "Come on lad, let's find Jess and check on our ewes, then we'll get ourselves some grub."

As they approached the main gate to the Villiers estate, the Faraday party merged with a steady stream of people from the village. Grooms were on hand to help with the horses and carriages and the wrought-iron arch spanning the main entrance gate was festooned in bunting. There was a carnival atmosphere and even Jake was beaming widely now, unable to hide his excitement at seeing Alice once again. Along with all the other visitors they made their way down onto the lawn in front of the terrace where a quartet was playing a selection of chamber music on the very spot where Jake and Indy had sat having lunch all those months ago. There were tables laden with all kinds of pastries, fruits and meats, to which they were encouraged to help themselves. Wine and ale flowed freely, servants weaving amongst the guests to ensure that all were catered to.

Jake spotted Alice at the same moment she saw him. She had on a dress of the palest yellow which floated around her form in the breeze like yellow gossamer. She looked absolutely lovely and brought to mind the stories of wood nymphs that Ma had told him as a child; of their golden hair and gossamer wings glinting in the sunlight. She left her group of companions and hurried over to him. "Oh Jake, you cannot know how much I've missed you." She squeezed his hand, tears filling her eyes.

"Me too! these last few months have been the most miserable I can remember. Where have you been? Why did you stay away so long?"

Looking over Jake's shoulder Alice saw her father approaching with the obnoxious Robert Shorcross and a couple of his cronies. "Oh bother, Papa is coming. I can't talk to you now but come to my room at two o'clock. I will say I am unwell or something and excuse myself. Go to the kitchens at two and I will send my girl Sarah to show you the way up the back stairs."

Jake's jaw dropped, "But…"

"Sshh, ah Papa, look who is here." Lord Villiers nodded to Jake, not meeting his eyes. He introduced him briefly to his companions then took Alice's arm.

"Come along my dear, we need to mingle. Nice seeing you Jacob, do help yourself and enjoy the festivities."

Jake did just that. He was over the moon. He discovered an appetite that had deserted him some time ago and tucked into all that was on offer. He supped some ale but not too much as he wanted to keep a clear head for his Alice. At just before two he wandered around to the side of the house keeping an eye out for Sarah. He leant against the wall adjacent to the kitchen door watching the stream of servants coming and going carrying trays and platters for the crowd.

He saw Sarah stand in the doorway then lean to one side feigning exhaustion. When she spotted Jake she sidled over and said that she would beckon when it was all clear. She told him that just inside the kitchen there was a door to the left behind which was the servant's staircase. When she beckoned he was to nip inside the door and through onto the staircase where she would be waiting. If anyone saw him he was to ask for a drink of water as he felt unwell. He nodded and watched her amble towards the kitchen door once more. For what seemed an age she did not appear but, just as he was beginning to think it would never happen, the procession of waiters stopped, probably because the music had ceased and he could hear voices as Lord and Lady Villiers welcomed their guests on this their special day.

Sarah poked her head out and beckoned Jake, signalling him to hurry. He ran to the door, ducked through into the stairwell and followed Sarah, tiptoeing so as not to make a noise on the wooden stairs. The door at the top of the stairs opened onto a thickly carpeted corridor, with mirrors and flower decked occasional tables along its length. Sarah knocked quietly on the third door that they came to and opened it ushering Jake inside.

He had been so excited at the thought of getting Alice

alone but was totally unprepared for the sight that met him. The curtains were drawn almost to a close so that the diffused light bathed Alice in shadow. She stood completely naked with her arms thrust out towards him smiling at his obvious surprise. Her hair was loose and tumbled down her back to the small indent at the base of her spine. Her skin was like alabaster, the pink nipples and areolas of her taught breasts and the small brown triangle of hair between her thighs contrasting with the whiteness. Her hips curved out from her tiny waist and her firm, rounded thighs tapered down to shapely slender calves and perfect tiny feet. She was so beautiful that Jake could hardly breathe. He felt his breeches tighten as the fire burning within him took hold. He wanted her so badly it was painful. His heart was racing, blood pounding in his throat and ears. "Please Jake, hold me. I have wanted to be together with you like this for so long and I began to despair that it could never be. Please Jake, come to me."

Not trusting himself to speak he walked into her arms and kissed her, pressing his lips hard against hers, his groin hard into her body. Using all his willpower he pulled away and managed to say "We shouldn't, if we got found out...." but Alice put her hand over his mouth.

"Jake, before we went away you asked me to marry you and I dearly want to be your wife, so if Papa refuses to allow it I will be your wife in deed if not in name. I love you and no matter what, I always will." They kissed again and unable to resist the tide of passion that overtook him, Jake tore off his breeches and carried her to the bed. It was so right, so natural. Their bodies melted into one with small gasps of wonder escaping as they experienced feelings of such exquisite pleasure that neither could ever have envisaged possible. They gave themselves up to each other kissing, caressing, writhing until they reached a crescendo of blinding ecstasy that had them crying out, all fears of discovery forgotten. When they were both satiated they lay in each others' arms panting, lost to the world outside, floating on a sea of contentment.

"I have something to tell you Alice. I was going to keep it to myself for a bit longer but now, as we are you could say already man and wife, I will tell." Jake went on to explain about his fateful meeting with Harry and the fortune that had been recently bestowed on him, which meant that now there could be no objection to their union on her father's part. He told her about the changes being made to Spinnakers and of his arranged voyage to find and collect Kwashi. Alice leant up on one elbow and looked into his eyes.

"Jake, that is wonderful news but I want you to know that I would love you rich or poor. I wish you weren't going away so soon but I'll wait for you, however long it takes. Perhaps then I can be free of the endless round of dreadful soirees that Papa keeps arranging, and of having to socialise with Papa's dreadful friends, especially that awful Robert Shorcross who seems to turn up wherever we go. I'll wait for you forever Jake, I promise. Just make sure that you return to me, that's all I ask." She lowered her lips to kiss him and slid her body over his, guiding him so that he entered her, and once more they took off to that place called paradise.

They were startled by a quiet knocking at the door. "Some of the guests are leaving and your father is asking after you Miss Alice, what am I to tell him?"

"Oh, tell him that I'm feeling a little better and will be down soon. Can you give me few minutes please Sarah, and then help me to dress?'"

"Yes Miss Alice."

Jake threw on his clothes, gave Alice a lingering kiss then made for the door. "Take care that no-one sees you my love and I'll tell Papa that India has told me about your good fortune and that I love you."

"And I will call round tomorrow to ask for your hand my Lady Alice. Are you sure you won't mind being plain old Mrs. Faraday?" Alice picked up a cushion and threw it playfully.

"Just go, and make sure you come back tomorrow – I can't wait."

On the all-clear from Sarah, Jake slid from the bedroom and made his way downstairs and back out through the kitchen. He saw Ma and Pa deep in conversation with Lady Catherine and found India passing time with Anne Feeney, the Cooper's daughter. "Oh, 'ere you are Jake. I was just telling Anne 'ere that we are gonna need lots of little tubs to bring back our plants in." Jake flashed a look at Indy, their mission was supposed to be a secret. "It's alright Jake, I was saying we're gonna look for cotton plants to grow round 'ere ain't we." Relieved that Indy had not spilled the beans, and now full of bonhomie he could not be annoyed, he slapped Indy on the back.

"That's right my old mate, cotton, cotton, cotton."

As a slightly chill breeze began to replace the afternoon sun the garden party came to an end and the clearing up began. The Faradays meandered home contentedly, both Lizzie and John feeling sleepy having eaten and drunk their fill. Indy was musing on the merits of Anne Feeney, "she's real pretty ain't she? And ever so funny; gawd she made me laugh so much, and that's a turn up I can tell yer. By the way did you get to see your Alice? I never saw much of 'er, someone said she was feeling ill." Jake was in a world of his own. Indy, not knowing how his friend had really spent the afternoon, thought that the foolish grin he was wearing was from too much ale. He shook his head and tutted, "might as well talk to me bleedin' self. I reckon I'd get more sense out of old Prince there than you!"

Jake was up and dressed with the lark. He had on his best clothes once again and could hardly contain himself over breakfast. "Where are you off to lad? You look like you've lost a penny and found a sovereign; what's brewing?" Jake had meant to keep things to himself until he could announce the good news but now it all came spilling out, with the exception of their love making.

"So, now that I can keep her as she's used to, I'm to see Sir Edward this morning to ask for Alice's hand. I want to make her my wife." Jake had expected his father to be pleased for him but instead he was met with silence. "Well don't look too pleased will you! I thought you would be happy for me. I love her and she loves me. You know we've been sweet on each other more or less since we first met."

John pursed his lips and put a hand on his son's wrist. "I am pleased that you've found someone Jake. There's nothing better than having the love of a good woman, believe me; but you aren't one of them folk. I know you are wealthy now but you wasn't born to it. I just don't think you should rush up there expecting to be taken in with open arms. I know his lordship thinks a lot of you – he's told me so, but well, you just aren't high born and that might make a difference."

Jake snatched his wrist away, angry and disappointed at his father's reaction. He left without finishing his meal and took off at a gallop, not knowing where he was going, but knowing that Pa was wrong and he couldn't wait to show him.

Eventually he calmed down, dismounted and led Prince to a stream to drink. When they had both rested he set off at walking pace to the Villiers Estate. He trotted up the drive watching out for Alice who would surely come to greet him. He rode right up to the house and, as there was no hitching post, dropped the reins leaving Prince to wait for the groom who would normally be in attendance. He knocked on the door which was opened by Morton the slightly imperious butler. "Good morning I'm here to see Sir Edward and Miss Alice."

"May I ask the nature of your visit Sir?" This was not at all what Jake had been expecting.

"I, well I need to speak to Sir Edward about something private."

"Just one moment Sir, his lordship is in the study, I will see if he is receiving. Please come inside whilst I make enquiries."

Jake stepped into the familiar grand hallway and watched as the butler coughed respectfully and entered the room. Jake heard muffled voices then Morton appeared and beckoned him, "this way if you please Sir."

Jake entered the oak panelled study noting the absence of Alice. "Ah Jacob, do come in and make yourself comfortable." Jake was suddenly feeling very nervous. It had all seemed so simple yesterday with Alice in his arms. "Now Jake let's not beat about the bush. Alice tells me that you have come into a fortune – the Throgmorton Estate no less, and that you wish to make her your wife."

"Well yes sir. I have the highest regard for her, in fact I love her very much and…"

"That is as may be but you are both very young, and even though she says you are now a man of means I'm afraid that I just cannot allow it – ever."

"But…"

"There is no point in discussing it further young man; the answer is no - not now, not ever. Now, I have a number of things to deal with as we are off the London for the season, so I will wish you good day. Can you see yourself out?"

Jake was incensed. "So, what Pa said is true then. I'm just not good enough for your precious daughter because I'm low born. Well I can tell you I'm just as good a man as you and your kind. Why, my Pa is worth ten of someone like you! Don't think this is the end of it, not by a long chalk. Me and Alice are meant to be together and it'll take a better man than you to keep us apart. I can certainly find my own way out, and I'm glad to be leaving." Jake turned on his heel and marched across the hallway pushing past Morton who had opened the door in readiness for his rapid exit.

Smouldering with fury he nudged Prince into a trot, wanting to get off the estate as soon as possible. As he approached the gate he met Robert Shorcross sauntering across the grounds who acknowledged him with a wave. "Goodbye old chap; better luck next time what. We are all off to London tomorrow, shame you can't join us. Alice is longing to get back to civilization you know, away from all you country types. Wish I could say I will miss the country air, but I won't."

Jake contemplated climbing down to wipe the smirk off of that undeniably handsome face but thought better of it. He was ashamed and embarrassed to the core and brawling in public would only add to his humiliation. He hacked across several fields until alone and out of sight he burst into tears. Today was supposed to be one of the happiest of his life but all he could feel was abject misery. Oh Alice,

had she meant what she said? Why didn't she stand with
him against her father? He was totally confused. Pa had
been right of course; those people just stuck to their own
and paid no mind to ordinary folk. He remembered Harry's
words; how it had taken losing everything before he
realized that all men are equal. He spent a while gathering
himself together before making his way home and was so
grateful that his father who, after embracing him said only,
"Jake Faraday, you are one of the finest human beings alive
and there's many not fit to lick your boots, and don't you
ever forget it."

....

Lady Catherine had endured a sleepless night knowing
that Jacob intended to call upon her husband to ask for
Alice's hand. When his daughter had approached him the
previous evening he had shot her down in flames, refusing
point blank to listen to her appeals or to give her any hope
for the future. Catherine had remained silent, watching
helplessly from the sidelines, knowing that her daughter's
heart had been broken. That morning she had hovered at
the top of the stairs when Jake arrived and heard the raised
voices as his proposal was rebuffed. She watched him
stride out, the look on his face conveying more easily than
words, the grief that he was feeling.

She dug her fingernails into the palms of her hands. This
was just so wrong, so unfair; she resolved then and there to
take some action. Hurrying back to her bedroom, stepping
around the trunks being prepared for their journey, she sat
at her writing bureau and after a few moments thought put
pen to paper. She wrote two letters, one to India Mason and
one to Jacob.

Dear Mr. Mason

I have asked Sarah to hand this note to you in secrecy before you embark on your voyage. I have enclosed a letter to Jacob in an effort to explain the unhappy events that took place here today and, for his own safety, it is imperative that he does not receive it until you have been at sea for at least one week; in other words, until it is too late for him to turn back. Believe me, I have his best interests at heart or I would not have taken this, what may seem to you, curious course of action.

I know you to be a true friend to Jacob and can only hope that you care enough for him to trust me and comply with my entreaty to put his safety above all else.

Yours very truly,

Lady Catherine Villiers

My Dearest Jacob

Please do not be angry with your friend for delaying the delivery of this letter to you. I beseeched him to do so as I feared you may be driven to act rashly and put yourself in danger upon reading the contents.

Where to start? Firstly I beg you not to be angry with my dear Edward. There is no doubt that he was at first alarmed that his only daughter seemed to be smitten with someone not in our circle and by taking her away to London he felt he was acting in her best interests. However, it soon became clear that our daughter was not to be deterred and that you had qualities that set you apart from ordinary men. In fact Edward had decided that, should you ask for her hand he would agree, on condition that you could prove yourself capable of looking after her adequately. He even went so far as to consult several of his

colleagues with regard to finding you a position in the city should you
have needed it. All this, I hasten to add, before we had any idea that
you had means of your own!

So why did my husband refuse to accept your suit this morning? Put
quite simply, it was because we are being blackmailed!

Robert Shorcross, with whom I think you are acquainted, somehow
found out that I played a major part in helping dear Harry to escape
to France after the duel during which Robert's father was shot and
killed. The wretched man has threatened to make it public unless we
agree to him marrying Alice, whom he has admired for some years
now. Upon the marriage he also wants us to grant him a half share in
the whole estate.

The news of my involvement in Harry's escape came as a shock to my
dear Edward but he has proved a true and loyal husband even though
the shame and scandal could ruin him, and of course the fact that I
could go to prison is just more than he could bear. Alice knows nothing
of this and is heartbroken to think that her father is so uncaring, which
is in turn breaking my dear Edward's heart. All any parent wants
for their child is happiness and now, thanks to Robert Shorcross, all
Alice knows is despair.

You must see now Jacob, why I did not want you to know of this
before you set sail. I fear you would have acted rashly, possibly at
great cost to yourself and your family. Robert Shorcross and his
mother are very influential people and both cut from the same malign
cloth, and they will grasp at any opportunity to destroy others, indeed
they relish doing so. I do feel it best therefore that you go away for
some while so that we will all have time and space to give thought as to
how we can resolve this problem.

We are off to London and then France for an extended tour which
will enable us to defer any plans that young Shorcross may present us
with. Once you are home again we can face our troubles together
whatever the outcome as then Alice will have you by her side, and

The Throgmorton Legacy

Edward and I know that we could not ask for anything more.
I wish you good luck and God speed on your journey, and remain
yours truly,

Catherine Villiers

Catherine sealed the letters and went to find Sarah with strict instructions that they must be handed secretly to India Mason only. She knew Sarah could be relied upon as she loved her young mistress almost as much as she did herself.

"Sarah my dear I have arranged for one of the grooms to drive you down to the Faradays' cottage with all the food left over from yesterday. Please ask Mrs. Faraday if she would be good enough to distribute it amongst the villagers as she sees fit, after taking what she wants for herself of course. Also, and this is important, I want you to take these two letters and make sure that you give them to India Mason only, and I don't want anyone else to know that he has them so keep them hidden in your pocket until you can get him alone. It really is important to all of us Sarah, especially Alice. Can I rely on you to do exactly as I ask?"

Sarah promised to do as she was bid, she was excited to have an excuse to speak to India, and she would do anything for Alice. She smiled to herself as she thought of how she had helped her mistress and that handsome Jacob to meet in secret. This was turning into a very good day. She had got out of packing Alice's trunks, a job she loathed, and she got to get first pick from all the lovely leftovers. She sat up top with the driver, munching a delicious game pie, watching the dappled sunlight dance on the horses' glossy coats as they trotted beneath the elms and hazels that lined their route, and listening all the while to the beautiful birdsong. Yes, this was going to be a very good day indeed.

India was trying to engage a sullen and withdrawn Jake in conversation when she arrived. The two friends were sitting on hay bales in the yard each with a tankard of ale in their hands. When he saw Sarah and the Villiers' coach Jake threw the remainder of his ale onto the ground and disappeared into the house. Sarah raised her voice when she addressed Indy in an effort to allay any suspicions that she may have an ulterior motive for visiting.

"Lady Catherine sent all this food down to Mrs. Faraday asking if she would be so kind as to pass it on to any folks who needs it. She hasn't got the time herself as we are all going to London again. She said for Mrs. Faraday to help herself first though, and just pass on what's left like. So if you can help us carry it into your parlour we would be much obliged."

India, a little dismayed at the volume of Sarah's speech nodded his willingness to help and selected the biggest basket. Sarah carried two game pies wrapped in cloths which she held high in her arms and from behind which she whispered to Indy. "I got an important message for you from Lady Catherine and it's to be a secret. I got something to give you but no-one else is to see." India was confused but intrigued.

"Right you are, I'll take you to see our new lambs when we've finished 'ere." They finished unloading, accompanied by Lizzie's oohs and aahs as what amounted to a banquet was piled up on her kitchen table.

"Now then young Sarah, another new lamb was born yesterday, would you like to see it before you go?" Sarah, who genuinely would like to pet the lamb, agreed enthusiastically. They walked across the yard and disappeared into the barn. She took the letters from her apron pocket and handed them to India.

"I dunno what's going on at the big house but Lady Catherine seems real upset and she said I'm to give you these in secret and you'm not to show them to anyone else; and you gotta promise me you won't or I'll get into trouble." Sarah, who loved to gossip, was on the brink of telling him that Miss Alice had been crying non-stop since yesterday, but her instincts warned her against confiding too much in him.

India of course knew that this was all to do with Jake's rebuffed marriage proposal but said only. "Well I better promise then ain't I? Don't want to get a pretty little girl like you into bother do I?" Sarah blushed from tip to toe and left the barn grinning like the proverbial Cheshire cat.

The letters were burning a hole in Indy's pocket but he fought the urge to open his until he had helped Lizzie divide the food into fairly even sized packages for the needy families that she had in mind. He and Eli loaded up the pony and trap and waved John and Lizzie off as they left to share out the fruits of Lady Villiers' largesse. He took the stairs two at a time and was grateful to find that the bedroom he shared with Jake was empty. He sat on the bed and took out the letters, hurriedly opening his. It took him some time to read, his brow furrowing in concentration. When he had absorbed the contents he tapped the sealed letter addressed to Jake on his knee deep in thought. He was now in a real dilemma. He hated the idea of keeping a secret from Jake as his loyalty to his friend was paramount, on the other hand Lady Catherine's letter left no doubt that Jake could be in real danger if he didn't. Before he had more time to think things through he heard footsteps on the stairs. He thrust the letters under his mattress just as Jake appeared.

"Your Ma's gone into the village with all that food from the big 'ouse. Where you been?"

"I just went out for a walk – couldn't bear to be anywhere near anything to do with bloody Villiers! It's shameful, we aren't good enough to be their equal but we're good enough to dump their leftovers on. I expect it makes the good Lady Catherine feel saintly passing on her crumbs to us poor lowly bred folks."

India was shocked to hear the bitterness in Jake's voice and he decided that maybe it would be best to let things lay a little, at least until Lord and Lady Muck had gone. She had hinted in her letter that it would be safer for Jake to get right away and maybe she was right. In the state his friend was in, Indy could well imagine that he could land himself into a whole lot of trouble so he decided to keep the secret. He would risk Jake's wrath when they were well out to sea - greater love hath no man.

Chapter 34

Repairs to the Elizabeth were completed by the end of May, Martin Coleman having made sure that all works had been carried out to the highest standard. He had organised the loading of provisions and managed to round up most of his old crew which had actually been no hardship, the new master being fairly generous when it came to their pay. Since his confrontation with Lord Villiers, Jake had thrown himself into organising their voyage, and wanting to get away from Poundsmill, had joined the ship at Bristol for a brief naming ceremony. He had then set sail along the coast and anchored off the village where he had a few last minute details to attend to. On the short journey he had put the ship through her paces and been very impressed with her handling and turn of speed. She was everything that Martin Coleman had promised she would be.

The influx of fresh blood caused great excitement in the village. The women were all a flutter and the men were appreciative of the extra money that was suddenly in circulation; none more than Big Eddy at The Jugged Hare who was doing a roaring trade. The Elizabeth was still two crew members short but, there being very little work around, Jake was content that he could easily find them amongst the villagers.

One hundred small barrels had been ordered from Sam Feeney, the cooper, in anticipation of finding and transporting the Kwashi plants. Sam was overjoyed to have received such an order and it has to be said that India was more than happy to check up on the cooper's progress, and of course was not averse to spending time with his daughter Anne. Eventually one hundred miniature barrels, bound with shiny metal hoops were stacked on the quay waiting to be loaded on The Elizabeth. At long last all was ready, the ship only awaiting the crew and a few fresh supplies to be taken aboard on the morning of departure.

....

Jake, Indy, Lizzie, John and Eli sat around the old wooden table in the semi-renovated parlour of Spinnakers eating in silence. Lizzie's chicken stew and fresh baked bread were delicious but all were lost in their own thoughts and on this occasion were unable to do the food justice. John and Lizzie, although proud of their son and the reasons behind his quest knew that his voyage would not be without danger and both remembered vividly how desolate the house had been when he had left as a boy; the fear that this time he may not return was uppermost in their minds although neither would ever have admitted it to the other.

Eli was a troubled man. Knowing that an experienced sailor would be an asset to any crew, Jake had invited him to join their expedition, but he had chosen not to. He was still haunted by dreadful visions from the past and could not bear the thought of re-visiting the islands where his nightmare had begun. He felt he was letting the family down by not protecting the boy's back but he knew he was damaged and that his fear and the horrors that woke him dripping in sweat most nights would render him useless in any dangerous situation. No, he would be of much more use helping out at Spinnakers; at least that is what he kept telling himself.

India was dreading the whole voyage. He was no sailor and even thinking of being surrounded by nothing but water for weeks on end, and imagining what may lurk beneath in the murky depths made him shudder so that he now regretted latching onto Jake's idea of harvesting Kwashi with such enthusiasm. Tomorrow they would set sail and if they found Llenanda, he wondered if he could deal with the heartache of seeing Narntech and his family again. A vision of his dear Nancy swam before him and his eyes welled up at the thought of her loss. He took a long swig of ale and felt every last drop as it struggled to get past the lump in his throat.

Jake sat looking at the spoon pushing his food around his bowl. He felt his head was fit to burst like an over-ripe tomato; it was so full of so many conflicting thoughts. Overriding everything was the constant pulsating mantra in his brain that Alice had gone. He was going away for the Lord knew how long and he may never see her again. He was still so confused. How could she have lain with him if she did not love him? She must love him it had been so real, so perfect, but why had she not come to him? Why had she abandoned him and left him to be insulted and humiliated by her father? All he knew was that his heart felt like a stone weighing heavy in his chest and that he would go mad if she had gone from him forever.

He snapped to when Indy banged on the table with his tankard. "'Ere come on you lot. We should all be dancing round and celebrating. Blimey. What's up with us? Jake here is as rich as yer like. Lizzie's 'avin a new 'ouse - more or less, and John's 'avin new workshops and tommorer me and Jake are off to get some Kwashi what will probably make us all even more rich - remembering that Jake's motives at least were altruistic - and of course it will help so many sick folks. We got nothing but good things to look forward to and we're all sitting 'ere like we was at a wake. Blimey, things are a lot different than when we fetched up 'ere last time, eh Jake. Come on now, let's all 'av a good drink together. Indy's pep talk shook them out of their melancholy. They raised a glass to one another and fell into lively conversation making the most of the time left, all knowing that the day after tomorrow the boys would be gone.

Slightly regretting the one too many he had downed, Jake sat in the yard of Spinnakers watching the sun come up. Jess, sensing a change, tentatively came out join him, nuzzling his knee. He looked down at her now grey muzzled face and adoring eyes and was filled with melancholy at the thought of leaving her and those he loved for he knew not how long. He loved this place so much. It was so peaceful even the murmurings of the animals and the cock's crowing did nothing to dispel the calming atmosphere of the place. Indy had been right, they were all so fortunate, especially him. He was standing on the brink of a new adventure knowing that whatever happened, all those dear to him would be cared for all of their lives. As for Alice - well in the morning calm he realized that she must love him and he reasoned that, once she was of an age, no-one could stop them being together, no-one.

Fondling Jess's ears he looked across the field at the lambs gambolling in the morning mist. Yes, in the clear light of day the future was full of promise, everything was fine – so why could he not shake off the feeling of unease that tingled along the length of his spine, the sense of foreboding. Harry's voice came back from the past *"you've got good instincts lad, listen to them."*

He stood turning his face to the emerging sun and smiled "Everything is fine Harry, just fine. I'll not let you down - don't you worry about that - I'll never let you down."

Epilogue

Big Eddy stood behind the bar of The Jugged Hare studying the well dressed young man silhouetted in the doorway. "Good day stranger, what can I do for you?"

The stranger turned his head nodding towards the Elizabeth anchored off shore. "I hear they are looking for crew for yon ship."

"That's right. She'll be off any day now. Plenty volunteering though! I hear pay's good, but if you'll excuse me sayin' so, you don't 'zactly look like the usual folks who come looking for work."

The young man merely smiled. "I'll take a room for a few days then if you have one, and a bowl of your mutton stew and a pitcher of ale."

"Right you are Sir. We've a nice room at the front. I'll get young Fay to show you up." Pointing to a small table next to a window overlooking the quay, "I'll put your food on yon table."

"Thank you, I'll be but a minute."

The young man followed Fay up to his room, thanked her and closed the door. He sat on the bed placing his valise beside him. He opened it and carefully drew out an enamelled miniature of a dark haired man who stood, hands akimbo, head thrown back laughing; his shirt open to the waist exposing his hirsute chest and a heavy gold chain and crucifix. The black eyes shone out from a strong face, the smiling mouth exposing a set of near perfect dentures, save that is for a pronounced gap where a front tooth had been broken.

The young stranger touched the picture gently to his lips. "I've found them Charlie and I'll make them pay. I promise." Sighing, he placed his dead lover's likeness carefully back in the valise before closing the door silently behind him and making his way downstairs eager for his supper and with vengeance in his heart.